Sister of Saidnaya

Sister of Saidnaya

A Syrian Immigrant's Tale

Rose Ann Kalister

Boyle
&
Dalton

Book Design & Production
Columbus Publishing Lab
www.ColumbusPublishingLab.com

This is a work of fiction. Names, characters, places, and incidents
either are the product of the author's imagination or are used
fictitiously, and any resemblance to actual persons, living or dead,
business establishments, events, or locales is entirely coincidental.

Print ISBN: 978-1-63337-181-1
E-book ISBN: 978-1-63337-182-8

Printed in the United States of America

1 3 5 7 9 10 8 6 4 2

In memory of my brother Charlie, Charles Ellem

Saidnaya, Syria

1921

Nadra pressed herself against the closed door so she could hear her parents.

"You go, we all go," Lila shouted at Sami.

"I don't have money for the whole family."

"You had enough to go twice yourself!"

"Too much money, Lila, too much money!"

"You get me pregnant then you leave!"

"*Habibee*," (Beloved) he said as he stroked her hand.

Lila pulled her hand away. "First a year. Then five years. Five years, Sami!"

"World War I wasn't my fault, Lila! Traveling back was dangerous, impossible! Then President Wilson was changing the rules, making us get passports and—"

"You go we all go!" Lila said as she stepped closer to Sami.

"I can't afford to take us and the four girls!"

"Two of them can stay behind. Mama offered to care for them. *Sitto* (Grandmother) is convinced we will return. We can send for them when we're settled."

Nadra crept away quietly, but her heart was shouting, *take me, please.* She didn't want her big sisters to be left behind, but if someone had to stay, she didn't want to be the one.

Since his return to Saidnaya, Sami was the center of a circle of men who wanted to know more about America. Whenever she could slip by her watchful mother, Nadra sneaked into the edge of the circle to hear Sami's magic words. Sami often caught her topaz-brown eyes, which were the same color and intensity as his, and winked ever so slightly.

Nadra never tired of listening as her father, handsome, debonair, with a beautiful mustachio, seduced his listeners with images of the New World. He might open a performance by stretching his arms toward his audience, then wider and beyond them, proclaiming, "America! A huge fertile land where the rain comes often, where the crops kiss the sun. Where farmers till the soil with machines. Not donkeys, not cows! In America the houses have water. You pull a cord and you have light. A generous land, my friends, a generous land! In America a man can earn more money in a year than he can in ten years in Saidnaya. In America you can leave your sons land and money!" Eventually Sami would grow silent, stroke his mustachio, scan the riveted eyes and whisper, "In America they do not have to fear the Turks or put up with the French! Here a Christian can hardly call his life his own. In America we Christians can find liberty." His voice rising, "In that rich beautiful land everything is possible!"

Nadra thought her heart would burst with longing and hope. In the morning she would ask her mother; she would beg to be chosen.

∽

At dawn, the villagers began their trek to the *karms*, the vineyards and fig orchards, where they gathered their crops in *sullas*, baskets. When the sullas were full, they returned. Lila would send her oldest daughters, Nesrin and Feheema, to the springs for the family's water. Nesrin would put a pad on her head and balance the water jug on top; Feheema carried the jug on her shoulder. Like their mother, Lila, those daughters were tall and strong. Nadra was strong but petite.

Sitto taught Nadra how to make the family's bread. Because Nadra learned quickly and mixed the dough well, Sitto declared that her granddaughter had golden hands. Nadra always asked to make the dough; if nothing else, it kept her out of the way of her angry mother. Today she wanted more than anything to please her mother.

Because Lila scolded her if she spilled flour on the kitchen floor, Nadra set the huge *khalkeen* on a chair which she took outside to the patio. Nadra poured many pounds of flour into the khalkeen, and then she dissolved the yeast into warm water. Pushing the flour to one side, she added the yeast, water, oil, and finally, the *mahleb*, a spice from the pit of the sour cherry.

She worked the flour into the wet mixture little by little, mashing the lumps and scraping the dough from the sides of the bowl with her hands. Sami's stories about America echoed again and again as she thrust her fists into the enormous mound of dough and pounded it. Curving her fingers over the mound, she pushed down with the heels of her palms, gave the dough a quarter turn, folded it over and pushed down again. Over and over again, loving the feel of the magic in her hands as she kneaded the simple ingredients to a rippling round of satin. She sang as she worked, old songs that Sitto had sung to her. "Fly away, fly away, beautiful bird."

Returning from the springs, Feheema saw Nadra's behind bouncing up and down as she plunged her fists into the mixture. She alerted Nesrin and together they mocked, "Bread jinni, bread jinni!" Nadra didn't care; she was determined to get the dough satiny smooth, to please Lila, to be chosen for America. Satisfied with the dough's consistency, Nadra greased it with a little olive oil so it would not stick to the khalkeen, then covered it with a cloth. Once the dough rose sufficiently, she would carry it to the *khubbaze* who would form and bake the loaves in the wood-fired *tannour*.

Suddenly Lila came out to the patio.

"Good morning, Mama."

Without responding, Lila raised the cloth to look at the dough. Nadra feared her mother's mood. Just yesterday Lila seemed happy to have her husband back, but some days she was suspicious, watching Sami, noting every smile, every word that he said to other women. Yesterday she even followed him, Nadra running behind her, Lila motioning her to the side or against doorways lest he see them.

"Mama, I very, very much want to go to America with you and Papa."

Nadra tried to hold her tongue, but she couldn't. Her desire was too great.

Lila finally looked at her daughter, with what seemed slightly more interest than she had shown the dough. "Keep your mouth shut. I have enough to deal with." Then she left.

Nadra regretted her outburst. Had she ruined her chances? Her heart flapped and fluttered, a trapped bird attempting to escape its cage. She broke into a sweat. She wasn't sure if it was she or the world that felt unreal. She bolted.

She ran through the enclosed central courtyard around which her home was built, past older adobe houses, past mud brick homes with flat roofs for sleeping and storage. She rushed past the women at the springs. She sped over the narrow donkey trails where children collected dung to form into patties for fuel and fertilizer. She passed the *fellaheen* tilling the land with heavy iron hoes and plows drawn by cows. Running up the slopes lined with grape vines and fig trees she came finally to the town's edge. Panting, she began the steep climb up to the mountain which overlooked the village, to the Monastery of Our Lady of Saidnaya.

Exhausted and sweaty, she welcomed the cool darkness of the monastery. Once inside the huge building, she made her way through small rooms and narrow doors to her destination. The holy shrine of Our Lady was a small dark room, lighted by wax candles; more light came from the many oil lanterns that dangled from the ceiling. Nadra took off her shoes. Behind a silver grid hung the sacred icon: the Virgin Mary holding her Child on her lap.

Kneeling, Nadra crossed herself and began praying the Rosary. She had no beads so she used her fingers for the ten Hail Marys in each of the five decades. "Hail Mary, full of grace. Blessed art thou among women…"

Calm at last, Nadra felt again the one thing she never wanted to lose—hope. She left the shrine, making her way carefully down the rocky climb, trying not to tear her clothes. Lila was looking for her when she reached home.

"Where have you been? The dough has already risen."

Lila thrust the baby at Nadra. "Change Tina." Almost as an after-thought, she added, "Papa and I will take you and Tina to America this coming year. Your sisters Feheema and Nesrin will stay here with Sitto until we have more money."

Hugging the baby, Nadra screamed and danced with joy. Tina's diaper leaked on Nadra's dress. Lila frowned. "Change yourself also and carry the dough to the khubbaze."

Nadra whispered a thank you to the Virgin.

❧

Once he completed the advance travel arrangements, Sami spent his mornings teaching students. The only child of a wealthy merchant, Sami had been educated in schools run by the Jesuits and Christian Brothers. His teaching manual was a black book emblazoned with gold lettering. Lifting the book above his head like a priest in ritual, he would intone *Al-Bakoorat Al-Gharbeyat Fee Taleem Al-Laghat Al-Englezeyat, The First Occidental Fruit for the Teaching of the English (and Arabic Languages).* Quoting from the preface, he liked to explain that the manual contained, "An elaborate Arabic and English vocabulary of the most useful and important words arranged in groups...enabling anyone conversant with either language to master the other." He added that he was thoroughly conversant in both. His students seemed impressed; he didn't see those who snickered behind his back.

Nadra wanted desperately to be one of her father's students so she could be ready for America. She begged him to teach her, begged to be one of his students. He always smiled, saying, "One day, *eyunnee* (apple of my eyes), one day." He taught her a few expressions but overall put her off saying, "We will have plenty of time when we cross."

Evenings Sami continued describing America to the Saidnayans—that huge country with magnificent forests, miles of paved roads, automobiles that people could afford, radios and movies, New York and Chicago competing to see who could build the tallest skyscraper. The endless opportunities. Sometimes he flung his arms toward the men and shouted, "*Yalla*! (Hurry, let's go!)"

Sami had honed his styles and delivery during his years in America. He took advantage of Americans' fascination with the Middle East. The Orientalist fantasy, which had begun many years earlier, was fueled by consumerism, marketing, and film. Sami did not work in the many shows and entertainments about "Life in the Moslem East." Instead he billed himself as a Scholar from the Holy Land, speaking in churches, community centers, and wealthy homes. Many of his lectures were about Christianity in Syria, focusing particularly on the Monastery of Our Lady of Saidnaya, built 1,500 years ago. He told those gathered the legend of the Virgin Mary appearing to Emperor Justinian asking him to found the monastery. Slowing his pace to intensify the gravity of his words, he added, "Within is the Chapel of the Virgin. The walls are covered with icons, one said to have been painted by Saint Luke. Our Lady of Saidnaya is the second Christian place of pilgrimage after Jerusalem! Visitors go there for worship...and healing."

Then he bowed solemnly toward a side table full of icons cast in metal, carved on stone, and embroidered on cloth, adding, "You are welcome to purchase any of these copies of the sacred icon—the Virgin Mary holding the Child."

Sami was the only Christian to work the Arab circuit.

❧

The day of their departure in 1922, twelve-year-old Nadra's anticipation was marred by sadness as she watched her older sisters Feheema and Nesrin retreat to the house after saying their good-byes. When Sitto stopped crying, she gave Nadra a silver amulet depicting an open hand. She said it was *hamsa, Kef Miryam* (The Hand of Mary). Pressing it into Nadra's hands, Sitto said, "It will protect you and it will bless these golden hands."

Clothed in long dark dresses, head scarves, and shawls, Lila and Nadra carried bags with baby items and valuable keepsakes. As they left, Lila handed one-year-old Tina to Nadra and locked her arm in Sami's, saying, "Yalla!"

The family traveled to the capital, Damascus, and from there to Marseilles, France where they boarded a steamship to Boston, Massachusetts. Sami had the experience and money to book a good transatlantic crossing. He knew that steamship voyages to Boston were shorter, focused on passengers rather than ocean freight, and offered better accommodations. The Zahirs had a four-person cabin on the main deck with a private bath. The journey would take about ten days.

When they arrived in Marseilles for the transatlantic crossing, it would take hours to board all the passengers and goods for the journey to Boston, Massachusetts. Lila sent her twelve-year-old off the ship to find a bakery and buy bread. Excited and intrigued by sights vastly different from her small village, Nadra ran down the streets. Her nose led her to a shop and a sign reading "Boulangerie-Patisserie." She found herself in a warm appetizing heaven.

A beautiful young woman with black hair and almond-shaped brown eyes asked, "*Madame, vous desirez?*" Nadra could only smile. Finally, realizing what the gorgeous girl was asking, she pointed here and there and there to different kinds of breads. The girl put them on the counter, and Nadra carefully removed the French coins from her pocket. Spreading the coins on her palm, she offered them to the young woman. The young woman selected three. Then she touched Nadra's hand and arched her brows quizzically, asking: "*Comment vous appelez-vous?*"

Understanding, Nadra replied, "Nadra Zahir." Smiling, the girl patted Nadra's cheek. It had been a long time since Nadra had experienced such tenderness. Recovering some composure, Nadra arched her brows quizzically in return and pointed to the girl.

Laughing, the girl replied, "Aurelia." Wanting desperately to stay but knowing it was time to leave, Nadra kept smiling. The girl said, "*Attendez,*" and glancing to the side and back to make sure no one saw her, she wrapped a butter biscuit and an almond macaroon in paper and handed them to Nadra, softly saying, "*Au revoir.*"

Burdened, but happy, with several loaves of bread and the two delicate cookies, Nadra ran all the way back. Knowing (hoping, actually) that her mother might be watching for her from the ship's deck, she stopped, backing into a hidden corner. She unwrapped the cookies. The fat round macaroon had a crisp crust and a soft interior; the delicate shortbread cookie left a butter stain on the wrapper. For a brief moment she thought about giving some of her prize to her baby sister, Tina, but the gift was so small, so unexpected. Inhaling the tantalizing aromas, she nibbled the corner of the macaroon and the butter cookie. She rewrapped them and hid them carefully in her pocket. The gifts, the gesture, could not really be shared.

The Zahirs finally landed in Boston, Massachusetts. When the North Atlantic steamships, the biggest man-made spectacles of their time, arrived in the booming Boston Harbor, thousands came to see them. Among the crowds when the Zahirs' ship landed were the Mensore brothers—Joseph, Michael, and Charles—and their friend John Hanoun. They often came from Lowell, where they worked in the textile mills, to see the ships and to greet new immigrants from their homeland.

When the men greeted the Zahirs, John Hanoun kept staring at the happy girl with black curls and golden brown eyes. He gave her mother a bouquet of flowers and began conversation with her father. Lila and Sami let John know that he would be a welcome visitor in their new home.

Noting the pains he was taking to ingratiate himself, the Mensores teased him. "Be ashamed, John! She's still a child. Get over it!"

"A girl like that could keep a man young forever," he said.

Laughing they said, "You have at least four years to save your money, John!"

Sami booked them into a small hotel offering deals which immigrant families with money could afford. From there the Zahirs toured and tasted their way through some of the historical and ethnic parts of the city. Sami read them the significant sections of the brochures about the Freedom Trail, Faneuil Hall, and other historical sites. What fascinated Nadra most was the beauty and vastness of this New World. The subways amazed her; the Boston Public Gardens delighted her.

Afternoons when Lila and little Tina napped, Nadra and Sami sneaked out to visit Revere Beach and the Museum of Fine Arts. On the way she frequently stopped to stare at the Boston Traffic Squad, the man on a motorcycle, another in a sidecar. She wished to ride in such a contraption. Sami took her on the streetcars and let her deposit the nickel. He also taught her a little English.

To Nadra, the variety of food was just as fascinating as the funny talking people. She especially loved the hot dog. When they went to Cambridge and strolled around Harvard Yard, they saw students lining up in front of the dog carts. Bold and curious, Nadra joined the line to get a better look at the attraction. Intrigued by the sight and smell of the meat nestled in a long soft roll, she asked Sami to buy her one. Imitating the students, she doused the steamed hot dog with relish and ketchup. She scarfed it down quickly and begged to have another, which she doused with mustard. Nadra loved all that was new and different.

After one morning foray to have breakfast along the sea, father and daughter returned to find Lila closing the large valise.

"Get all your things together, Nadra."

"We're leaving?"

"Yes. Tomorrow we move on," Lila said.

"To our new home?"

Turning to Sami, Lila said, "You didn't tell her?"

Sami said, "Not yet."

Beaming, Nadra said, "I can't wait to see it!"

"It's not close," Sami said.

"Where is it?" Nadra asked.

"West Virginia," he replied.

Alarmed, Nadra said, "You mean Boston isn't home?"

Lila looked at Sami. He patted Nadra on the head.

Hedley, West Virginia

1922

What Boston was, Hedley was not. But it was what Sami expected and wanted. He had no desire to live in one of the Syrian ghettoes in big cities like Boston, New York, or Cleveland, let alone break his back in one of their dirty iron or steel industries or deafening textile mills. He ushered the family to a boarding house while he hunted for a building that could house a store and a home.

He found a two-story building one mile from Hedley's main intersection of Route 50 and Market Street. The town's inter-loop trolleys split in the middle of the intersection, each going in a different direction and passing each other at a switch line. Most of that block consisted of storefronts housing drugstores, tire shops, pawn shops, shoe repair shops, fruit and vegetable markets, and other such establishments. Many owners lived upstairs.

The first floor of the brick building would be their store. To get to their second-floor home they would have to climb twenty-one steps to a landing and a small porch. The only door, made of wood and glass, opened into a long hallway. On the left a long living room facing the side street. At the end of the long hallway two small bedrooms that faced Route 50. Behind those bedrooms, "A large kitchen for Mama!" announced Sami. Lila's response was her usual frown. Behind the kitchen a long narrow bathroom big enough for a toilet, wash basin, tub, and washing machine. Behind that two adjoining bedrooms.

The side street ran down a steep hill to the Baltimore and Ohio Railroad. That street was one of the main accesses for the railroad workers.

Once they were unpacked and reasonably settled in their new home, Sami took Lila and his daughters Nadra and Tina to buy "store clothes." Dazzled by the variety of new ready-to-wear clothing available in a variety of sizes and colors, Lila chose short loose cotton dresses and light cardigans for Nadra and Tina. For herself she chose to wait and study the many alternatives in the Sears Roebuck and Montgomery Ward catalogs. Sami pressured her to decide, insisting it was important to blend in, not stick out. He backed off when she stopped wearing her hair long and twisted it back to the nape of her neck in a smooth chignon. He treated himself to more 8 panel flat caps that all men and boys were wearing. He frequently wore a suit.

The small Syrian community in Hedley became a part of the Roman Catholic parish Saint Peter's. The Anglo-Saxons in Saint Peter's ranged between curious and friendly. Some nationalities, like the Irish and Italians, vied for leadership and influence within the parish. Those outside the church weren't sure what to make of this unfamiliar Syrian breed and were often suspicious.

The Syrians and all immigrants and minorities had to be careful. The times were influenced by the Red Scare, fear of foreigners, race riots, and terrorist attacks. These factors and others led to the resurgence of the Ku Klux Klan. The Klan promoted itself as protector of traditional values and opponent of minorities. A big 1920's revival occurred in West Virginia in places like Clarksburg, Parkersburg, and Williamson. There the Klan opposed Catholics, Jews, immigrants, labor unions, and blacks. The Klan demanded that several Catholic and public school teachers in West Virginia be fired.

The Syrians themselves were friendly but polite; they kept their distance until invited in. Though most of them were illiterate, they spoke good English and were friendly and gracious. Amongst themselves they usually spoke Arabic. Sami paraded his learning credentials and the Syrians embraced him enthusiastically, realizing they had another letter writer and reader for their communications to the old country. Sami prodded Lila to be outgoing and friendly.

While settling in his family, Sami was also observing what products might do well in his confectionery. Coca-Cola's immense marketing machine was screaming, "Drink Coca-Cola Cola!" so Sami offered it as the machine directed: "At Soda Fountains and in Bottles!" He also took advantage of the increasing popularity of chocolate and candy bars. When Curtiss Candy Company claimed that the Baby Ruth candy bar was named for President Grover Cleveland's daughter, Sami made sure everyone knew and cut samples for the children. Also among his store's offerings were sweetened dried fruits and spices.

Proud of his confectionery, Sami hired a photographer. Sami stood on the left, Lila on the right. The two large glass windows were imprinted with SAMI ZAHIR. The right window offered "Home Made Gandies" (Sami had trouble with the English "c"), "Ice-Cream and Soda"; the left window read "Wholesale and Retail, Foreign and Domestic Fruits." Outside the store on the extreme right stood a large four-wheeled contraption with a handle—a nut roasting machine.

Lila was determined to avoid getting pregnant soon. At night as Nadra lay in her room next to the wall adjoining her parents' bedroom, she could hear Lila telling Sami, "Leave me alone." When it became obvious that he was not leaving her alone, Nadra moved her twin bed and Tina's cot to the center of the room.

At first Nadra was not only disappointed but also scared of her new home. All these Amerikan seemed to be driving something—angry men in horse-drawn buggies, fourteen-year-old boys in light truck delivery wagons, and conductors starting and stopping street-cars which ran up the center of the streets. Angry drivers with no training or licenses added to soaring traffic deaths and injuries. Disembarking streetcar riders had to run a gauntlet of racing cars, trucks, motorcycles, and buggies. Trying to cross the intersection one day, Nadra barely missed being struck by a car. Relieved, Sami hugged her and took her upstairs. Angry, Lila slapped her.

In the 1920s the National Safety Council tried to control driver behavior through laws, signs, and signals. In the 1930s manufactur-ers began correcting design and safety flaws.

Nadra missed Saidnaya, that small, poor, hilly village. In the garden of her memory Saidnaya blossomed. The boughs of the fig trees bent with the weight of the fruit, the grapes ripened in the vineyards, the farmers shook the pistachio nuts off the bushes. She longed for her Sitto's loving touch. She wore the amulet, Kef Miryam, often saying a prayer to the Virgin.

Nadra missed her sisters Feheema and Nesrin. She remembered the nights when they slept on the roof under the stars, cooled by the mountain breezes, gossiping, drinking *shy* (tea), and eating strips of *amariddine* (dried apricot leather). She craved their light-hearted laughter, their wicked teasing. Nadra didn't know how to write; Sami only occasionally asked if she wanted to say anything to them in the letters he wrote.

When she could, that is, when Lila wasn't watching, Nadra would run down to Main Street to peer in the stores. She also soon discovered the two hospitals, one public, one Catholic. Happy, confident nurses went in and out, teasing and laughing with each other. Watching them in their crisp white uniforms and caps, Nadra dreamed of becoming a nurse. There were no nurses in Saidnaya. She also liked standing on the corner of Tuppen and 9th Street to watch the children playing in the school yard. That night when she was making tea for Sami and Lila in the kitchen, the only warm room in the apartment, the thirteen-year-old demanded, "When can I go to school?"

Lila ignored her.

Smiling, Sami said, "In time. In time. Now we need you here."

"What about my sisters? They could help. When are you bringing Feheema and Nesrin here? You're making money now."

"Money isn't the problem," Sami said. "The New Immigration Act cut the number of Syrian people who can come here."

"My sisters can't join us?" Nadra asked as she poured the tea.

"Papa already told you," Lila said as she took a cup of tea. "The government won't let them."

Sami added, "Feheema might marry..."

"Who?" asked Nadra.

"Karim Makdoud."

Making a face, Nadra asked, "Why?"

"…and Nesrin is not well."

"What's wrong with her?" Nadra asked.

"We don't know," Lila said.

"We do what we can," Sami said as he patted Lila's hand.

Seeing that Lila's frown had changed to tears, Nadra said, "At least she has Sitto."

❧

Lila had Eva in 1923, a year after their arrival in Hedley. Sami bought a rocking baby cradle.

One evening when Nadra was stringing beans for supper while simultaneously rocking Eva's cradle with her foot, she overheard Sami teaching Lila. After Sami left and she and Lila put Tina and Eva to sleep, Nadra said, "Why do you have the privilege of being taught, Mama?"

"So I can do more of his work."

"I would gladly do that work, Mama," she replied.

"You would gladly shut your mouth."

❧

Lila had her first son in 1925. She insisted they name him Theodore, gift of God. They called him Teddy. Teddy would be followed by Millie.

Eventually it became Nadra's job to open the store in the early morning. Sami promised to relieve her so she could go to school.

He never came down in time. She pleaded with him, so they set up a system. When it was time for her to leave for school, she would climb on a chair and knock on the ceiling with a broom handle. Hearing her knock, he was supposed to come down immediately. He never did. Mornings, Nadra's world was the confectionery, afternoons it was the apartment. She was assigned storekeeping, housekeeping, and more childcare.

Such were Nadra's first four years in the New World.

The Suitor

1926

This was the year Nadra Zahir, a turn-your-head beauty, turned sixteen. Slim and tall, but not as tall as Lila, with full breasts and a cream complexion. Her black hair was thick and curly, the topaz glint in her brown eyes dazzling when it wasn't overshadowed by melancholy. She had a sweet smile, but tethered to an aching heart, she seldom smiled. Locked in a cage, her spirit pined for release, for the freedom to live a life of her own, to fly away, to soar. She expected little from Lila, who took for granted her good behavior and willingness to work, yet Sami's stories gave her hope, hope for a new and happy life in America.

This was also the year John Hanoun could begin his eager pursuit of Nadra Zahir.

When John came to Hedley he stayed with his friend Michael Mensore. John, Michael, and his brothers Joseph and Charles were in the living room of a small house in a modest neighborhood. A coffee table in the center of the room was flanked by a long sofa and two armchairs.

Michael brought out a bottle of *arak*, a pitcher of water, a carafe, and an ice bucket.

Joseph, a swarthy man with jet eyebrows and a growl for a voice, sprawled across the sofa staring at John. He straightened up when Jeannine, Michael's wife, entered with a plate of meze. "*Shukran* (Thank you)," he said politely. As she left, Michael looked at the men and pointed to the appetizers saying, "Please."

"It hasn't been the same since you three left Lowell. I've been worried that the mills will close completely," John said as he helped himself.

As he popped olives in his mouth, Charles, the smaller light-skinned brother who always seemed amused, said, "So this was news to you? You didn't know why we were leaving?"

"I wanted to wait," John replied.

"No reason to wait now, the little beauty has grown up," Joseph said as he grabbed some cheese.

Michael was carefully pouring arak from a bottle into a carafe. He followed that with twice as much water, then poured the cloudy liquid over ice. He gave each man a glass.

"Do you see her?" John asked.

"Once in a while. She works the store," Michael said.

Lowering his dark eyes over a large pickle, Joseph said, "Hope you didn't spend all your time just saving your money. Those girls in the mill were taken with you."

"He's smarter than that," Charles said.

"I don't think so," Joseph growled.

"How do you know?" Michael asked.

"He was always frowning," Joseph said.

Laughing, Charles said, "Leave him alone, Joseph." Patting John on the back he continued, "If she won't have you, we will adopt you."

Michael raised his glass to John and drawled, "To-mor-row John makes his pil-gri-mage to the Za-hirs!"

Every day John meandered to the Zahirs' confectionery. The good-looking and respectful suitor never failed to elicit an enthusiastic invitation to dinner from Sami and Lila. Soon after those visits, however, Nadra made it clear to her parents that she wasn't interested in older men.

Incredulous, Sami said, "He's a young man, a handsome young man."

"He's at least, at least, twice my age!"

"I don't think so, eyunnee, I don't think so."

So Sami asked his age and John said he was twenty-nine. Everyone knew he was lying, but no one was going to be impolite and say it. Nadra realized that Lila and Sami didn't care anyway. But she cared.

With a smile, John said, "I know that to someone so young, and beautiful, twenty-nine seems old."

Nadra tried not to look into his warm brown eyes smiling at her, tried to ignore his tall slim physique, and tried to tamp down her ever-growing, irresistible interest in sex.

John was invited for the holidays. On Easter Sunday, he brought gifts for everyone. A pan of *baklawa* for Sami and Lila, Raggedy Ann dolls for Tina and Eva, and a teddy bear for baby Teddy. John was proud and amused to bring a teddy bear for Teddy. For Nadra he brought heavy gold serpentine bracelets, enshrined in a crimson velvet case. Sami examined them closely, and determining that they were fourteen carats, meticulously wrought, nodded his approval. The little sisters begged to try them on.

Whenever John arrived from Lowell, the Zahirs came to attention, pleased to greet him, delighted to share their table with him, keen to offer up Nadra to him. Lila even cooked. Nadra's little sisters adored him and ran to greet him. Little Teddy raised his arms in anticipation of being picked up for a ride in John's strong arms. John was forever smiling, cordial, and solicitous. He was so eager to have Nadra, so eager to marry.

Nadra had to be polite to John. How could she be otherwise? But in spite of her good manners, John picked up on her refusal to look him in the eye and her strained responses. He asked Sami and Lila if something was wrong. Sami laughed at him and in a booming voice turned his question against him. "What could possibly be wrong!"

Speaking softly, Lila said, "John, can't you see? She's young, shy, and a little nervous. She's never been away from us."

"I didn't say I wanted to take her away."

"Wonderful! I may have a deal for you," said Sami. "You can make a good living here. Look at your friends the Mensores."

"But does she want me?"

"What's not to want, John?"

Nadra decided she would try to make John not want her. She stopped combing her hair and only put on her worn clothes, not that she had any pretty new ones. That didn't seem to help so she doubled her efforts to ignore him. Short of being rude, she paid him little attention when he visited. She barely glanced at the gifts he brought her. She tended to her little sisters and brother; spent time in the kitchen, putting away the leftovers, washing the dishes.

Giving up the possibility of an education, let alone her ambition to be a nurse, Nadra even declared that she wanted to be a nun. Lila and Sami found that amusing. So she decided to plead, to beg.

Lila had three little children to care for now—Tina six, Eva four, and Teddy two—and no doubt was soon to be pregnant again. Yes, Nadra would appeal to her mother, not directly of course, but indirectly, letting her know that she would happily continue to lighten her burden. Hadn't she already been more of a mother to Tina and Eva than Lila? With her continued help, Lila would have more time for Teddy, her gift from God. That was it, she would make an impassioned appeal to Lila, sell herself as her mother's slave. Permanent slavery, better than marriage.

Or perhaps she should talk to her father? He possessed what Lila lacked, a tender heart, softness, a desire to please. Hadn't he referred to her as eyunnee, and to her and her sisters as his pretty girls, caressing and kissing them often? She decided. She would put her hope, her rescue, in her father's kind hands.

Nadra put the little ones to bed and Lila was out, so Nadra was fortunate to catch her father alone. He was in the drafty living room, in his reclining Morris chair, a muffler draped over his chest. He was reading the current newspaper from the pile on the table next to him. As always, he smiled when he saw her. He pressed the push button to bring his upholstered chair upright. She removed the pile of newspapers and in their place put tea and his favorite, *kaik*—cookies stuffed with dates and walnuts. She sat close by, ready to bring him more hot tea. When he was satiated and relaxed, she looked directly at him and spoke softly. "Baba?" He looked at her inquisitively.

"Baba, please, I don't want to get married."

"Eyunnee, you don't have to be afraid. John is a good man."

"I'm not afraid. I want to go to school, Baba. I want to learn, I want to be smart, I want to be like you."

"You're just a young girl. You are meant to raise a family."

"I want to go to school first. You know I work hard. I have a good mind."

Smiling, he said, "You are like me."

"I want to be part of this new world. I want a place in it."

"You don't know how lucky you are, Nadra. John is a handsome generous man. He's saved a few dollars. And those bracelets he had made for you, they're easily worth…"

"I don't care."

"You should care."

"I don't want a man now."

"How can you not want such a man?"

"I have other dreams." Fighting the tears welling in her eyes, she added, "Baba I'm just not ready to marry. Please. I'm too young."

As she saw his look of surprise change to sympathy, waves of hope crested in her heart. He beckoned her to him and caressed her tenderly, murmuring, "Eyunnee." He said he would consider her petition.

Nadra had no more than said, "Thank you, Baba," when they heard Lila entering the apartment, calling, "Sami? Sami!" She entered the living room, removing her scarf and coat. Lila surveyed the scene curiously, like a feral animal unsure of its prey. The waves of hope plunged to despair as Nadra watched Lila's eyebrows contract and the corners of her mouth dip into a scowl. As the brown eyes darkened, Nadra realized that she had made the wrong choice.

"Nadra says she is not ready to marry."

Lila's eyes slowly traversed an imaginary path from father to daughter before she announced, "You are a young woman now. You will marry."

Her face flushing with anger and her voice rising with resentment, Nadra shouted, "I will not!"

Calmly eying her, Lila asked, "Where will you go?"

Nadra's eyes widened as she struggled to comprehend the question. "Where will I go?"

"Yes. Where will you go?"

Stunned by the question, Nadra looked at her father for support. He avoided her gaze as he left the room.

Without looking at Nadra again, Lila picked up the teacup and plate of cookies and followed Sami. Nadra was alone on a glass path, having fallen on the broken shards. She would feel the cuts forever and remember the lesson. She had based her trust—and hope—on someone else.

The next day Lila talked to John privately, saying sotto voce, "It's time to take Nadra away from this house." Together they set a date for a summer wedding.

In despair Nadra retreated to her room. She stayed there. It was the only way she could contain her disappointment and rage. *I've been betrayed*, she thought. *They brought me to America to wait on them, to work for them, to clean up after them! I care for the children, I run the store! And now they give me to a man I don't want.*

She had no one to turn to. No one to talk to. Neither Sami nor Lila came to her. Little sisters Tina and Eva, however, tried to open the door to talk to her until Lila caught them. Finally they eluded Lila, sneaked in, and threw themselves on Nadra, crying. Rocking them she brushed away their tears, all the while holding back her own.

≪

Capitalizing on John's promise not to move Nadra from Hedley, and also knowing that millwork was steadily declining in Lowell, Sami proposed a deal to John. He suggested that John give up being a laborer and start his own business, one similar to his own. If, for example, he should be interested in starting an ice-cream parlor or a confectionery, he, Sami, just happened to have the equipment and fixtures that John would need—for a fair price of course. John need only find the place or, better yet, John could take over Sami's present location. After all, he added, it was already home for Nadra. Sami would rent another building, farther down on Route 50.

"Thank you, Sami. I will think about it, maybe talk to—"

"Think about it? I thought you were keen to have her?"

"I thought we were talking about fixtures, Sami."

Laughing lasciviously, Sami replied, "Of course."

John rushed back to Lowell, ready to hire the jeweler again. In keeping with American tradition, he commissioned a diamond ring. In keeping with Syrian tradition, he commissioned an engagement belt—several inches of black velvet holding French gold coins decorated with tiny filigreed fans and a detailed ornate closure.

It was not long before John was back in Hedley with his precious gifts. When he presented them, Lila hooked the engagement belt around Nadra's tiny waist. The little sisters laughed; Sami smiled; Nadra felt that she was being roped. Lila gave Nadra a nudge and a look. Nadra's lips said thank you to her fiancé, John, while her heart cursed her mother, Lila.

Lila was busy and pregnant again, so the matron of honor, whom Nadra barely knew, took on the task of helping her buy some new clothes and choose a dress for her wedding. Her matron of honor was the wife of John's best friend, Michael Mensore. Unlike Michael, Jeannine was not an immigrant. A savvy Syrian-American with a good education, Jeannine Mensore was a take-charge business woman. Well dressed, gracious and smiling, she picked up Nadra in her Chrysler Imperial and headed for downtown.

Jeannine did not know the circumstances of the betrothal, but she saw the young bride's sadness. She tried to lighten the mood, adding several dollars of her own money to the meager allotment Lila had given her for the clothes. They chose a fashionable wedding ensemble: a calf-length dress of cream silk. Below the round neckline fine pleats ended in a dropped waist encircled with delicate embroidery. Over the dress a long-sleeve matching coat. The wedding veil flowed from a silk-flower cap. Sheer nylons and white Mary Jane shoes. Looking in the mirror, Nadra smiled in spite of herself.

To celebrate the end of their successful shopping, Jeannine took her to a new café, a first experience for Nadra. As they finished their meal with coffee and cake, Jeannine asked, "Nadra, has your mother talked to you?" Nadra found the question confusing. Lila seldom talked to her. Noting her quizzical expression, Jeannine clarified, "About the wedding night, about being married."

"Only that I am to let him do what he wants."

After a moment's hesitation, Jeannine said, "Nadra, you will like what he wants to do."

Nadra's reaction was bitter surprise.

Smiling, Jeannine added, "John is a good man and he's kind."

Nadra did not respond, so Jeannine added, "And he's devoted to his mother. A man who is good to his mother will be good to his wife."

"*Inshallah*, Jeannine."

"You know, of course, that Mary, John's mother, will be living with you."

"No, I did not know that."

Hesitating but still smiling, Jeannine patted Nadra's hand and said, "Well, you will have two mothers in Hedley. Mary can't get here in time for the wedding. She has to pack everything and you can imagine how much there is. She and John were in Lowell for years, and of course there are other matters to settle, and friends to say goodbye to. She will be here when you return from your honeymoon."

"Is there anything else I don't know?"

"Nobody refers to her by her first name. She prefers to be called *Um-Hana*."

"Mother of John."

Discoveries

Nadra didn't know anything about men, had never been alone with a man, had never kissed a man or touched or been touched. Other than Lila's nightly demands that Sami leave her alone, the only talk about men and sex that she had been privy to were the random comments, conjectures, and gossip of her two older sisters Feheema and Nesrin. John had yet to touch her, though Lila and Sami didn't hesitate to leave them alone. Those occasions were awkward. Even though John was all smiles, as usual, and brought a gift, Nadra was silent. Tina and Eva liked to sneak around and peek at them, until Lila caught them and shoved them back into the kitchen. On one such visit, John told Nadra that he was taking her to Boston for their honeymoon.

That news made her feel better. Obviously John remembered her comments about loving Boston. Perhaps Jeannine's description of him was true.

Still, Nadra was depressed and afraid. She began talking to herself. *Can living with John possibly be worse than living with Sami and Lila? Especially now when I'm filled with hate? They robbed me. They knew what I wanted, what I needed, and they didn't care. They robbed me of my hopes and dreams and gave me away to a man I don't want. A life I don't want!*

But I can't hate John. After all he didn't do anything. Yes, better John than Lila and Sami!

On the day of the wedding, Tina and Eva sat on Nadra's bed to watch her dress. Eva could not resist fingering the cream silk of the wedding dress and Tina took on the role of helper by holding each garment up so Nadra could put it on without wrinkling it. When Nadra placed the silk-flower cap on her head, both sisters cried, "Wait until John sees you!"

Pregnant Lila broke the spell when she waddled into the room, grimacing from the exertion of carrying yet another child.

"Isn't she beautiful, Mama?"

Surveying her daughter, Lila said, "Put on the gold bracelets."

"You mean the handcuffs?" Nadra said.

"Stupid girl, those bracelets are your bank account!"

Taken aback, Nadra didn't respond.

"You come with me," Lila said as she held out her hands to the little girls. As they left the bedroom, Lila said, "You are supposed to smile, Nadra."

Sami hired a black limousine and a driver from the neighborhood funeral parlor to take them to St. Peter's Church, an imposing Romanesque revival structure, in the heart of downtown. Upon entering, Nadra dipped her right hand into the marble holy water font and made the sign of the cross. She spied Jeannine, John, and his best man, Michael, in the vestibule. The men wore smart suits with notched lapel jackets and flat front trousers. Their high-padded shoulders gave them a well-set look. Spotting her, Michael nudged John who turned to look at her. Seeing the exchange, Sami said to Nadra, "See how eager he is, eyunnee." Jeannine said something to

John and Michael that made them retire to the side of the church. Then she came to Nadra. She held the bride's hand and smiled.

Saint Peter's Church, open and vast, filled Nadra with wonder. Huge murals in the center portrayed the hallmarks of Peter's life as apostle, denier of Jesus, and as first Pope. A mural on the right showed Peter, James, and John witnessing the Transfiguration of Jesus.

It was the mural on the left of the Coronation of Mary that held Nadra's attention, reminding her of the Icon of Our Lady of Saidnaya. The small dark room in Saidnaya lighted by candles and numerous oil lanterns.

As she did many times when she climbed to that shrine, she said a Hail Mary. In Saidnaya the humble Virgin held the Child on her lap. Here Mary stood crowned Queen of Heaven. Perhaps this great church, this triumphant Mary, was promising a richer, fuller life.

Jeannine let go of Nadra's hand and nodded toward the ornate white Gothic altar in the middle of the sanctuary. Nadra was able to say a second Hail Mary before Sami extended his arm in preparation for the giveaway to John.

At the small reception, Nadra tried to be happy, tried to smile while John brimmed with pride, loving the gorgeous black hair that framed his bride's oval face. Loving her luminous eyes and long lashes. Interrupting his reverie, his friends clapped him on the back and congratulated him. Jeannine hovered by Nadra, steadying her and smiling.

Nadra wasn't sure whether to feel relief or dread when they finally left for their honeymoon. She felt like a little girl leaving home for the first time. John held her hand whenever he could and sometimes even raised it to his lips.

Aware of her virginity and apprehension, he moved slowly. Their first night he folded her into his arms, kissed her forehead and her eyes, and whispered that he would wait until she was ready. He lay next to her, his arm around her waist, his breath warming her neck. For the first time in a long time she felt loved, protected, and wanted.

The next day they visited Boston Common. John explained that it was the oldest public park in America and delighted in showing her Fenway Park and Harvard Square. Once again Nadra was overwhelmed by the variety of shops, cafes, museums, students, and street performers. When she saw the dog wagons, she stopped, hoping John would take the hint and buy her a hot dog in a warm bun. She was too shy to ask. He immediately assumed she was hungry, and taking her hand, he turned her in the other direction. "No, no, we will go someplace nice." She was disappointed, but she enjoyed a cup of clam chowder and shared his fried fish sandwich.

When they went to Newbury Street he insisted on buying her a gift. She chose something small, an embroidered French handkerchief, and was embarrassed to hear the high price. John ignored her concern and offered to carry it in his jacket pocket. From there they boarded the ferry for the Boston Harbor Islands. On the way back to the hotel they stopped in an Italian bakery and bought cannoli.

In their room he laughed at the greedy way she was wolfing down the cannoli. He offered her the French handkerchief, but instead of using it, she held it to her heart. So he bent down to lick the traces of cream from her lips. When she held his face in her hands and looked into his eyes, he kissed her, first tenderly then passionately. As he slowly undressed her, he caressed every inch of her, in between licking, kissing, and sucking her breasts. When her longing reached the intensity of his, he took her, gently, careful to avoid the pain he feared she might be feeling. But passion thrust against pain as they moved slowly together in shared need and ecstasy.

∾

To Nadra and most people, John seemed quiet and reserved. But once comfortable and relaxed with each other, she discovered otherwise. It was like someone finally uncorked a bottle of shaken seltzer. He wanted to tell her about his coming to America. When she asked how old he was at the time, he was quick enough to do the math correctly, adding, "I didn't lie to you about my age."

"Of course you didn't," she said with a smile.

Returning her smile, John told his story. Unlike Sami, he was shy—a man unused to being the center of anyone's attention. He was like a gentle father telling a story to a beloved child, leaving the narrative only long enough to check her attention.

John and his parents came to the New World for several reasons. His father, Boutros, was a camel driver in a caravan operating between Damascus and Aleppo by way of Homs, Hama, and their neighboring desert villages. He hoped for a better station and a better living. The two oldest sons remained in Saidnaya while John, the youngest, came mainly for work and to escape conscription under the Turks.

"Years my father and I worked for the money to come over. But there was never enough for a cabin so we came steerage." John bowed his head, shuddering at the memory. "Bad food, sickness, fear. Sixteen days we slept smashed against each other in small bunks. When we finally reached Boston, they herded us together like animals, to look at our papers and to examine us. My mother walking between me and my father, we followed the crowd, holding on to each other, holding on to our papers. Relief and joy pounding our hearts! But that didn't last!"

"What happened, John?" Nadra said as she took his hand.

"They wouldn't let my father in! They said he had the eye disease."

"Trachoma?" Nadra said.

John nodded. "Our sponsors, the Mensore brothers, tried to help, but it was no good. They made him go back. I still see his eyes, the disbelief, the disappointment."

"Your mother stayed."

"The Mensores took us to Lowell."

It was obvious to Nadra that there were parts of the history that John wanted to leave out. Whether Mary left Boutros standing on the dock in Boston or waiting at the house in Saidnaya, her parting kiss was evidently the last one he received. But Nadra was determined to learn the rest of the story. If she had to be tied to John for the rest of her life, she would learn all she could.

"The Mensores got me my first job in the wool mill where they worked. And you know what those son-ma-guns did?"

"Tell me."

John loved her twinkling amused eyes. "Before I learned English they taught me to say, 'Good morning son-of-a-bitch' to the foreman."

Nadra laughed.

"For a long time my nickname was son-of-a-bitch."

"I hope you didn't tell your mother." Regretting her comment, she quickly added, "So this was your first job?"

"Fifty-four hours a week. Long, hard, and hot, but each week cash in a small brown envelope."

Laughing, John told Nadra he felt like a child, fingering the money lovingly, counting it over and over, totally taken with the new experience of having money—money to buy food and clothes and pay rent, money to give to his mother, money to enjoy a night out, money to treat friends. Money to send to his father and to his two older brothers.

Nadra wondered if he was still sending money to the old country.

When John bought the confectionery business from Sami, they agreed that while he and Nadra were away Sami would remove his personal items from the confectionery and the family would vacate the second floor. When they arrived back in Hedley, John went immediately to inspect the confectionery. Sami had left behind some, but not all the equipment and fixtures they had agreed on. Most of the expensive equipment was missing.

Nadra went upstairs to the apartment, climbing the twenty-one steps to the landing and tiny porch. She opened the wood and glass door into the long narrow hallway, to the place where she had lived as a teenager.

Blessed Mother, let my days here as a married woman be shorter and happier.

Walking down the long hallway, she went from the kitchen to the bedrooms. Sami and Lila left behind a table and three chairs, Nadra's twin bed, and their old double bed. She noticed that they had not cleaned up after themselves, but what had she expected.

She picked up some of the litter on the floor and made a mental note to see if they left the broom.

When Nadra entered the living room she found Um-Hana, her mother-in-law, standing like a lighthouse. No warning light glowed from her head, but she stood tall, solid, and powerful. Nadra wondered which of them should say welcome. Neither spoke. When John entered the room, however, both put on the good face. Um-Hana kissed him. Turning to Nadra, beaming, she pointed to the long wall where two huge tapestries hung, depicting leering camels and sanguine Arabs. "This is your wedding present."

John walked from room to room just as Nadra had, taking note of everything but saying nothing. Nadra followed him and finally asked him what was wrong. Obviously he did not want to tell her, but finally he blurted, "Sami left us this damn furniture instead of the equipment. He was sure we would need the furniture more."

"Give the furniture back to him."

"What?"

"Give the furniture back to him!"

"Where will we sleep?"

"In a hotel, on the floor! What's the difference where we sleep?"

"I'm not going to start a war, Nadra."

"Why not? He owes you. He owes us!" she said. But what she was thinking was, *Lila and Sami didn't rob me. They sold me!*

Gliding into the room, looking alarmed, Um-Hana asked, "What's the matter, Son?"

"Nothing is the matter, *Umee*."

Turning on his heel, he left, saying, "Time to get this place cleaned up, Nadra."

Nadra wanted to drag him back, to tell him to clean it up himself and that she would deal with Sami! Instead she turned to face another tall frowning woman, her second mother.

That night a phonograph kept playing in Nadra's head. One voice growled, "Leave me alone." The other insisted, "A man who is good to his mother will be good to his wife."

Nadra beat down her emotions. She reflected, evaluated, and planned. This new life could be workable. She would make it workable. Once she cleaned the apartment, she took an inventory of their wedding gifts and the things Um-Hana brought with her. Um-Hana brought very little. She explained that she sold much of what she and John had in Lowell so she could buy the two leering camel tapestries. Nadra was already directing her eyes to the short walls, to avoid looking at them.

Having determined what they required to set up their home, Nadra told John that she needed some money. Annoyed by his slight hesitation, she asked, "Don't you want me to make a home for your mother?"

Embarrassed, he gave her the money but as she took it, he stayed her hand. "I want you to make a home *for us*."

"The same difference, my love."

"Are you mocking me?"

Fearing that a sharp tongue might ruin her plans, she smiled and spoke softly, "No, John, I'm just eager to finish the upstairs so I can help you set up our store."

"I don't expect you to work in the store."

"What do you think I've been doing for the last four years?"

Enemies and Allies

John and Nadra's store was a grocery and confectionery. Having the experience of such an enterprise, Nadra knew what should be avoided, what could be improved upon, and what should be new. She encouraged John to dip into more of his savings, not only to replace what Sami had taken, but also to buy new tables and chairs and showcases. Buoyed by her help and enthusiasm, John was ready to follow all recommendations until Um-Hana's brother, his "'incle," as John referred to him, became a regular visitor.

Ike Hanoun was a tall, boney bachelor with a huge nose that occupied the greater part of his face. The only thing that could match the grandeur of his attitude was his nose. His ringleted hair was black and his eyebrows bushy. He affected an expression of disdain as his brown eyes scanned the environment. He always wore a suit and over that a raincoat. He was educated and came to be one of the Syrian community's scribes. If a letter was to be sent to the old country, he was often the one who wrote it. If a letter came from the old country, he read it—in an officious nasal tone. Considering his education and stature, he felt veneration was his due. John obliged but Nadra was not so inclined. She hated to admit it, but she felt her father had as much if not more knowledge and certainly much more charm. In respect to his place in the family, John's Uncle Ike was called 'Am-moo Ike.

Nadra considered Um-Hana the permanent enemy occupier, but she hadn't had warning about 'Am-moo Ike. He would appear out of nowhere, as if camouflaged by the raincoat he always wore. In their confectionery he would slither around the construction mess, discarded items, and new purchases. Nadra came to regard him as a sniper, searching for his target, ready, and armed. Finally he took aim at the price tags on the handsome wood cases. Astonished, concerned, and irate, he fired, screaming at John, agitating him.

"You want to pay such a high price, John? Are you crazy? You want to go to the poor house?"

When John began his reply with a timid, "But 'Am-moo—"

Nadra cut him off with, "Yes, it will be very expensive, 'Am-moo. Perhaps you could help us."

"Help you?" he said.

"With some money," Nadra said.

"Nadra, we don't ask our family, or anybody, for money!" John said.

"John, 'Am-moo understands. He knows what it is like for people like us and he would like to help us."

John's annoyance was becoming outrage.

Nadra said, "We are all family and family always helps."

Incredulous, 'Am-moo screamed, "Help?"

"You understand, don't you, 'Am-moo?" she said.

"I have no money!" 'Am-moo shrieked as he headed for the door.

Angry, John yelled at Nadra. "Do you know what you just did, what you just said?"

Ignoring his concern and fury, Nadra said, "Of course" as she climbed a ladder to put decorative items on the shelf over the bar. Lining up the last items of the display, she asked, "How does it look, habibee?"

∽

Their first summer John hauled baskets and bins of fruit to the outside—grapes, peaches, melons, apricots. The store had two entrances with two large windows in between. In one window Nadra used a variety of jars, dishes, and decorative paper to display exotic dried fruits and nuts—pistachios, chickpeas, *halvah*, amariddine.

"The Syrians will love this stuff," John said as he popped Jordan almonds into his mouth.

"There will be nothing left to love," Nadra said as she pushed his hands away.

She moved to the other window and opened several cartons of American candy and used lists to verify their contents.

"How did you learn to read?" John said.

"This will be paradise for children," she said as she arranged Necco wafers, Boston Baked Beans, Mary Jane peanut-butter chews, Baby Ruth, Bit-O-Honey, and other kinds of American candy in the window.

"Did Sami teach you?"

To imitate Sami's mustachio, Nadra stuck a length of black licorice crossways in her mouth, inflated her chest, and mocked Sami's teaching stance and tone. "I used *Al-Bakoorat Al-Gharbeyat, Fee*

Taleem Al-Lughat Al-Engelezat." She added a little mincing step as she intoned, "*The First Occidental Fruit for the Teaching of the English (and Arabic Languages).*"

"You're too young to know so much, Nadra."

"I can't really read and write. He taught Mama! When I could I listened and watched. I did most of the work, so I got to know the American wholesale people. I can recognize the important words and I know how to make check marks."

She picked up a pencil and an order sheet to begin checking off items. "In February, John, we will buy candy valentines for the young Amerikan." Moving close to him, she playfully imitated the candy names as she said them: "'Kiss Me.' 'Will You.' 'Be Mine.'" John tried to grab her but she pushed him away as she said, "and 'Buzz Off'!"

He adored her and she knew it.

The couple realized that during Prohibition (1920-1933) their enterprise was the next best thing to a bar. At the left entrance they built a beautiful wood soda bar that ran all the way down the huge room. The bar was flanked by wire stools. The soda fountain had three chromium-plated brass spigots with black Bakelite handles. The center one dispensed tap water, the other two spritzed cold seltzer. John made a show of mixing the syrups with seltzer in tall glasses to make fruit drinks for the children. He mixed Coca-Cola Company syrup and seltzer for their parents. The Hanouns enjoyed watching their patrons' delighted expressions when they served them.

Behind the bar were glass shelves holding tall glasses for malts and milkshakes, footed glasses for ice-cream sodas, steins for root beer, and dishes for sundaes. Putting effort into making the displays as appealing as possible, Nadra spent time arranging bottles of syrup, cans of malt and cocoa, jars of nuts and maraschino cherries.

In the back were oak ice-cream tables on pedestals of wrought iron with matching chairs. Center spaced among them were two handsome wood cases with glass fronts. In them the Hanouns showed off their handmade confections: fudge, peanut brittle, nougats—all of which they made on a long marble table. John couldn't read the recipes but Nadra could a little. If she was uncertain or confused she would match the words in the recipe with the words on the labels of ingredients. She even mastered the glass cinnamon squares that were delightful to look at and delicious to eat.

For Fridays they initiated a grab bag for a nickel that lured the after-school children. When business started to lag, Nadra would make the peanut brittle before the front window; she drew a curious crowd of customers. She was proud of their work, proud of their successful store. They called it their happy business.

John's pride and pleasure in their success manifested itself on the day he excused himself early to go out with his friend Michael Mensore. Loud honking heralded their return. When she ran out to investigate, John was sitting behind the wheel of a new sedan with sweeping body lines, a spacious interior, and full balloon tires. Michael jumped out and announced, "It's a REO Flying Cloud, Nadra!"

"It's beautiful, Michael."

"Actually, it's like any other sedan, Nadra. The name's the charm! It's named after a clipper ship that set the world sailing record for the fastest passage between New York and San Francisco."

"Is it yours?"

"It's ours!" John shouted.

"You didn't tell me you were going to buy a car."

"Where would Mrs. Hanoun like to go?" John asked.

Astonished, she said, "I didn't even know you could drive, John."

Laughing, Michael said, "He can, barely." Michael helped her into the car as he said, "I'll watch the store."

"Mr. Hanoun, I would like to go everywhere," she said.

John laughed, adding, "Much as I'd like to, we can't chain Michael to our store." After a spin to the City Park, they returned to the store. Michael joined John and they headed for downtown. She was too happy for him, for them, to be miffed at being abandoned in the store. Their life was going so well. They were happy together. They had a good business; now they even owned a car. But he damn well could have said something about it first.

Nadra loved working in the store. It was her store now. And John's store. She poured her energy and ambition into candy making and marketing. And she got away from Um-Hana. She did realize, of course, that she did most of the dirty work. She wore a hairnet to catch the wisps of hair that meandered along her sweating brow, and a long white apron to catch the chocolate and food color stains. John wore a long sleeved white shirt with a tie and played the role of proprietor and cheerful greeter.

Even though she worked long hours in the confectionery, Nadra no longer felt anxious and deprived. She was no longer dependent and trapped. No longer the slave of the Zahir household. She was also now a married woman.

Yet at times she still felt like a young girl, a young girl still needing to be mothered. A young girl jealous of those schoolgirls who came to watch her making candy. A young girl having lost the friendship of sisters and others her age who giggled, compared clothes, and made comments about boys. She was grown up, and she hadn't had any fun. The other Syrian women eyed the youngster curiously, noted her incredible industry and mettle, then heard the beating of her heavy heart.

John was the first to spot the procession: three women and five children, walking single file. They were across the street. Coming toward him. The toddlers held hands, walked slowly next to their mother, and stopped obediently at the curb. The two bigger boys trailed behind, kicking and poking each other. The women told them when it was okay to cross the street.

The leader and the oldest was Dowla, a small pretty woman, her slightly graying hair in a bun, kohl rimming her eyes. Her delicate skin glowed, seeping kindness and goodwill. She greeted John and voiced her good wishes. She held out her arms to Nadra. "Hello, sweetheart." Delighted, Dowla greeted everyone with a smile and an embrace, as though they were an unexpected gift.

John began lavishing candy on the children immediately. Shanti, tall and formidable, glowered at her knee-scraped boys who were already stuffing their mouths with chocolate. Then she pinned John with her piercing green eyes and demanded to know, "When does

Nadra get a little time off?" Uninterested in his answer, she untied Nadra's apron and pointed to the door.

Sonya, plump and pleasant, carrying a baby and followed by two toddlers, smiled at John, saying, "Don't worry. We'll give her back."

They took Nadra home with them. There they treated her to Arab coffee, pastries, gossip, and bawdy stories about too-old men marrying young girls.

When Nadra returned home she was happy and still giggling over the outrageous stories. John and Um-Hana waited up for her, but Um-Hana, disapproval etched on her stone face, went to bed the moment Nadra arrived. John and Nadra sat together, talking quietly, his hand now on her knee. Smiling, he never took his eyes off her. She knew he wanted to take advantage of her happy mood. Holding her hand, he switched off the living room lights and led her to their bedroom. Nadra was wary of Um-Hana, sure that she heard everything. She pictured the old lady sitting in her room across the hall, her ear pressed against the wall. John assured his wife that the old lady was snoring. Exaggerating his movements to tease Nadra, he stalked her, creeping stealthily along the bed like a cat ready to pounce on its prey. Noticing that her tom cat was eminently capable of mating, she laughed and thrust her hips upward, ready to match her ardor with his. She had drunk enough coffee to keep her awake for a week.

The next morning the noise Um-Hana was making in the kitchen woke them. To Nadra's surprise, Um-Hana had already put on the coffee and was chopping green onions and parsley. Um-Hana ignored Nadra's greeting as she bustled between stove and refrigerator.

Yes, Nadra thought, *she did hear us.*

Um-Hana poured a little olive oil into the skillet, waited until it got hot and added the onion and parsley. As the ingredients sautéed, she cracked three eggs into a bowl. John entered—handsome, contented, a ready smile with an afterglow. Um-Hana's pinched expression blossomed into a smile.

No, Nadra thought, *she didn't have to hear us.*

Um-Hana gave John a cup of coffee. She beat the eggs and poured them over the vegetables. Once the omelet was set, she slid it onto a plate which she placed in front of him. Beaming, she announced, "*Ijee!*"

Digging in with gusto, John said, "Thank you."

"Maybe Nadra doesn't have time to make what you like."

Nadra thought, *I hope he chokes*, and started to laugh for thinking such a thing. As they stared at her, she poured herself a cup of coffee and settled in to watch the show.

I wonder how long she's going to live.

Nadra relished their business success. Reaping the rewards of her ideas and work suited her. Sometimes she even wanted to spend some of their money. Encouraged by her new friends, especially the flamboyant, free-spending Shanti, Nadra would go downtown to shop. She'd look for something pretty for herself, something to please John, something to swell Um-Hana's jealousy. Usually she returned with just an item for the apartment.

John liked being a businessman. He considered himself lucky to have found work in Lowell's woolen mills and to have been able to save money for his own business. Many Syrians who came to West Virginia before him found work in the factories, such as the glass plants—Blenko, Fostoria, and Fenton. Other immigrants migrated south and west to start new lives as pack peddlers, bringing goods to areas with sparse population and few stores. They sold "needles and notions," souvenirs of the Holy Land, laces, embroidered linens, silk goods, and even the recently invented perforated toilet paper. John was happy to escape that fate. That work was too much like his father's work in the Syrian caravans.

Once the Saidnayans accumulated enough money as peddlers or laborers, they would often open a store or buy property. Andy Rahbone bought a small hotel that he was renovating. Simon Metrey opened a grocery store in the south end. Once Charles Mensore saved enough money from working double shifts in the glass factory, he began buying property. His brother Joseph Mensore had a small scrap yard.

The Syrian Americans, the first generation, were ahead of the immigrants. The well-established Jabirs were wholesale grocers by day and gamblers at night. Their sister, Jeannine Jabir, married to Michael Mensore, John's best friend, managed the grocery business. The Syrian women liked to say that Jeannine knew how to sell but not how to cook. By the time Michael married Jeannine he had invested his money in a used car lot. All were family men.

The only other bachelor in the group, other than John's Uncle, 'Am-moo Ike, was Farid Ferris, a handsome amiable bachelor who opened a restaurant in hopes of satisfying hungry Syrians and curious Amerikan. He called it The Oasis.

John and Nadra rented their store and apartment. Nadra was looking forward to the day when they could buy property, particularly a house, a real home where they could raise a family.

A year into her marriage Nadra was pregnant with their first child. That same year her mother, Lila, was pregnant with her last child. Nadra felt conspicuous being pregnant the same time as her mother. But at least now she would have her own baby to care for instead of Lila's, and a happy burden it would be. When Nadra started showing, Sami embraced her saying, "Look at my pretty girl now. Good job, John, good job!" As she pushed away from her father's arms, John saw anger in her eyes. He took her hand and led her away.

Nadra was happy to ignore her parents and be ignored by them, but her affection for her little sisters and brother never waned. Tina and Eva would come to the confectionery often, one holding Teddy's hand, the other carrying baby Millie. They loved to watch Nadra make candy. They also loved John, who continued to be generous to them. They could hardly wait for the Hanoun baby to be born.

Nadra's first son was born in 1928 and was christened George. Lila's last son was born the same year and christened Wasim. The two boys would become best friends.

1929

Nadra and John Hanoun saw the reality of the Great Depression each day. The fathers who used to direct their children through the candy displays no longer had jobs. The couples who used to sit at the counter to order sodas or sundaes stopped coming. The mothers who bought treats for parties would survey the store windows and move on.

As the land of opportunity became increasingly the land of desperation, the Hanouns did all they could to bring in the customers. They understood each man, woman, and child's lust for a little sweetness. They used to highlight their handmade candies. Now they tried to attract the worker who managed to earn an extra dollar and was willing to spend the change on penny candy for his children. They displayed the candies showing what five cents would buy, ten cents, fifteen cents, or twenty. The first Mounds bar was a single bar for a nickel. When Mounds made it two bars without increasing the price, Nadra had her friend Shanti make a sign reading: "Mounds! Now 2 bars for each couple!"

Nadra knew that Heath promoted their candy as a health item and sold the one-ounce bar for five cents. Heath bars were only sold for home delivery by a Heath dairy salesman. She tried to create a similar candy bar that they could sell in their store. She soon found that the quality ingredients—toffee, almonds, and chocolate—plus the time and cost were prohibitive. She stopped trying when John said, "Enough, Nadra, you're costing us money."

Nadra had already given up filling grab bags for the children and demonstrating the making of peanut brittle in the storefront window. But occasionally the children still came by to stare in the windows. Touched by their skinny frames and hungry eyes, Nadra would open a roll of Necco wafers and distribute it one-by-one. More and more children came. She knew she had to stop, especially when John insisted she was only making the children's plight worse. She agreed and went upstairs, away from the pleading eyes.

Soon the ordinary clientele who had once been the backbone of the business dwindled even more. Now those people could barely sustain their families, let alone buy ice-cream and phosphates and handmade candy. They were the have-nots. Only the haves would occasionally come to buy the groceries or fruits, nuts, and handmade candies.

John became Nadra's biggest worry. At times she felt his anxiety was veering close to panic, but she knew he was not unique. Dowla's husband never managed to earn more than minimal wages. Eventually it was his four daughters, all unmarried, who kept the household going. Nadra suspected that Sonya's husband, Simon, a known miser, took out his money worries on Sonya and the children.

Nadra never gave up. Hope was her wellspring. She went into overdrive to sustain herself, her family, and most of all, her husband. But she was not able to spare John the pain of having to sell his beloved REO Flying Cloud. She wanted him to wait. But he felt that the car was a foolish and unseemly luxury. John didn't know anybody who could afford the car, but Michael did. The REO Flying Cloud went to the home of a bootlegger.

⏳

Nadra's second son, Billy, was born in 1930, and the third, Tommy, in 1932. When she was pregnant again in 1934 she and John were hankering for a daughter. Nadra told John that she wanted to call her Aurelia—for twelve years Nadra had carried that beautiful French girl's gentle touch and loving eyes in her heart.

Aurelia.

⏳

Nadra's baby was born at home on a beautiful day in April. As in her other births, for George, Billy, and Tommy, Nadra's mother, Lila, and her friends Dowla, Sonya, and Shanti were there. Dowla was on the right side of the bed, holding Nadra's hand; Shanti was on the left wiping the sweat dripping into Nadra's eyes.

"All's good now, Mrs. Hanoun," Dr. Crooks said. "Your cervix has dilated to ten centimeters. Nice contractions…steady and increasing…steady and increasing…just like we want them."

Sonya inched her way to the bed to pat Nadra on the shoulder.

"The baby's head is moving toward the vaginal opening. Don't push. Just relax and breathe, Mrs. Hanoun, re-lax…re-lax…re-lax…" Keeping a firm hold on Nadra's hand, Dowla breathed with her, blowing air in and out steadily.

"You're fully dilated now. Let's push. Push!"

Nadra was becoming breathless and fatigued.

"The baby's head is crowning. Push more gently now. Baby's head and body are emerging. Push more slowly now…gentle…head and body are out…"

The room was suddenly quiet. Too quiet. Nadra pulled herself up immediately. She saw the doctor hand the baby swiftly to Lila.

"What's wrong!" Nadra shrieked.

"She's stillborn, dear," Dr. Crooks said.

"Stillborn?"

"The umbilical cord is wrapped around her neck, Mrs. Hanoun."

Dowla and Shanti kept their hands clamped on Nadra.

Sonya cried, "There will be another, Nadra. There will be another."

When Lila moved toward the door, Nadra screamed, "Where are you taking her? Let me have her!"

Dr. Crooks tried to calm her. "Don't worry, dear. I'll hand her to you. Let us wash her first."

Dr. Crooks turned his back to Nadra, shielding the baby from her view as he removed the umbilical cord.

Dowla and Sonya cleaned the baby, wrapped her in a blanket, and Dr. Crooks put her in Nadra's arms.

The baby was still warm. Marveling at her black hair and perfectly formed features, Nadra pressed her against her breasts, wishing that she could feed her, infuse her with life.

"Look how beautiful she is." Nadra kissed the eyes that would never open and smoothed the tiny curls, crooning, "*Ya Rouhi*" and "*Ya Hayati*" (My Soul, My Life). She began keening, rocking backward and forward.

She told Shanti and Dowla to bring her the delicate white gown, coat, and hat she had made. When she was dressing the baby John came in.

"She's an angel, John, an angel. See how perfect she is."

He tried to smile but his expression turned to sorrow as he touched his child.

"She's cold now." Nadra put the coat on the baby. As she surrendered her to the waiting arms, she sang, "Fly away, fly away, beautiful bird."

Nadra lay there for two days, tears pouring from her eyes, milk stopped up in her breasts. Dowla, Sonya, and Shanti took turns at her side, often with hands fingering their Rosary beads.

Nadra longed for Sitto, wanting desperately to tell her of her loss. *But why share grief,* she thought. Sitto had enough worries with Nesrin's illness and Feheema's rotten husband.

But Nadra had no more time to dwell on her sorrow. When her three boys, ages seven, five, and three, peeked in on her, she could see their concern and fear. How could she expect the little ones to understand? She had to move past the loss.

Since Um-Hana's help was limited and grudging at best, Nadra had given up most of her work in the store. Raising three little boys in an upstairs apartment was full-time work. There was a yard but it wasn't a convenient or safe place for the boys. To reach it, they had to descend from the second-floor apartment and walk along the left side of the building past the cellar.

The only pleasant part of the journey was the huge display of morning glories that Nadra planted under the staircase. On wash days she carried overflowing baskets down the stairs so she could hang clothes in the sun. John tried to anticipate her descent so he could carry the baskets for her. The apartment was at the top of a long steep hill leading from the Baltimore and Ohio Railroad. At

3:00 p.m. the railroaders, lunch buckets in hand, would climb that hill as they headed home. Nadra couldn't help but wonder what kind of homes they were going to. Did they have houses with lawns and gardens? Were they awakened by the shrill steam whistles of the trains where they lived? She heard the wailing melancholy sounds of the whistles all hours of the night. Sound and soot. She learned to live with the sound but often longed for the clean air and the cool nights in Saidnaya, when she and her sisters slept outdoors on the rooftop under the stars.

She had to rearrange the apartment for her growing family. Um-Hana remained in her original bedroom, but Nadra and John gave up their bedroom for the boys. The couple slept in the large living room. It had two doors. Door one opened directly into the company and sitting area of the living room which was furnished with a large horsehair sofa, two side chairs, an ornate glass-topped coffee table, and, facing the front windows, a long black sofa table holding cacti and ceramic animal figures. On the walls hung the huge tapestries that Um-Hana gave them as a wedding present. Door two opened into the other end of the living room, revealing the couple's bed and a square bedside table on the far wall. There was seldom any real privacy, but John and Nadra pretended there was when they closed both door one and door two. As they grew older, the boys called them the sacred doors.

The kitchen was at the end of the hallway. The family ate at a wood table and six chairs painted white and decorated with bright Meyercord decals of mixed fruit. In the good years a tall narrow storage cabinet held a storehouse of Middle Eastern ingredients like olive oil, chickpeas, sesame seed, and fava beans as well as wholesome American food. Nadra, like all the Syrian wives, bought the Middle Eastern ingredients from Mr. Amour, the itinerant salesman from New York who came to town about twice a year.

The long wall was dominated by a white Hoosier cabinet, an essential in kitchens with no built-in cabinets. The base held pots, pans, and bowls. Two side drawers housed utensils. The base also included a sliding countertop on which Nadra loved to leave the snacks she prepared for the children.

The top portion of the Hoosier was shallower with several smaller compartments with doors and drawers. The feature that Nadra loved most was the swing-out flour bin with a sifter that could hold twenty-five pounds of flour. When Nadra had time to bake, the porcelain pullout shelf would hold numerous loaves of Syrian bread, the big thin kind or the smaller pocket variety called pita. She took pleasure in sharing the bread with friends and with those who had little, like the old lady across the street, Latifa.

Nadra's pleasure was not even diminished when Um-Hana commented snidely, "You like to be generous."

Nadra's ingenuity was as strong as her generosity. When the pantry dwindled, she relied on the grocery items in the confectionery. When they had the money, they were able to buy more wholesale. In the process she mastered American food. Even though Betty Crocker wasn't a real person, Nadra paid attention to her "Starve the Garbage Can Campaign," which provided helpful hints on how to conserve food and eliminate waste.

No one missed the butter when they devoured Nadra's delicious cornbread. When they were fortunate to have a chicken come to Sunday dinner, it appeared again with noodles on Monday and in a pot pie on Tuesday. Velveeta cheese, ground and blended with pimentos and mayonnaise, adorned white bread. Boston-style beans made from scratch left the oven with flaky biscuits to join crisp slaw. Corn Flakes and all the right spices transformed a middling portion of ground beef into a splendid meatloaf. The children were especially fond of Home Front Macaroni.

The kitchen led into Um-Hana's bedroom, which faced Route 50. Just inside the bedroom were two huge trunks that she and John had brought with them from the old country. When Nadra had the ingredients to make extra pastries for the holidays, which she gave to friends and relatives, she often stored them on top of those trunks, covering them with waxed paper. She was sure that Um-Hana helped herself. Crumbs on her bodice and the floor gave her away.

Lila owned a Singer sewing machine she never used, so she gave it to Nadra who immediately took advantage of the Singer in-store lessons. She learned how to make the hand-me-downs fit the children. She made the long, gathered skirts and blousons that Um-Hana wore. She could transform three yards of anything into a Sunday dress. She even turned marked-down remnants into cobbler aprons for Sonya, Shanti, and Dowla.

Though Shanti wasn't inclined to wear aprons, she exclaimed, "Lord, she cooks *and* sews!"

Nadra smiled when Dowla asked, "Sweetheart, did you also sew for Um-Hana?"

"Of course," Nadra said.

"Sure she does, but it takes five times as much cloth," Shanti said.

Life was hard but Nadra felt they were managing as best they could, until she made her discovery.

Speculations

Nadra left the children playing upstairs long enough to fetch some cardboard from the store. In the confectionery, John and 'Am-moo Ike sat at one of the ice-cream tables, writing a letter. She was not surprised. 'Am-moo Ike was probably just doing his scribe duties. What was alarming, however, was the money next to the envelope. In his usual way, 'Am-moo Ike barely acknowledged her presence. John, however, was clearly unnerved. 'Am-moo Ike folded the stationery, put the money inside the fold, and inserted it into the envelope.

"Where's that going?"

Neither man answered.

Finally, John said, "To my father and to my brother, Yusuf."

"Why?"

Nadra knew John held an untenable position. He was being interrogated by his wife in front of his uncle. But she didn't care. Ignoring her completely, 'Am-moo Ike stood up, pushed his chair to the table, put the letter in his pocket and left.

She sat in 'Am-moo Ike's chair, searched John's eyes, and asked again, "Why?"

"It's just a few dollars, Nadra. No big deal."

"It's a goddamn big deal!"

"Watch your mouth!"

"I'm using cardboard to line Billy's shoes where the sole wore out! It's called Hoover leather—did you know that? Tommy is due for his vaccination! George needs a winter coat!"

"Stop shouting!"

"I thought you had more sense than to be sending money to the old country!"

"They have nothing."

"We have nothing!"

Devoid of words, John looked down at the table. Nadra couldn't take her eyes off him.

"It was just a few dollars."

"Like the few dollars you are *always* giving your '*incle*?"

Biting back, he said, "Maybe *I* like to be *generous* sometimes!"

Nadra sat down and stared at John. "*Generous*! That word seems to run in the family now."

John looked away, ignoring her comment. Finally he said, "We made a little more money this month, Nadra."

"How much?"

"I can't say exactly, it was...better..."

"You have become close about the money, never telling me anything, always hiking it to the bank as soon as you can."

"I have been years working and saving money!" John said.

Leaning over the table, closer to John, Nadra said, "Maybe I didn't bring any money, but I was years learning and managing my father's store! My knowledge and experience were no small part of our 'happy business'!"

John said, "I know! And I kiss your hands and your feet for that knowledge and help, Nadra! I really do, I..."

Nadra's stare silenced him. Then she rose from the table as she said, "Well, you can kiss more than my hands, John. You and your mother and your 'Am-moo Ike!"

After the money episode Nadra was sure that 'Am-moo had relayed the situation to his sister, Um-Hana. Now when Um-Hana crossed Nadra's path she had a way of angling her head to the side in obvious disapproval and defiance. Nadra could no longer abide her. Having few friends and few places to go, Um-Hana was always there. Because she was always there, Nadra felt that she couldn't ever complain about the old woman, let alone scream and rage. Because she was always there, Um-Hana was an ever-tight band around her heart.

Um-Hana was taller than Nadra but round and wore a long black skirt and blouson top. Um-Hana parted her hair in the middle and wore it pulled back into a knot, framing a blank face. To Nadra the old woman was a solid block of limestone topped with a powerful beacon—a lighthouse that lit up all Nadra's flaws and faults. Were they in the old country, Nadra would have to follow behind her and pay her the deference and respect she thought was her due.

John's financial worries were much greater than his concerns about the battles between his wife and mother. He needed money.

Confections and ice-cream were no longer sustaining them. Even though his better-off friends continued to buy nuts, dried fruits and candies for holidays and family occasions, he was still not making enough income. He decided to stay open longer, particularly on weekends when he saw people headed for The Cinema down the street. He bought popcorn in bulk, set up a popping machine, and began selling popcorn. He could produce a fifteen-cent box for three cents, a nickel bag for a penny. He had eleven-year-old George make a large sign: *Going to the MOVIES? STOP here first.* Selling popcorn also had the advantage of bringing those with extra coins inside his store.

All was good until the movie theatres made the same discovery, the neighborhood ones like The Cinema as well as the larger ones. What was a sustaining sideline for John was becoming big bucks for The Cinema as well as the bigger theatres downtown. Those theatres added stands inside their doors and eventually made more money in concessions than in their price of admission.

When she calmed herself, Nadra wondered if some kind of guilt was motivating John to send money to the old country. She had once asked Dowla if she knew why Um-Hana's husband had never again tried to come to America and why she chose never to return to him. But Dowla wouldn't tell her. Why the big secret?

Sonya and Nadra's Perennial Question

Nadra loved the Syrian community. After the day they abducted her from the confectionery, she was closest to Dowla, Sonya, and Shanti. The four liked to meet in Dowla's kitchen on Friday mornings. The kitchen's back windows looked out at Dowla's grape arbor. In good weather they sat outside in the grape arbor at the picnic table.

This Friday Dowla had leftover pancake batter from breakfast so she added extra flour, a little sugar, and vanilla to bake her version of sugar cookies. Using a crocheted pot holder, Nadra removed the cookie tray from the oven.

Dowla handed a trivet to Shanti. "Here, put this under the tray." Dowla stayed close to Shanti, smiling.

As Shanti did what she was instructed, she read the message on the trivet. "When did you become a comedian, Dowla?"

"I found it."

"Since when did you learn to read, my Irish friend?"

Simultaneously Nadra and Sonya asked, "What does it say, Shanti?"

"Irish Blessing—May you be in Heaven a half hour before the Devil knows you're dead."

Nadra laughed and lifted the cookie sheet to look at the trivet.

Looking at Sonya, Shanti said, "You finally smiled, even laughed."

"What do you mean?"

Pinning Sonya with her eyes, Shanti said, "You know what I mean. Tell us what's wrong, Sonya?"

"Nothing's wrong."

"Liar!" Shanti responded.

As she set a saucer and cup in front of each woman, Dowla said, "Be kind, Shanti."

Moving closer to Sonya, Shanti said, "I only want to know how is Merry Mary?"

"I'm okay," Sonya replied.

"No," Shanti said, "our Silly Sonya is changing."

Nadra poured the coffee.

Dowla poked Shanti as she placed the milk and sugar in front of her.

"We want to know what's going on," Shanti said.

As she put the cookies on a plate, Nadra interrupted, "*Shanti* wants to know. The rest of us are minding our own business."

"Sonya is one of our own!" Shanti barked back at Nadra. "What's troubling you?" she asked Sonya.

"I don't want to talk about it."

"Simon?" Shanti asked.

"Simon is depressed, afraid, he isn't making any money."

"Is that really the case?"

"Of course."

"How do you know?"

"He doesn't give me much."

"He never did!"

"Leave it, Shanti," Dowla demanded.

"I worry about you. We're all worried about you."

"I told you, Shanti, he's under pressure and sometimes it gets the best of him!"

"I think he's mean and cruel," Shanti said.

"Maybe I don't care what you think!" Suddenly Sonya rose from the table, almost tipping over her chair. After taking her coffee cup to the sink, she headed for the door.

"I'm only trying to help you," Shanti said.

"I don't need help and I hate your nosey eyes!" Sonya said as she slammed the door.

Dowla ran after her and saw Sonya's youngest boy sitting on the porch steps. Alex was the child who wouldn't stay home, the child who followed Sonya everywhere. Dowla returned to the kitchen and shouted at Shanti, "No matter what a man is, you don't say it in front of his wife!"

Shanti shouted back, "We're all thinking it, Dowla!"

"But we are not the ones living with him."

Shanti shoved the plate of cookies away. They sat in silence, Dowla wringing her hands, Shanti scowling.

Nadra felt a sense of foreboding, but she tucked the feeling away. It was best to change the subject so she asked Dowla her perennial question.

"Dowla, why did Um-Hana never go back to Saidnaya?"

Shanti began pacing but stopped abruptly to listen to Dowla's answer.

"She likes it here."

Laughing, Shanti added, "What's not to like, living with a daughter-in-law who would like to lynch her!"

"Why didn't she want to be there, with her husband, with her other sons?"

"Too many locusts, too much sheep shit!" Shanti said.

"Shut up, Shanti! Why won't you tell me, Dowla?"

"Dowla likes to keep the peace," Shanti said.

"Why is it such a big secret?"

Exasperated, Dowla replied, "It can hurt people."

"Um-Hana? John?"

"Leave it, leave it."

"I'm sorry."

Nadra dropped the matter. Perhaps some things were best left unsaid.

1937

Nadra hadn't wanted to be married. She did not want to live in the same dingy apartment she inhabited as a teenager. She did not want to live in Hedley, West Virginia. Most certainly she did not want to be living with her mother-in-law. But she wanted to give birth to this constantly kicking baby, her fifth. Having lost her daughter, she was now incapable of setting aside her worry and anxiety, even though her first three pregnancies yielded healthy boys. The three of them were now driving her crazy. She was still scraping congealed egg yolk off the plates when they started their row. She tried to ignore them, but their small, over-the-store home made that tough.

"Come on, give me half!" George, the oldest, shouted at Billy.

"No!" Billy responded.

Using his broad shoulders to back his younger brother into the wall, he demanded, "Hand it over!"

"No!"

Butting in, seven-year-old Tommy said, "You're supposed to share."

"You're supposed to keep your mouth shut, snot!"

"Don't talk to our little brother that way!" George said.

"Yeah!" said Tommy.

"Ah, shut up, both of you!" Billy said.

"Come on, Bil-lie."

"No, Georg-ie."

Nadra dried her hands and lumbered to the living room, plant-ed herself in front of them and stared. "What now!"

"Nothing," Billy said.

"Yeah, nothing," George agreed.

"Billy won't share his money!" Tommy explained.

"You have money?" Nadra asked Billy.

"Billy?" she asked again.

"I got a few quarters."

Nadra held out her hand. Billy reached deep into his pocket and pulled out the quarters. Nadra slipped them into the pocket of her apron.

"I worked for them."

Nadra pointed to the side chair. Glowering at George and Tom-my, Billy crossed the room and threw his lanky frame on the chair. She nodded at George and Tommy and pointed to the large horse-hair sofa. They took their places at opposite ends. "You stay there!"

She then trudged to the kitchen and continued scraping the dishes as she tried to figure out what could be done with the boys for the rest of the day. John could give the older boys chores to do in the store, but someone had to keep a constant eye on the impetuous Tommy. She could trust George and Billy to do that, but only up to a point.

"*Zabra,*" George sneered at Billie.

"You're the prick," Billy sneered back.

Turning to Tommy, George added, "And you're the *hamour!*" (jackass)

"Right!" Billy shouted at Tommy. "Why did you have to tell her about the money?"

"Now nobody has it," George added.

Nadra returned to the living room. "George, you take the trash out then sweep the steps."

"All of them?"

She wanted to smack her firstborn, but instead she pinned him with her topaz-brown eyes.

"Billy, you run the sweeper. Tommy, you get a rag and dust the living room."

"I don't know how to dust."

"Billy, show your brother how to dust."

When she left the room, Billy clipped Tommy along the side of the head, at which point Tommy let out an impossibly painful scream.

"Mom, there's no dust," Billy declared.

Billy was the only one of the three observant enough to see that.

She went again into the living room, which doubled as the master bedroom, and told Billy and Tommy to take the ceramic animals and cactuses off the long black table. Next she had them place the ceramic pieces in the cardboard box that she handed them. She had them carry the cactuses to the porch. What they called the porch was actually only the landing at the top of the twenty-one steps that led up to the apartment. She saw George loitering on the landing, broom in hand. When his brothers bent over slowly with the prickly cactuses, he hit them in the butt with the broom. Tommy screamed again and Billy tried to throw George down the stairs.

"Stop it! You stop it or I will tell Baba!"

That got their attention. She seldom told John about their disobedience, but when she did that meant the belt.

"Now get into the living room! You two keep dusting. George, you move the long black table away from the window and closer to the bed."

"How come?" he asked.

"Just do it!" she barked. "Then dust!"

"I gotta dust too?"

She held her breath. "E-v-e-r-y-b-o-d-y has to dust."

She heard a tap at the screen door and a hesitant inquiry: "Nadra?"

Tommy went to the door and stuck his tongue out at Eva, Nadra's younger sister. Nadra pushed Tommy back into the living room and let Eva in.

"What are they doing?"

"Looking for dust."

Eva followed her into the kitchen.

"You want some breakfast, honey?"

Eva responded with a halfhearted, "No."

"Oh, well, I'll just get you some milk and cookies."

"Nadra, I don't know anyone who cooks and bakes more than you do."

"I don't either."

"Mama never bakes."

Mama doesn't cook much either, Nadra thought, but she didn't say it. She put another cookie on Eva's plate.

Looking around, Eva said, "Where is Um-Hana?"

"This is her bath day."

"Alleluia."

Nadra smiled in spite of herself. Several cookies and two glasses of milk later, she asked, "Eva, you think you could—"

"Sure, I'll keep an eye on them."

"God bless you."

Nadra took a small coin purse from her apron, slipped Billy's quarters into it and gave it to Eva, who was impressed with its weight.

"I'll keep them out of your hair."

Eva went into the living room and smiled malevolently at the boys.

"Come on, monsters, follow me!"

Thrusting his shoulders back, George snorted defiantly. "I don't have to!"

"So, hang out here with your mommy," Eva responded.

As he ran after her, George asked, "Where are we going?"

"We are going to the park and after that—a super surprise!"

Now that her three boys were out of the house and Um-Hana, her mother-in-law, was in the bathroom for her big wash, Nadra hurried to the bedroom to sit and put her feet up. Peering over her swollen breasts and big belly, she turned her legs as much as she could to study the varicose veins that had started popping in both legs. Her back ached and her ankles were swollen. This child never stopped kicking, as if it couldn't wait to escape from the confined space. *The kicking's a good sign*, she kept telling herself.

But the last baby had also kicked. The painful memories returned, a black and white film running permanently in her memory. That beautiful baby looked like an angel sleeping peacefully, her life over before it began.

"Please, God, let this baby be born alive. Please, God, soon," she whispered as her eyes closed and she surrendered to her fatigue.

She was soaring high above the apartment, beyond the railroad tracks, into a gorgeous glade replete with meadows, streams, and budding trees. Sweet singing birds beckoned, guiding her higher and higher, closer and closer to a beautiful nest. Suddenly a black buzzard with rounded head and tail and broad soaring wings circled round, blocking her path. Her heart thumping, she woke with a start. Um-Hana passed by Nadra's door, dressed in her blouson top and long black skirt, her gray hair in a bun as tight as her face. Nadra figured Um-Hana was going to Dowla's. Nadra sighed and, touching Kef Miryam, begged the Virgin Mary to protect her unborn child.

She knew her time was close. Her uterus began contracting, but the contractions were not yet more regular and more painful. She had prepared herself and the family and the apartment. Each horizontal surface, whether low or high, dusted and scrubbed. Kitchen sink spotless, fruit bowl full of oranges, grapes, and bananas. Lemonade in the refrigerator. Had she forgotten anything?

The laundry and ironing were done. She had made two more outfits for Um-Hana—lightweight black skirts in cotton, long ones of course. She even talked the old woman into letting her make the tops to match in short sleeves, four of them, with an embroidered one for Sundays. Um-Hana nodded her approval, but never made it to an audible thank you.

Though money was still scarce and food precious, she spent the week preparing as many meals in advance as she could. She made a large meatloaf, using Corn Flakes as filler, *tabouli*, and a quart of *laban* (yogurt), which John loved to have with marmalade and bread. She hulled the last of the season's strawberries to go with her orange-flavored pound cake. She crammed so many oatmeal cookies into the green ceramic jar, its lid sat askew. Knowing how the boys would wolf them down, she hid the extras in the tall cabinet, behind the cracked wheat. The cooking and baking relieved her irritability and tension. She knew John also worried, but then John worried about everything.

When Nadra felt the thick, stringy, blood-tinged discharge from her vagina, she knew her time had arrived. She cleaned away the bloody show. After that she began preparing what she hoped would be a sterile environment, if there could be such a thing for a woman living on Route 50 and only yards away from the Baltimore and Ohio Railroad. She retrieved the clean sheets, towels, and pads she had stored in old pillowcases to ward off dust and debris. She wanted whatever would come in contact with her and her newborn to be immaculate. She changed the marital bed into a birthing bed. She carefully wiped the black table, arranged the diapers, baby soap, bottles of antiseptic, sterile cotton pads, rubbing alcohol, nasal syringe, ice packs and super absorbent maxi pads. (Nadra saved money for months so she could afford sterile pads from the drugstore instead of having to rely on homemade rags.)

The doctor would be using the square table at the right side of the bed. She cleaned it thoroughly and placed packs of sterile cotton pads on it. She draped a large cotton towel over the table. Taking one of the bottles of antiseptic with her, she was ready to move into the kitchen to place the required pots and pans next to the kettle, but she stopped. The contractions were more regular and painful; she hadn't expected them to be that soon. She knew it was time to call the doctor and tell John. Once she was off the phone, she went to the porch and bellowed for John. He ran out of the store and raced up the steps before she stopped him, saying: "I called the doctor; you can tell Mama."

It took him a minute to connect, and when he did, he nearly fell down the stairs.

"Be careful, John. My baby needs a father."

"You're okay?"

"Hurry now."

"Sure, sure."

She knew that her friends would be there in minutes. They were all in the neighborhood and they were all attuned to each other. She went back to her chair and put up her feet.

Her tall, stern mother, Lila, arrived first, frowning as usual. For Lila birthing was more of an annoyance than an event; she herself had already birthed seven children. Noting the rug that Nadra had placed under her chair, she asked: "Your water didn't break yet?"

"No."

Lila inspected the bed and table. Nadra was going to tell her that she hadn't taken out all the kitchen utensils for boiling water, cleaning, and sterilizing, but she decided not to bother. Lila would leave that to somebody else anyway.

Dowla was the next to arrive, smiling broadly in eager anticipation. Um-Hana trailed behind her, then stood to the side, fluttering nervously. Dowla knelt next to Nadra's chair, took her hand, and asked if the contractions were coming on regular and strong. Biting her lip, Nadra answered affirmatively. A knowledgeable mother of six who had helped numerous younger women, Dowla also asked if the contractions came at shorter intervals.

Nadra said no and told Dowla that the kitchen wasn't completely prepared and pointed to the bottle of antiseptic. Dowla picked up the antiseptic, took Um-Hana to the kitchen, and told her to finish the preparation.

Um-Hana's first task was to set the kettle and pots of water boiling. Hands shaking, she banged all the pots and pans she touched. Nadra worried that Um-Hana might drop something on the floor, that she might forget to use the antiseptic, that the doctor might not get there on time.

Nadra thought she heard someone on the stairs. She prayed that it was the doctor. Sonya Metrey sneaked into the room like a menacing cat with a raised paw that was about to pounce on Lila. Lila was not amused. Changing from a tiger to a Cheshire Cat, Sonya purred, "*Salaam aleikum.*"

"Hello to you too," Lila replied. "Now come in and be quiet, Sonya."

Sonya made a face at Lila then went to Nadra, smiling, kissing her and squeezing her hand. "Hello, *um,*" (mother) she said. Nadra adored Sonya; her loving nature, robust sense of humor, and unfailing optimism lightened Nadra's worries. Yet Sonya lived the hardest life of them all. Her husband, Simon, was still beating her, particularly when she became pregnant. She already had nine children, and when she gave birth, she never had a doctor, nor did she have all of the things that she needed for her personal care. Her husband would not even give her money for the maternity pads. But the ladies were in attendance and they made sure Sonya had everything that was needed. With their help all of her children entered the world safely and in good health.

"Everything good here, ladies?" asked Sonya.

"Everything is good," Lila replied. "You can be the runner, in case we need anything..." Lila didn't want to say, "In case something goes wrong."

Nadra was closing her eyes and gritting her teeth from the intense pain. Lila moved a straight chair close to Nadra, placed her hands on her stomach and asked her daughter if she wanted to move to the bed.

"No," Nadra answered irritably. "I want the doctor. Everything is moving faster this time."

"Sure it is. This is your fourth," Lila replied.

"This is my fifth," Nadra corrected.

Nudging Lila out of the way, Dowla said, "Get her some water." She sat in the chair and took Nadra's hand. "When it gets bad, squeeze my hand, hard." Sonya stood behind Nadra and gently massaged her neck and shoulders.

Meanwhile, Lila went into the kitchen. Before getting the water she made it a point to appraise Um-Hana's work. They didn't speak. Lila nodded. A small gesture of approval. As she exited from the kitchen Um-Hana said, "*Alla yerzo' shee Sabee.*" ("May she be blessed with a son.")

Lila replied, "Inshallah."

Nadra's water broke just as Dr. Crooks arrived, a tall graying man with warm hazel eyes. Surveying the room and beaming at the women, he asked, "Do you ladies really need me?"

Without missing a beat, Sonya responded, "No, but we want you, honey!"

"Good afternoon, Mrs. Hanoun," he said to Nadra. "Let's get you into bed. This one will probably go fast."

Sonya planted herself in front of Nadra so that she could hold and support her as she rose. Lila and Dowla helped her onto the birthing bed and propped her up on her back. Then they moved back, like obedient school children, deferring space to the doctor. Sonya assumed a watchful position on the outskirts.

Dr. Crooks went to the square table and unpacked his Gladstone bag, setting out various obstetrical instruments, suture materials, cord scissors, a pediatric sucker for removing mucus from the baby's mouth, and a portable baby scale. All eyes were on him. Um-Hana did not bang or drop anything. Everyone watched; no one spoke.

Upon examining her, Dr. Crooks found that Nadra's cervix was almost fully dilated. The women seemed to come to attention. When dilation was complete, Dr. Crooks said, "It's time to get your baby through the birth canal, Mrs. Hanoun. It's time to start pushing."

Each time Dr. Crooks told Nadra to push, Lila, Dowla, and Sonya told her to also, in Arabic. "*Dfu-shee, ya haibeete, dfu-shee!*" ("Push, my love, push!")

Even Um-Hana would duck out of the kitchen long enough to encourage, "*Dfu-shee, bintee, dfu-shee!*" In spite of her pain, this made Nadra laugh. This was the first time Um-Hana called her *bintee* (my daughter).

While Dr. Crooks was saying, "Put your chin to your chest and push. Push, push as if you're having a bowel movement—the biggest one of your life!" Lila was praying to St. George, out loud. And Sonya was saying the Rosary, out loud. Worried that the children might return at any point, Nadra was careful not to scream. "Oh-h, oh" were the only sounds she made, but that became increasingly difficult as the baby's head crowned then disappeared again. Dowla wiped the perspiration from Nadra's forehead and told her it was okay to scream.

"Take a little rest. You are doing real well, Mrs. Hanoun."

"You always say that, Doctor."

"That's because you always do real well."

"Now, push with all your might, Mrs. Hanoun. That's my girl!" As the baby's head eased its way out, Lila handed the doctor the sucker so he could suction any mucus from the nose and the mouth. He helped guide the baby's shoulders and torso out, the legs next. The sounds of a crying baby filled the small apartment.

"She's a screamer!" Dr. Crooks rose with the baby in his arms, like a high priest before the altar. Peering over the sheets at Nadra, he announced: "It's a girl, dear."

Spontaneously, Sonya and Dowla began applauding. Then, taken aback by their own joyous reaction, they laughed and hugged each other.

"This is my second girl, Doctor."

"I know, honey." He went to her side so she could better see the baby. "That's all right, you're allowed to cry."

Sonya said, "Every woman deserves a daughter!"

Dr. Crooks cut the umbilical cord and placed the baby into the towel that Lila held. As Um-Hana dashed back and forth from the kitchen with pans of clean hot water, Dowla and Lila wiped away the amniotic fluid and wrapped the baby in a blanket as fast as possible. As Lila held her, Dr. Crooks put ointment into the baby's eyes, opened the blanket, and checked her well before placing her in Nadra's arms.

"One more little push, Mrs. Hanoun, and the afterbirth will

be out." With Dowla standing next to him holding the pan that Um-Hana brought in, Dr. Crooks removed the placenta to the pan. Um-Hana took it into the kitchen, wrapped it in paper and put it into the trash. She began crying.

Dr. Crooks examined Nadra, listened to her heart, and took her blood pressure. "Take it easy now, Mrs. Hanoun, and give yourself a little time." He packed his Gladstone bag and bowed to the ladies. "Don't know what I would have done without you."

"Thank you, Doctor," Dowla said.

"Enjoy your little girl, Mrs. Hanoun."

As Lila and Dowla tended Nadra, washing her, changing her clothes and putting the maternity pads between her legs, Sonya paced with the infant in her arms, singing a lullaby. The children could be heard galloping up the steps. Um-Hana ran immediately to block their entrance. She did let John come in.

Sonya put the baby back in Nadra's arms. Bending to kiss his wife, John said, "We have our girl now."

"John, I want to call her Aurelia."

"Whatever you want," he responded as he kissed her hands. Harrumphing, Um-Hana swept out of the apartment.

"What's wrong with her?" Sonya asked.

Lila said, "We wanted a boy."

"She's already had three."

In time, Eva and the boys were allowed to enter. Eva said, "Look at all that black hair and it's curly." The boys were amazed. Nadra resisted laughing.

Finally, George said, "She's nice, Mom, real nice."

Nodding, Billy added, "Yes, we like her."

Tommy asked, "Are you going to give back Billy's quarters?"

"I gave them to Eva, along with my money. I think she has something nice planned for you." They danced and hooted, enjoying the benefits of having a sister. But their joy ended when Lila insisted that her daughter Eva go home because she had chores at her house, so the boys were put in Um-Hana's charge for the rest of the day. Um-Hana did not allow the boys to go to The Cinema to see the new Hopalong Cassidy movie, *Heart of Arizona*. That was to have been Eva's super surprise! Their expectations dashed, they spent the rest of the day pushing each other around while howling the movie's tagline: "Fightin' Mad and Rarin' to Go!"

❧

From that day on, John and Nadra's first living daughter and last child was referred to as *l'bint*, the girl, and in more affectionate moments they called her Aurelia.

Relieved and contented, the women gathered chairs from the kitchen and sat round the birthing bed watching Nadra and the nursing infant. They were pleased. Nadra did well. They did well. The doctor did well. Dr. Crooks had been the insurance policy. After Aurelia suckled at Nadra's breast then drifted off to sleep, Lila rose to take the baby.

"No," Nadra responded. "Let her sleep with me now. But tell John to go to the cellar for the cradle."

"I'll get the cradle," Sonya said.

"Sonya, it's heavy."

"Sonya big and strong, especially after hauling around the twins."

"John would be insulted if you carried the cradle up those steps."

"I forgot. You were one of the lucky ones who married a gentleman."

All the women laughed and Sonya left the room bellowing, "John! John!"

In less than fifteen minutes John lugged the bulky wooden cradle into the room. Like a proud salesman demonstrating his prize ware, John swung off the large white sheet, revealing a sturdy cradle made of solid pine. The women gave him their full attention, as though they had never seen a cradle before. Pressing his hand against it, the cradle rocked smoothly and gently, guaranteeing to help the infant fall asleep. He also demonstrated how the swing locking device was also a locking pin for safety. He wheeled the cradle about the room, demonstrating the casters. When Nadra told him where she wanted the cradle, he obeyed her command, pointing to a second locking pin on the casters, saying, "For safety." He found the cradle when Nadra was first pregnant in 1927. He hid it in the trunk of his beloved REO Flying Cloud. As a surprise he hauled it up the twenty-one stairs into the apartment, beaming and proud.

"It's spotless," Sonya remarked.

"She went down to that cellar to clean and disinfect it."

"You sure she wasn't meeting somebody there?"

The older women told Sonya to be quiet. Embarrassed, John still managed a smile. He exited hurriedly, explaining that he left George in charge of the store.

"Hurry, John, before he eats your entire inventory!" Sonya shouted.

Nadra told the women where to find the one-inch mattress and linens for the cradle. As Sonya and Dowla prepared the cradle, Nadra dozed off, in spite of herself. Sonya took the baby from her, placed Aurelia in the crib, and rocked it gently.

"I have to go," Lila declared. Smiling, Dowla and Sonya waved her off.

Making sure Nadra was still asleep, Sonya asked, "Think she's worried about Sami?"

"Probably," said Dowla.

"Wonder who he's into now?"

Noticing the flicker of Nadra's eyelids, Dowla whispered, "Keep quiet, Sonya." Rising from her chair, she added, "I'm leaving now, but I'll return soon."

The baby began whimpering. Hearing her, Nadra lifted her head from the pillow to look at her. It was time to nurse, but before Nadra could move from the bed, Sonya stopped her and handed her the baby.

"You should be home, Sonya."

"Would you want to be home with nine kids? Don't worry; the older ones always help."

Smiling, Sonya watched as Nadra moved herself up, resting her back against the bed, cradling the baby in the crook of her arm. Loosening her gown, she compressed her right nipple slightly; making sure the baby hooked on, the whole of the ring in her mouth. Both women laughed as they heard the baby's eager sucking sounds.

"You're going to need some food too," Sonya said as she left for the kitchen.

"I won't eat alone!" Nadra shouted after her.

"I'm not bashful."

"I don't have to plead with you three times?" Nadra said.

"I'm too hungry to play that game. I know you have cookies somewhere."

"In the green ceramic jar, on the table," Nadra said.

Sonya went to the kitchen and returned after a few minutes. "Guess they moved," Sonya said as she returned with a tray holding water, two small dishes of laban, bread, and strawberries. After she spooned some strawberries into one of the dishes that she handed Nadra, she said, "Neither one of us needs a cookie."

"Did the boys eat, Sonya?"

"Um-Hana fed them."

"She was mad, Sonya."

"Do we care?"

They both laughed.

"Really, Sonya, she will be mean to the boys."

Mixing strawberries into her yogurt, Sonya said, "So? They will learn the difference between a woman and a dragon. Do you want something else?"

"Just a little water."

As she was drinking, Nadra glanced toward the door. "Someone is coming."

Appearing in the doorway, Um-Hana appraised Nadra and the baby then announced: "Lila will let Eva watch the boys for an hour while I make lunch for Hana." Um-Hana liked to use John's Arabic name.

"You don't have to make anything. I made—"

Ignoring Nadra, Um-Hana left for the kitchen, declaring, "Hana is hungry."

"How come you haven't put arsenic in her coffee?" Sonya said.

"Waiting to get her and the 'incle at the same time."

Nadra shifted the baby to her left breast.

Watching her, Sonya remarked, "Dowla is coming back in a little while."

"To make sure I'm doing it right?"

"Your first-born almost starved."

"Don't be mean, Sonya."

"I'm just teasing you." Assuming a gentle, persuasive manner, Sonya added, "Now Dowla and I have a plan, Nadra. She will come in the morning, I will come in the afternoon, and Shanti in the evening."

"It isn't necessary. I will be fine."

"The doctor said to take it easy for a few days."

"The doctor always says that. And Um-Hana hates Shanti!"

"We know, we know!" said Sonya as she giggled. In spite of herself, Nadra laughed also.

"I don't need trouble, Sonya."

"When Shanti comes, Um-Hana will disappear!"

"You're wicked, Sonya."

"Practical, Nadra, practical."

Hearing footsteps, Sonya turned to inquire: "John?"

"Yes."

"What are you doing with the cookie jar?"

"The boys were eating them all, so I took them to the store."

"It's empty?" Sonya asked.

Embarrassed, he nodded yes and ducked into the kitchen. John never saw Nadra nurse, only revealing herself in front of her close women friends.

"You going to tell the hungry one where you hid the rest of the cookies?" Sonya asked.

"In the tall cabinet, behind the cracked wheat."

"Knew there had to be more."

"I'm suddenly so tired, Sonya."

"Of course you are. It was the worry more than the birth." Sonya gave her a tissue to wipe away the tears. "I'll burp the baby. Drink a little and take a couple of bites then sleep."

"I'll be all right. By tomorrow I'll be all right."

Once John finished his lunch and extracted himself from the care of his mother, he peeked into the bedroom and found Nadra asleep with Sonya at her side.

"Someone watching the store for you?"

He nodded.

"Sit. I'll return tomorrow afternoon." Sonya surrendered her chair and left him with his sleeping wife and daughter.

∽

When Nadra awakened, she found John asleep. *How peaceful he looks*, she thought, but she knew the serenity wouldn't last. Before long he would reflect that there were now seven to care for: himself and Nadra, the four children, and his mother. She knew that John never doubted her ability to care for them all, but his humble beginnings and lack of education had eventually caused more doubt than faith in his ability to make a living. Judging from the stories he told her, he was not like that when he first came over. He thought the early days in America, the good days, would last forever. Even though they had come safely through it thus far, the Great Depression had redoubled his fears and anxiety. They had all come in pursuit of a better life, and in the beginning most of them had found it. Now many, like John, questioned if they had. But she had no doubts. They would have a good life, here, in America. She said a prayer to her mother, the Virgin of Saidnaya, as she drifted off to sleep again.

When she awakened, John was still there, smiling, clutching a small box, a bouquet of yellow sweetheart roses on the square table. He kissed her hand and gave her the white box.

"For me or Aurelia?"

"The flowers for you, the box for Aurelia."

She opened the box to find a fine gold necklace holding a delicate heart.

"How did you manage this?"

"I have my ways."

"How did you know we would have a girl?"

John smiled. She wanted to chastise him, to say, *we can't afford such things now*, but she did not. She was happy that he had been as hopeful, and as pleased, as she was.

From door one came a shy but somewhat officious voice declaring, "I have come to see Nadra and the child."

"It's my 'incle," John said.

Dark brown eyes peered down from a frizzy black dome and broad forehead as 'Am-moo Ike bowed ever so slightly to Nadra. Amused, she bowed her head, ever so slightly, sarcastically offering the deference she so abhorred.

"*Kayf haalek?*" he asked.

"I am doing very well. And how are you, 'Am-moo?"

'Am-moo waved his palms in dismissal while contorting his face in pain. Nadra was about to ask what hurt when John cut her off. Extending both hands as though offering a buffet table of delicacies, John indicated the cradle. 'Am-moo Ike approached the cradle carefully, studied the infant intently, lowering and angling his head from one position to another. John hovered close to him, anticipating his reaction.

"She doesn't look like anybody," 'Am-moo said.

"Thank God!" Nadra responded irritably.

"You will name her for your mother."

"We have already named her, 'Am-moo."

"You named her Mary, for your mother."

"We named her Aurelia," Nadra growled.

"What the hell kind of a name is that!"

"It's French."

"Who's French?"

Before John even had time to be nervous about what might come next, Um-Hana came in door two and ushered 'Am-moo to the kitchen.

Nadra swung her legs over the bed, ready to get up.

"What are you doing? What do you need?"

"Hand me the baby! Gently now. Support her head."

John handed her Aurelia, but wasn't sure what to do next. "Are you going to nurse her?"

"I just want to hold her."

Smiling at them, John said, "She's a beautiful baby, Nadra, a good baby."

"Of course she is."

⤚

"All right, John, move yourself on out!" a voice barked from door one. "Benny and my boys are downstairs with your boys."

"Hello, Shanti."

"Congratulations."

"Thank you," he answered as he tried to rush past her.

Grabbing him, she said, "Now, John, there's something I want you and Benny to do, and maybe a couple of the other men too. You and Benny come up here in a little while and I'll explain."

John left.

"Sorry I wasn't here, Nadra, I was at the grocery store. Next time you check with me before you start labor."

Imperious Shanti surveyed the room before she began a thorough but benign inspection of the new mother and child. She took Aurelia from Nadra and swayed with her in her arms. "Thank God she doesn't look like Um-Hana!" she bellowed as she convulsed with laughter.

"Shanti, *ibe alikee* (shame on you)."

"Whatever you say. Lord, I'd like to have a little girl."

"What's stopping you?"

"When was the last time you looked at Benny? Jesus, you have to do something with that prim face of yours, Nadra! Now listen. Sonya, Dowla, and I have a plan to chuck Um-Hana for a while!"

"Shanti, I don't want trouble."

"It will be okay. We're just going to keep her busy. The Diocesan priests are having their big powwow Saturday over in the parish hall. They are all coming, and of course the ladies will have to feed them."

"That will be a job."

"Guess who is making Syrian food for them?" Shanti laughed again, adding, "The Italians and the Poles are doing their thing and Um-Hana will do ours. Dowla's in your kitchen now, telling Um-Hana all about it."

"Um-Hana can't cook, Shanti."

"Maybe she can't cook like you, but she knows how to roll cabbage and grape leaves. Someone else will make the filling. She will be doing a lot of rolling to feed that crowd."

"It will take her forever."

Laughing again, "You got yourself a two-day furlough, honey. We figured you would prefer that to another baby blanket."

"I hope the fathers like her food."

"They're priests! Food is all they've got!"

The baby began whimpering so Shanti gave her back to Nadra. Handling her gently, Nadra checked the baby's diaper.

"Sonya won't be here tomorrow afternoon."

"Good. She already has enough to do without coming here to help me."

Shanti watched Nadra change the baby's diaper and cradle her lovingly in her arms as she crooned a lullaby.

"That's not why."

Nadra stopped humming. "Shanti, don't tell me that…"

"Yes, the bastard began hammering her again the minute he got home."

"I hope she's not pregnant."

"That's not why."

"Something set him off?"

"Everything sets him off! He's a moody, suspicious, nasty man! Before he just treated her shabbily, embarrassed her, insulted her, lashed out!" Shanti began pacing, seemingly in an effort to contain her emotions.

"Now Sonya is his punching bag!"

Wheeling around to face Nadra, she shouted, "That's right! Nothing like marriage to intensify a bully's violence!"

"I hate him!"

"We all hate the miserly mean son-of-a-bitch!"

❧

Through door one a young woman slipped quietly into the room, straightening her shoulders and lifting her head. Walking carefully like a nervous bride negotiating the aisle. She wore a simple off-white summer dress with symmetrical stitches under the bust and over the shoulders, emphasizing her figure. The wasp waist ended in sinuous folds that stretched over the round contours of her body. She wore wedge heels; hard-to-get 15 denier nylons enhanced her legs. Her black hair sleek and upswept, her complexion dark, her brown eyes dazzling, impressing Nadra, amusing Shanti. "Well! If it isn't the Zahirs' femme fatale!"

Smile on face and gift in hand, Nadra's sister Tina whispered, "We finally got us a girl, Nadra," as she kissed Nadra and Aurelia. She ignored Shanti.

Shanti moved closer to Tina, raising her finely tweezed eyebrows as she said, "Who's the lucky man?"

"You don't have to ask. You are the first to know everything."

"I'm behind, sweetie, I'm behind."

"Andy. Anything else you need to know?"

"Andy! How did you manage that? Did you throw Peggy off the Sixth Street Bridge?"

"Benny and the boys are looking for you, Shanti."

Coming close to Tina, Shanti remarked, "You're the dark one

of the family, aren't you?" Pinching Tina's cheek, she continued, "Add another dab of rouge to brighten those sultry eyes, sweetie. Bye, for now. I'm coming right back, Nadra." Shanti exited through door one.

"What's the bitch up to now?"

"I don't want any trouble."

"Shanti's nothing but trouble. I'd like to throw *her* off the Sixth Street Bridge."

"She's helping me out, Tina."

"What do you need her for?"

Smiling, Nadra pointed to the chair.

Tina sat, then said, "I was going to come by in the morning, see if you needed anything."

"I'm fine," Nadra said as she opened Tina's gift. "A silver spoon."

"Somebody in the family deserves to be born with a silver spoon in her mouth."

"Thank you."

"Don't mention it. Of course it's for when she's ready to eat on her own."

"It's beautiful."

"I'll come by in the morning, in case you need anything."

Nadra reached over and squeezed Tina's hand. "You look really nice, Tina."

"Thank you. Papa liked my dress, but it was obvious Mama wasn't impressed, not that she's ever been."

"Her approval isn't what counts."

"You think I'm as good looking as Peggy?"

"Better, sweetheart, better."

"Really?"

"Really."

Tina stood and turned toward door one. "I have to get out of here before the witch gets back."

At that moment Shanti entered. "The witch is already here." Shanti bowed and waved Tina out, but she remained by the door until John and Benny entered.

"What do you expect us to do, Shanti?" Benny asked.

"What I would expect any good *ibn Arab* (son of an Arab) to do!"

"It's not our business! She's not our wife!" Benny said.

"Simon Metrey is a mean wife beater," Shanti said.

"We know, but he is her husband," John said.

Dumbstruck, Shanti glowered at the two men, lowered her voice and asked, "And does that make it all right?"

Embarrassed, John responded, "No, of course not."

"Maybe if someone beat the hell out of him," Shanti said as she moved menacingly toward her husband.

"Are you crazy?" Benny asked.

Shanti stopped in front of the tapestries to reflect. "How about this? Threaten to stop doing business with him. When he wants his wholesale goods for his store, say no."

"Sure, Shanti, then how are his kids going to eat?"

"They barely eat as it is!" Shanti said as she backed Benny into the horsehair sofa.

As he pushed back, Benny said, "That's right, so let's make it worse for them!"

'Am-moo entered the room from door two to ask, "Why is everyone shouting?"

"Shanti thinks we can make Simon stop beating Sonya," Benny said.

As the number of contenders grew, they edged into the bedroom space.

"She's his wife," 'Am-moo said.

"That's the point, old man!" Shanti growled.

"No man can interfere with another man's family!" 'Am-moo shouted back.

"Get out of my bedroom!" Nadra snarled.

"Shanti, think about it, if we interfere, he may well do her more damage," John said as he edged the contenders back to the living room space.

"You're afraid to talk to him?" Nadra said.

"No," John said, "I'm saying if we do, he may do her more damage?"

Nadra turned away from him.

"No man can interfere with another man's family!" shouted 'Am-moo again. "Now, John, why does this child have a French name?"

"I insisted on it!" Nadra said.

Looking like a dumbfounded pasha encountering a disturbed slave, 'Am-moo was temporarily at a loss for words.

Entering door two with Dowla trailing her, a hand-wringing Um-Hana demanded, "Look, these poor hands! I not able to roll cabbage and grape leaves!"

Shanti nailed Um-Hana with her eyes. "You roll them at Dowla's house, I've seen you!"

Recovering and looking askance at the disturbed woman, 'Am-moo asked John about Nadra. "Whatsa matter with her?"

Five boys crashed through the sacred doors, John and Nadra's three and Shanti and Benny's two. Each camp shouting that they had been scammed, they cried for their parents to intercede. When the parents tried instead to determine the reason for the conflict, the five boys began belting each other.

"I'ma not gonna do thousand cabbage and grape leaves for buncha Irish priests who do nothing for Syrian people!"

Adding her voice to the ever-widening melee, Aurelia began crying then howling, choking on her sobs. So began her introduction to life with the Hanouns in the Syrian community of Hedley, West, by God, Virginia.

Aurelia

Aurelia was an enormous delight to her mother and a mewling annoyance to her big brothers. In the frigid winter, when the baby cried, Nadra would swaddle her tightly in receiving blankets and sway with her as she walked the floor in front of the hallway stove. After Aurelia's first birthday, when the summer heat enveloped the apartment, she began crawling, attempting to lift herself up. Nadra would help her stand and take tentative steps as she sang, "*Hday-ya mday-ya.*" Nadra coaxed her baby to take one, then another step. Continuing she sang,

"*RuH-naw jeena.*" ("We went and we came back.")

"'*Aa ij-ray-na*" ("On our journey")

"*Shuf-nal-ma-ma*" ("We saw Mama")

"*Te'lee 'dhaama.*" ("Roasting chickpeas.")

"*Tay-na shway-ya*" ("Give us a little bit")

"*La-lub-nay-ya.*" ("For the baby.")

She began tickling her as she chanted the last line—

"*Au-lat 'cromma, cromma, cromma!*"

Aurelia would laugh with delight.

Nadra thought, *If only Sitto could see her. This is the song she sang to me.*

❧

Aurelia was indulged as much as any child could be during, and in the aftermath, of the Great Depression. Mixing what precious sugar she had with milk, Nadra made her rennet puddings; she bought remnants of material and sewed her pinafores which she adorned with meticulous handwork, sweet lambs or ebullient bunnies peering from the yoke. Um-Hana liked to feed Aurelia the sweets she swiped from Nadra's holiday stash, amusing herself with the way Aurelia dropped nuts and slobbered rosewater syrup on her white pinafores. Her aunts Tina, Eva, and Millie bought her little girly things, hair ribbons, plastic barrettes, tiny bracelets. One time they bought her delicate silver studs and asked Nadra if they could have Aurelia's ears pierced. Finding out about their plan, John erupted with volcanic fury. "What are you trying to do to her? She's just a little girl!" That would be but a prelude to a mindset, a crusade that he would keep until Aurelia became an adult.

The first word Aurelia was able to say was "Baba," so the term came to be used for others, as in all Arabic families. For Aurelia and her brothers it meant father; for John it was an affectionate term for his children, particularly Aurelia. Saying, "Hello, Baba," John would bend down and pat her on the head. To tease her, he would touch her nose, pretending to take it, then force his thumb through his fingers, showing her the stolen nose. Even after she caught on to his trick, Aurelia continued to show alarm and surprise, so delighted to have her father's attention.

When she was old enough to walk the distance, John would take her to see the circus parading into town just after dawn. Bleary-eyed but happy, she was as eager to see the "March" as he was. Sometimes she had to run a few steps to keep up with his pace.

Fronted by the high school band, the crier led the "haul," the move between the circus train and the show lot, warning the "natives" to "hold your hosses the elephants are coming!" Horses and camels thundered down the street, followed by the slogging-along elephants. Those elephants, wearing tutus, would balance on their hind legs later in the show, when their masters jabbed them with the bull hooks. Ornate wagons hauled the big cats—the lions and tigers that would be forced to jump through burning hoops. Bears held onto the wagon bars and stared; later they would be riding bicycles under the big tent. Chimpanzees flitted back and forth as though anticipating the motion of their motorcycle act. The spectators' eyes were riveted on the caged animals.

Transfixed by the animals' desperation, Aurelia clung to her father's leg and began crying. He picked her up as she said, "I'm sorry for them."

He soothed her saying, "Baba, they are just animals."

Other criers, talkers, followed, exhorting the onlookers to, "Follow the parade to the show grounds! Big free exhibitions on the show grounds immediately after the parade." Hawkers were everywhere, selling souvenirs, pennants, whistling birds, canes, and whips.

But such trips with her father were infrequent. John was even more anchored to the confectionery, always looking for an opportunity to make another dollar. Comic books, then magazines were the current answer. John fanned out copies of *Superman*, *Batman*, *Captain Marvel*, *Captain America*, and *Tarzan* in his store's large front window.

When Aurelia was a toddler her brothers found her cute and amusing. They gave her whatever they no longer wanted—a broken balsa wood plane, a yo-yo, and occasionally, a piece of candy that they pilfered from the store when John wasn't looking. She accepted them but came to realize such gifts were pay-offs as the boys vaulted out the apartment to more interesting places.

No longer a toddler, Aurelia was still on her brothers' heels, wanting to be a part of games, exploits, or fights they engineered. They were forever chasing her away, rejecting not so much her company as the responsibility for her. To avoid her, they even had to sneak out of the apartment, which was difficult considering that there was only one exit. When they avoided her or ran away from her, she was hurt. She howled with indignation. It was not long before she was dubbed The Cry Baby. Her aunts considered her backward. Those descriptions miffed Nadra.

Nadra understood Aurelia's longing, so she took her daughter out often, pushing her in the old worn stroller. In the cool mornings of the summer they traversed Route 50, passing the businesses, pizza joints, and motels that lined the first mile until Route 50 reached the park. There they wandered past the large white fountain that graced the park's entrance to the lily pond and to the children's play area. When Nadra pushed Aurelia in a swing, she sang to her. The trip to the park was Aurelia's favorite.

On fall days they often went where Nadra liked best, the neighborhoods. Directly across from the apartment was another world—Miller Street. Two- and three-story houses with porches and ample front yards lined the street. Most houses were frame, interspersed with a few red brick and buff bricks. Grass everywhere. Trees gloried in fall colors of red and gold. Flowers that had begun growing in summer were still in bloom, salvias, daylilies, goldenrods, tiger lilies, and sunflowers. Marigolds in rich colors of yellow, orange, and deep red soaked up the sun. Nadra envied the women who knelt at their flowerbeds, adding flats of chrysanthemums. Nadra said good morning to all of them, and they often left their planting to comment on her pretty little girl and to chat.

With Aurelia, Nadra could be a kid, something she was never allowed to be before. They went everywhere and when they could afford it, they went downtown to Krenek's where they ate hot dogs, but of course they never told John or the boys. It was on their honeymoon that Nadra discovered that John hated hot dogs. He would not allow hot dogs on their table. He liked to hold forth on the gross things that butchers put in them. But if any of that were true, Nadra was sure that ample amounts of relish and mustard would kill the threat.

Some days Nadra would complete her housework early. Taking Aurelia by the hand, she would go to her friends who lived close by, spending an hour or two before it was time to head home and make supper.

One such trip would prove ominous.

Sonya

Nadra told Aurelia they were going to see Sonya Metrey.

Aurelia jumped up and down. "I love Silly Sonya!"

"So do we all. Now, can you put on your shoes?"

"'Course, Mama." As she sat on the floor and struggled with her shoes, Aurelia said, "Are we going to take cookies you hid from Baba and the boys?"

Surprised and amused, Nadra said, "Yes."

She watched as her four-year-old dragged a kitchen chair to the tall cabinet and opened the door. She pushed aside the cans and boxes to get to the coffee can filled with cookies. Giving Aurelia a bag, Nadra said, "Put the cookies in here." Aurelia did as instructed but left two cookies in the can.

"What about those?"

Aurelia simply smiled and put the top on the can.

If she had them, Nadra took sweets or fruit to Sonya's house. Everyone knew that Simon gave Sonya very little money. Most days the family survived on *imjadra*, lentils cooked with *bulgur* or rice. On good days they ate bulgur with added bits of chicken. On bath days the children bathed in the same shallow bath water, the tub rimmed with the dirt from their bodies.

As they were walking to Sonya's, they were surprised to see her husband tear out of the house. Simon Metrey was a tall muscular man with a square face and prominent square jaw. Aspects of his features seemed a play on the square. The black furrowed eyebrows sat below the black hair that he flattened across his square head. The slightly open hard-set mouth. Hostile brown eyes that dared others to meet them. He was usually smoking, a cigarette dangling from his fingers.

Nadra nodded to him, grasped Aurelia's hand more firmly, and walked deliberately past his house. She felt that he was watching them so they continued walking in the other direction.

Aurelia was trembling. She clutched the bag of cookies to her body and inched closer to Nadra.

"I want to go home, Mama."

Only after they walked several blocks did Nadra feel safe to turn and look. Her worried thoughts sped her breathing, making her heart race and her muscles tighten. As they turned back toward Sonya's house, Aurelia gripped Nadra's hand tighter. Nadra realized that Aurelia was shaking. Nadra patted her gently, "Don't be afraid."

"But you're afraid, Mama."

When Nadra tapped on the front door, no one answered so she pushed her way in, calling for Sonya. The atmosphere was quiet, unnaturally so. Three children were huddled together on the living room sofa. The littlest one was sobbing; the other two were white-faced, their frightened eyes darting everywhere.

Nadra released Aurelia's hand and nodded toward the children. Aurelia joined them, sitting next to the sobbing child, patting him. When his sobs subsided, she motioned for the other two to move closer, and she opened the bag of cookies.

As she left Aurelia with Sonya's children, Nadra's heart cried, *May God protect all our children.*

Nadra looked for Sonya. When she saw her son Alex crouching outside a door she knew she had found her. She was in the bedroom, weeping. Neither spoke. Nadra sat next to her and held her hand, her eyes surreptitiously scanning Sonya's face, arms, and legs. When Sonya stopped crying, Nadra leaned closer and gently unbuttoned Sonya's blouse. When Sonya tried to stop her, Nadra shushed her, but had to hold herself back when she saw the bruises and welts on Sonya's chest. She examined her back and found more of the same, including a long bloody trail where she had been scratched. *Sneaky devil! Now he's abusing her in places where the bruises and marks won't show,* thought Nadra. Nadra returned to the living room and shooed the children into the backyard. She searched the bathroom for Mercurochrome and washcloths. Returning to Sonya, she cleaned the long scratches gently and covered them with the antiseptic. Together they went to the kitchen where she wrapped ice cubes in a thin tea towel and pressed them to the bruises on Sonya's chest and back. Eventually Nadra placed the icy cloth in Sonya's hand so she could hold it on her chest while Nadra made tea. The children were peering in the window, their eyes big with fear and worry. Nadra's heart screamed, *May he be thrown into a black cave where armed fiends push and shove and hit him each second of his remaining life. God damn devil!*

Half crazy with rage, Nadra raced home, Aurelia running behind. Struggling to contain her cursing, she told John. Then she called Shanti. Shanti told her to come to her house. The men were meeting there in the evening to play cards.

Another Man's House

Shanti lived in a large brick house in an established neighborhood. One of those Anglo-Saxon houses with mantles and mirrors in which all the furniture matched. White sheers with floor to ceiling draperies hid the outside. Nadra felt she should wear her better clothes when she visited. She tried to make her face friendly and reasonable, to better plead her case.

After greeting Nadra, Shanti led her to the dining room where the men sat at the table with their drink glasses interspersed with Blenko glass bowls of pistachios and roasted chickpeas. Cigarettes and a box of cigars were also on the table, items Sami brought from his newly established Smoke Depot, which was housed in his tavern's adjoining room.

The women faced Shanti's husband, Benny, 'Am-moo Ike, Sami, Farid Ferris, and John.

"We want to talk to you," Shanti said.

The men looked at the women quizzically but continued playing.

"Simon is at it again," Shanti said.

Sami was about to deal another hand when Shanti slammed her fist on the table. "Simon's at it again!"

While still holding their cards, they turned toward the women.

"He's at it again! Nadra saw what he did. Sonya has bruises and bloody scratches on her bosom and back. She was weeping when Nadra found her. The children were terrified."

Nadra said, "You have to help her."

After a long and awkward silence, John said, "We don't know what to do."

"In time Simon will mellow," Sami said.

"What the hell does that mean?" Shanti said.

"Hold your tongue, Shanti."

"Don't tell me what to do, Benny. You tell me what you can do to help Sonya."

Sami said, "He's still a young man, with a big family, a business. When life is better he will mellow."

"Like ripe fruit, he's going to grow soft?"

Ignoring Shanti's sarcasm, Sami smiled. He passed around the box of cigars.

"She will be dead by then," Nadra said.

"We have no business in another man's house," said 'Am-moo Ike.

Nadra almost choked when he said that. When he caught her eye, she refused to release him. He looked away.

Gazing around the room, Nadra said, "You don't want to help her, do you?"

"It's not that, Nadra," said Benny as he took a cigar.

Sami said, "It's not our way to tell another man how to run his family." Sami cracked a few pistachios.

"You can't talk to him? You're smart men, you have done so much in your lives, your businesses."

"We don't know what to do," John said again.

"Nadra shames us. She is right. *Ibe*, ibe on us," said Farid Ferris.

As Sami lit a cigar, he said, "You can't understand. You are not a married man."

"What's that got to do with it? It's okay to beat up a woman?"

John rearranged his cards. 'Am-moo Ike tried to peek at Benny's hand as he repeated, "We have no business in another man's house."

Barely controlling her voice, Nadra hissed, "You sit there with your cigars, smoking, talking, laughing...while Simon pounds and scratches Sonya. *Ibe alikun!*"

John shouted at her, "We don't know what to do that won't make it worse!"

Nadra glared at him before she left the room.

"Let's not fight, friends," said Benny. "You have coffee, Shanti?"

"No."

Shanti also left the room.

Together they slammed out of the house and sat in Shanti's car.

"What else can we do?"

"Short of murdering Simon, not much, at least not much without harming Sonya too."

"Even when we shame them, they do nothing."

Shanti said, "They don't feel shame."

"I like to think John does."

"You like to think a lot of positive things, Nadra."

"I'm going home."

"I'll drive you."

"Thanks. I left Aurelia with the boys."

Shanti said, "Isn't Um-Hana there?"

"She's always there."

❦

Before Nadra arrived home the children gathered in the company and sitting area of the living room. Tommy and Aurelia sat on the horsehair sofa facing the coffee table, looking at comic books. Billy sat on one of the two side chairs, sketching. The other chair next to him held his favorite magazines, *Popular Electronics* and *Mechanix Illustrated*.

George entered from door two.

"You're not supposed to come in through door two," Billy said.

"So arrest me!" George said. He tossed two packs of Dubble Bubble to Tommy and Aurelia.

"Thank you!" they both said as they tore the wrappers. Billy grabbed Aurelia's funnies and began reading both his and hers. Then they began chewing.

"Say nothing about how you got them, snots!"

"What are you doing, Brain?" George said.

"None of your business, *Georgie*."

George tried to look at Billy's sketch. "They don't like you to waste paper."

Billy threw the *Mechanix Illustrated* at George.

George threw the magazine back at Billy. "Baba doesn't like you to use your left hand."

"Baba doesn't like anything I do."

"When he sees you, he'll smack you again."

Aurelia moved toward them to look at Billy's sketch.

"So what else is new?" Billy said to George.

Smiling, Aurelia said, "I like it."

Assuming an informed tone, George said, "Baba and 'Am-moo Ike say being left handed will make you stand out and look slow."

"I don't like you, *Georgie*! You're a show-off. You just like to speak Arabic with the old folks to show off."

"*They* like me."

"Most of those stories you tell are lies."

Aurelia edged closer to them. "Mama was really mad today."

George said, "Why is that, little one?"

"Simon hurt Sonya again."

"Doesn't surprise me," Tommy said. "I've seen him smack Alex more than once."

"She's going to tell Baba and all the men."

"Best of luck," Billy replied.

They were immediately silenced when they heard footsteps at the front door. Aurelia and Tommy hid the bubblegum wrappers in the sofa cushions and slid the gum to the side of their mouths.

Nadra came into the living room. "What are you all doing?"

"Nothing we shouldn't be doing," George said.

Eying them closely and surveying the room, she asked, "Grandmother is in her room?"

"Yes, she decided not to go out with her boyfriend tonight," Tommy said.

Nadra turned to glare at Tommy who retreated farther into the sofa cushions.

Focusing on the little one, Nadra said, "It's time for you to be in bed, Aurelia."

"Why?"

"Because I said so." She held out her hand and waited.

When Aurelia finally took her mother's hand, she said, "They always get to stay up. They always get to do everything!"

"Your day will come, Aurelia," Nadra said as she patted Aurelia.

"When? I want to know when!"

Eventually Nadra returned to the living room and told her boys, "I'm going back out again. To Mrs. Rahal's."

"When are you coming back?"

"Since when do I have to tell you, George?"

"Jeeze, just asking."

Nadra gave them one last look and left.

"Sounds like telling Baba and the men didn't work out," George said. Peering at Billy's sketch, he added, "How come you don't draw girls? You some kind of hermaphrodite?"

"Go strut someplace else," Billy said.

"You're weird, Brain."

"Your tits jiggle when you hurry down stairs, Georgie Porgie."

George lifted his hand.

From sacred doorway two pajama-clad Aurelia screamed, "Please don't hurt each other!"

∽

When Nadra returned she went to bed immediately to avoid having to talk to John. But she wasn't able to avoid Lila who summoned Nadra to the Zahirs' that morning. Nadra was surprised because mornings Lila usually worked in the Smoke Depot. Though he maintained control, Sami taught her how to manage their secondary business and keep the books.

Nadra took Aurelia with her.

Without asking, Lila led them into the kitchen and poured Nadra a cup of coffee.

"She drinks milk?" Lila asked.

"Of course she drinks milk," Nadra responded.

"I don't want any," Aurelia said. When Nadra looked at her, Aurelia said, "No, thank you."

"There are magazines in the living room," Lila said.

Aurelia went into the living room, reluctantly, and hid close to the door, listening.

Lila focused intently on Nadra as she asked, "What do you think you're doing?"

Nadra merely lifted her eyebrows.

"You know what I'm talking about."

"Then why are you asking?"

"You can't tell men what to do!"

"You can if they don't know enough to do it by themselves."

"And did you succeed?"

"No."

"Do you know why?"

"They said to stay out of other people's families. They told us it was none of our business."

"It *is* none of your business!"

Nadra leaned toward Lila and spoke briskly. "You didn't see the bloody lines on Sonya's back, the black and blue marks on her chest. The terrified children huddled on the sofa."

"No one likes the man. She was warned about him."

"Sonya is kind and gentle."

"Sonya hasn't yet learned to close her legs," Lila said.

"My God, you think that—"

"It doesn't matter what I think. You can't tell a man, any man, what to do. You never *ever* tell a man what to do!" Sipping her coffee, she added, "You only have to decide what you want to do."

Quietly Sami entered the room, belting his bathrobe tightly around his middle.

Lila looked at him, smiled, and rose immediately. "Pour your father a cup of coffee. I'm going to work."

"Don't forget to order the Lucky Strikes!" Sami shouted at her.

"Good morning, Nadra."

"Good morning, Papa."

"Ah, here's your pretty little girl," Sami said when Aurelia entered the kitchen, smiling at him.

Nadra poured Sami's coffee, gave Lila five minutes to get down the street, took Aurelia's hand, and left also.

Eruptions

Back in the apartment, George was sneaking around the boys' bedroom door. The fourteen-year-old opened it slightly to watch Billy as he worked on his model airplane.

"Playing with yourself or that airplane?" George said.

"Can't you ever shut up?"

Using his broad frame to thrust the door wide, George said, "Why don't you make me?"

Billy ignored George.

Swatting the plane, George mocked, "Why don't *you* make me?"

"Keep your hands off my stuff!"

"Keep your hands off my stuff!" George mocked as he reached for the plane.

Twelve-year-old Billy was not as broad as his brother, but he was taller and faster. He rose quickly and threw all his weight against George, knocking the wind out of him. Once George rallied, he grabbed Billy's arm and began twisting it. Billy kicked him in the balls, and when George began howling, he grabbed his leg and began pulling him toward the open window. Billy put all his strength into pushing George over the windowsill. George began bellowing, "Help! Help!"

Hearing the thuds and screams, John, 'Am-moo Ike, and

a customer immediately ran up the apartment stairs and into the bedroom.

"My God, my God, what are you doing!" John asked.

"He's trying to kill me, Baba!"

"I was just teaching him a lesson," Billy said.

"Lesson my ass!" George screamed.

"What did you do to your brother, George?" John asked.

"Nothing! I came to get my shirt. He's weird, he's just weird, Baba."

Enraged, John was ready to take his belt to both of them, but 'Am-moo pulled John to the side and began whispering. "The boy isn't going to learn through talk, John. He could have killed his brother."

Closing the window, the customer said, "Hey, John, boys will be boys."

"We need to take him to the jailhouse," 'Am-moo insisted. "Tell them to lock him up for an hour, scare the hell out of him so he straightens up."

Shaking his head at the suggestion, the customer retreated to the store.

Billy looked at them defiantly, then John quickly grabbed one arm and 'Am-moo the other.

Billy was kicking at the men's legs when Nadra came home with Aurelia and was intercepted by the customer who told her, "Mrs. Hanoun, your husband and uncle might be a little over the top. Your boys had a fight and they're gonna take the youngest to jail."

Nadra scaled the stairs, took her broom to 'Am-moo Ike who still gripped Billy's arm, and screamed demon-driven threats at her husband. Aurelia cowered in a corner, terrified but fascinated.

Nadra finished her invective with, "You're supposed to be a father, but you're acting like a hamour!"

Um-Hana came screaming into the room, "Don't you talk to John that way!"

"I'll talk to him any way I please! He's my husband—you left yours, remember?"

Rising on her haunches like a hound debating whether or not to attack, Um-Hana hesitated, then finally chose to retreat.

"Why did you have to say that?" John said.

"God help me, what have I ever been allowed to say?"

"You go too far, Nadra."

"You went too far, John, and you know it!"

John stepped closer and said, "I am the head of this house!"

"No, you're not! That old fart is! She is!"

'Am-moo Ike marched out.

"You have said enough!"

"You were going to put our son in jail!"

Nadra said nothing more, but she would exact full revenge.

Longing to get even, Um-Hana's antagonism became overt. She took issue with Nadra's cooking. She insisted the Lenten dish *immjadra* was to be made with lentils and rice. Nadra insisted the only proper way to make immjadra was with lentils and *burghul*, which she claimed was far more nutritious. While the warring women resorted to tradition and Allah to prove the authenticity and deliciousness of their recipes, the children declared immjadra a Syrian horror and proclaimed their hatred of both versions. They wanted Nadra's fried perch or baked cod with French fries.

Longing for peace, John was careful to eat equal portions of both immjadras. When he was asked which he liked best, he replied in a tremulous voice, "I like them both," at which point Um-Hana ladled another glob onto his plate. Nadra started to do the same just as he looked up at her. She withdrew the ladle, touching his shoulder gently as she moved away.

But Nadra's mercy was limited. She had already begun her bedroom withdrawal, which was difficult considering that they only had one bed. Usually she waited until John went to bed and was asleep. When that didn't work and he questioned her, she told him that she had more socks to darn as she pulled them from her sewing basket.

"All those socks have holes?"

"All these socks have holes… I don't have the money to buy new socks…for the children."

He turned away and went to sleep.

When Nadra ran out of socks and excuses, she was careful to situate herself as close to the edge of the bed as possible.

"If you move any closer to the edge, you will be on the floor."

"Perhaps that's where I should be."

"I'm not my mother!" he shouted as he sat up in bed.

"Yes you are. You're a mix of her and that old fart 'Am-moo!" she said as she rose up to face him.

"My God, Nadra, what do you want?"

"I want *us* to be head of this house. *I* too am head of this house!"

"What is my mother? A guest?"

"Yes!"

"You're getting like *your* mother, Nadra, sour and resentful, no good word for anybody."

"What about your mother?"

"She has more heart than yours, Nadra."

"Does she?" Shaking her head, she said, "I'm sure they have been running neck and neck, John. One frowns, the other glares. They have hearts of steel and hands of wood. Never have those idle hands prepared a sweet. Never has a kind word slipped from those pursed mouths. Every devil in hell could learn from them!"

John laughed.

"Shall I say more or are you tired?"

Ignoring her sarcasm, he said, "You exaggerate, but I'm listening."

"When I first came to America, I was happy and excited, dreaming of what I would see, what I could do, what I might have. Then we moved into this apartment, this damn apartment! I grew up here, John. This apartment was my prison for the first four years of my life in this great glorious America. I tended the store, watched the children, cleaned upstairs and downstairs, but no one ever cared what I wanted."

"What more do you want, Nadra?"

Taken aback by his question, Nadra struggled to contain herself, like smoke trapped in a burning house.

"I want a say, I want a voice! I will not live that way again. Like the Amerikan like to say, no one will be the boss of me. No one else will decide how to raise my children!"

"Our children, Nadra, our children."

"Really, John? Why were *you and 'Am-moo* ready to cart Billy to jail?"

"I was angry."

"And I am angry! And I am angry when you smack that youngster's hands."

"I don't do it out of meanness. I do it to change him."

"Why don't you go smack someone else—someone who really needs changing? Like Simon Metrey!"

"I do not smack Billy out of meanness. You know that."

"Do you know why you do it?"

"Obviously not, but you know."

Nadra spoke clearly and slowly, as one would do when speaking to a child, "You're still stuck in your old country ways. You do it out of ignorance, John. You don't know better."

He jumped out of bed and faced her. "My God, is there nothing you are afraid to say to me?"

"Why should I be afraid?"

He came as close to her as he possibly could without knocking her over. She did not move.

"You insult me, Nadra! Have I ever spoken to you in such a way?"

Chastened, she hesitated before she said, "Not your words. Your actions."

"Words can cut as deeply," he said as he turned away.

❧

Nadra was overwhelmed. She had two interfering in-laws, a husband who wasn't making enough money, two teenage boys who hated each other, an eight-year-old who didn't even fit into his brothers' hand-me-downs and needed a vaccination, and a daughter who was called backward.

In an effort to avoid feeling sorry for herself and to gain per-
spective, Nadra would reflect on her two sisters left behind in the
old country. One died at age twenty; the other was married to a
womanizer and drinker. Poverty-stricken, that sister often wrote to
her father, Sami, pleading for money. Reflecting on them, Nadra felt
grateful to have gotten away from Saidnaya.

Sometimes she thanked God she wasn't like Latifa, the elderly
lady who lived in the shabby apartment across the street. Alone, no
family, Latifa latched onto Nadra's kindness and goodwill. Aware of
the danger of slowly shuffling across Route 50, she positioned herself at the curb and shouted, "Yoo hoo, Mrs. Hanoun!" at least four
times a week. Nadra responded to her needs and also gave her what
food she could spare. When Latifa did make it across the street, Nadra's children dispersed, claiming Latifa's multi-decibel voice was
too much for them. Billy suggested she be fixed up with 'Am-moo
Ike, who deserved her.

Nadra needed someone to talk to. She could, but would never go to Lila, her mother. So she took Aurelia and went to see
Dowla Rahal.

Dowla

They found Dowla in the kitchen. Smiling, she embraced them. "Good morning, sweethearts!" Dowla walked in plain flat black shoes and wore a housedress covered with an ample apron. A hardworking mother who kept house for her adult children and did all she could to make them comfortable.

The Syrian community in Hedley included a small array of strong women, women often called strong because they were such a marked contrast to their husbands. Most were at least assertive, if not aggressive, but all were adamant and verbal. Nadra was drawn to Dowla Rahal who was the opposite of those outspoken harridans. Unlike the other wives married to weak and/or non-descript husbands, Dowla was quiet, gentle, and tolerant. She was also blessed with wit and imagination, often surprising those who thought they knew her. She was married to David, a small quiet man who began his career in America by pushing a wooden cart, selling vegetables and fruit. Unlike others who started with push carts, he never earned enough to start his own store. Later he became a custodian for a bar and grill, cleaning up each day after it closed and setting up before the start of business the next day. His friends liked to say that David's philosophy of life revolved around the belief that if you had a stomachache on Monday, it was because you didn't go to church on Sunday.

Nadra realized that Dowla had already accepted David as he was. Such knowledge may have made her sad at times, but it never made her round on David or others, like a battleship bringing guns to bear. Accepting his limitations and her own, Dowla said, allowed her to embrace those of others. Dowla insisted that we were all a package—of strength, weakness, craziness, and hope.

They had tea and cookies. Aurelia had milk and sugar cookies, and when she started getting sleepy, they lay her on the sofa, nestled against the plentiful pillows.

When Nadra confided in her, Dowla's kind eyes embraced her.

"You feel 'Am-moo Ike and Um-Hana have more influence than you."

"They're just using him, Dowla."

"Perhaps it's their way of being needed."

"We don't need them. They do nothing for us."

"Give them something to do. Use them."

"Why doesn't she go back to her husband in the old country?"

Anticipating the old question, Dowla was already looking away.

"I'm sorry. I promised not to ask again."

"We all have to work our way through this world."

"You're getting philosophical now."

"Practical."

"Practical?"

"You're going to figure it out, Nadra."

They were not aware of it, but the little one was listening.

You're going to figure it out. How simple that sounded, but maybe Dowla was right. After all, she did usually figure it out. Perhaps she should pretend to be like Dowla—patient, kind, soft spoken, helpful. She decided to change and learn how to "use them." Her frowns and glares became smiles. She managed warm good mornings to Um-Hana. Several times she had George take food to 'Ammoo's place. Then she suggested that John invite Ike to dinner.

On that occasion 'Am-moo put down his fork long enough to announce his new entrepreneurial scheme—potato chips.

"Potato chips?" John said.

"Yes, potato chips!"

"Everybody buys Conn's from Zanesville," John said.

"'Am-moo is not talking about regular potato chips, John," Nadra said.

"These will be special!" 'Am-moo said as he took another helping of *kibbe*. 'Am-moo emphasized his next sentence with a wave of his fork. "Fresh! Homemade by hand!"

Nadra beamed. "Syrian potato chips, John!"

John squinted at her. She patted his hand then handed him the salad. Smiling sweetly, Nadra said, "That's a lot of work. Perhaps George could help you. He could learn from you, 'Am-moo."

John almost choked on the olive he had placed in a wad of bread.

"Yes, it is my plan to teach him. He's likeable and he has a good mind, the Hanoun mind. I will teach him business and Arabic."

Ike had a storefront on Noble Street that he used for his business, though there was no sign of his business on the front. On the inside he had a potato peeler that he cranked by hand, plus a potato slicer apparatus. Before George arrived from school, he would have the sliced potatoes in a stoneware crock filled with water. Upon

George's arrival 'Am-moo would start up the French fryer. Once the chips were cooked, he spread them out to cool on a wooden table covered with oilcloth. George sat at the table, filled the bags, and handed them to 'Am-moo Ike. He sealed them and put them into a box. If George did anything incorrectly, like putting too many chips into a bag, 'Am-moo would gently tap or shake his hand.

All the time George was filling the bags, 'Am-moo was instructing him in Arabic; he only spoke Arabic the whole time. "*Alef, ba, ta, zheem, hha*" he would intone, and George repeated each of twenty-nine letters of the alphabet after him. Once he mastered the alphabet, he practiced the vowels and consonants. "Open your mouth as if you are saying *aah* and make the sound at the back of your throat. *SabaaH* (morning), *Tayyib* (okay)." Each time George opened his mouth, he threw in a potato chip. Eventually Ike planned to teach him to read and write Arabic. For pay he could eat all the chips he wanted. George always took a bag of potato chips home for Aurelia.

After production 'Am-moo Ike launched into distribution and sales. But he soon tired of walking all over town to peddle his potato chips to grocers and owners of gambling and beer joints. So he made an addition to George's duties.

"Okay, how much?" was George's response.

"What do you mean?" 'Am-moo said.

"You expect me to do it for free?"

"I'm educating you."

"You said the word *free* isn't in the Arabic language."

"You get to eat all you want and you always take some with you."

"Let's settle on a per-bag price, 'Am-moo."

"I can't afford that!"

Sidling closer, George spoke softly. "I won't tell them about the woman, *lady*, who didn't answer the door when I took dinner to your place. You know, when you were not there. I left the food. Then I hid and watched until she opened the door and picked it up."

Curbing his anger, 'Am-moo said, "Two cents a bag."

Incredulous, George said, "No, no, no, 'Am-moo!"

Pearl Harbor: December 7, 1941

The Japanese invasion of Pearl Harbor thrust America into World War II. Like all Americans, the Hanouns were part of the mobilization. Tommy rounded up tin, paper, and rubber for the scrap drives. Nadra saved cooking fat and toothpaste tubes. With the men off to war, teenagers like Billy found work readily. Vecchio, who did the school photographs, gave him a job in his photography studio. While others were listening to news, entertainment, and government propaganda on the radio, Billy was checking out television and learning how it worked. When Nadra took four-year-old Aurelia to see *The Reluctant Dragon* at The Cinema, they whooped along with everyone when "Draftee Daffy," "Russian Rhapsody" and "Daffy–The Commando" mocked Hitler, Tojo, and Hermann Göring. When the basket was passed around for the March of Dimes, Nadra let Aurelia put in what few coins they had.

In 1942, John and George went to register for the Food Rationing Program. John hovered on the side and had George do the talking and signing. As soon as they studied the books and tokens, it was obvious to the Hanouns that they would hardly have enough sugar for the family, let alone the business.

Even through the Depression years John had at least made a living in the confectionery, but now he was hurting and scared. He could no longer buy the amounts of sugar, fats, processed foods, and other ingredients he needed to make the peanut brittle, white cows, and nougats he used to sell along with the ready-made candies he purchased from wholesalers. He could not even afford the black market prices for the needed ingredients.

He was able, however, to purchase stock for the store and family from a wholesale grocer, Cameron Grocery. He began stocking more and more groceries, coffee, cereals, and canned goods. He installed a large deli case for wieners, sausages, sandwich meats and cheeses. But the only customers he attracted were those who needed an item in a hurry. He could not compete with the big grocers like the A & P and Kroger. Desperate, he told Nadra that he would ask the advice of his friends Joseph, Charles, and Michael Mensore.

∽

The Mensores came within a day of receiving John's plea for advice. Joseph and Charles arrived together. Michael trailed in just after them. They shook John's hand and embraced him.

"So how are you?" Charles asked.

"I have been better."

Charles laughed, patting John on the back. Joseph merely arched his jet eyebrows, taking in John and the store.

Inviting them to sit at a table, John said, "What will you have to drink?"

"Nothing," Charles said. Joseph waved off the offer also.

Sitting at a table, Michael said, "Maybe later."

While John watched nervously, Joseph made a lap around the confectionery. "It's still a classy place," he said as he walked past the wood showcases, oak tables, and wrought iron chairs. Then he checked out the restroom. "And it's clean."

Charles walked around also, looking at the display by the soda bar, picking up a milkshake glass and a sundae cup. "Too bad. Can't make any money from ice-cream and fancy candy nowadays."

"You need the beer drinkers!" Michael said emphatically when John joined him at the table.

Peering out the big window on the left, Joseph said, "You're practically on top of the railroad, John! When the railroaders walk up the hill, you have to nab them before they turn right and head for one of the other beer joints."

"That's right," Charles added. "None of them are as nice and clean as yours."

"How do you know that?" John said.

Laughing, Charles said, "We made a few stops before we came here."

"The problem is—" John started to say.

"What is the problem?" Joseph demanded as he turned toward John.

"I don't want to sell beer."

"What you want isn't the issue," Joseph growled. "Think of it as giving thirsty people what they want!"

"Turning the store into a tavern is my only option?"

"Some taverns sell food also—hot dogs, blue plate specials, that kind of stuff," Joseph said. "You only need to sell beer."

"You will be a beer joint!" Charles said.

"Put up a sign right away so they have something to look forward to," Joseph said. "When they crest the hill, go out there and make conversation—with a beer in your hand!"

Charles said, "When you open, do a welcome day. Maybe have a free treat, like popcorn."

"I used to sell a nickel bag," John said.

"So give everybody a free bag!" Charles said.

Sitting forward and smiling, Michael said, "John's Place! A clean friendly place where a man can relax with a couple of beers before he heads home!"

"Speaking of that, I've got to head home," Joseph said. "You call me anytime, John."

Charles patted John on the back again and left with Joseph.

When they were out, Michael said to John, "Let's have a Coca-Cola." When John returned to the table, Michael raised his bottle and said, "Don't worry about the money, John."

❧

That night Nadra left the children and went down to the confectionery to hear what John had learned. As though she were a guest, he directed her to one of the oval oak tables and poured her a Coca-Cola she did not want into a chilled glass. Using the bar towel to wipe moisture from the table and his brow, he reviewed the situation with her. As she listened, she heard the facts, felt his emotions, and faced the reality. Taking his hand, she said, "I know it's not the way we want to make a living, John, but we have no choice."

"You really believe that?"

"Yes, as much as you do."

"Selling beer, Nadra? Making money off people who like alcohol?"

"And *you* never touched a drop of arak, John?"

Mopping his brow again, he said, "Seldom, Nadra, very seldom, maybe on a happy occasion."

Her reply was spoken softly, but it made his head jerk up. "The world is not as steadfast as you."

Her previously sympathetic face was now totally devoid of expression, the clear tablet she presented when she was being careful not to offend. Faced with a mask of objectivity, he could accuse her of nothing.

"A beer license is not cheap!"

"None of them offered to lend the money?"

"Yes, Michael did."

"Good."

"Never before have I had to borrow money!"

"We will pay it back. Michael knows that. Inshallah this will be the only time."

"Of course it will be the only time. Yet I can't bear it, Nadra. Turning our place into a beer joint, selling beer to hillbillies!"

"Get off your high horse, John! Even the President drinks beer! Don't you remember what he said when he signed to repeal Prohibition?"

John laughed. "I think this would be a good time for a beer."

"That's right. Anheuser-Busch sent a team of Clydesdale horses to deliver a case of Budweiser to the White House."

Mopping his brow, John said, "We will be competing with other taverns."

"Of course, but ours will be nicer," she said as she patted his hand.

"Maybe it *will* work for us."

Squeezing his hand and smiling, Nadra said, "We will make it work for us, John."

❦

John began dismantling the confectionery so he could change it to a tavern. He gathered together everything he could no longer use. The soda fountain with its three chromium-plated brass spigots with black Bakelite handles, most of the oak ice-cream tables on pedestals of wrought iron with chairs to match, the handsome wood cases with glass fronts. He hoped to get a good price for them. He would keep the wire stools that flanked the soda fountain. When he went after the long marble table on which they made the fudge, peanut brittle, and nougats, Nadra stopped him.

"Can't we save it?"

"For what?"

"I don't know. Maybe memories?"

"You can't eat memories, Nadra."

Well, at least he's taking action, she thought to herself. All the same, she could not stand seeing the demolition of all they had created together—the joy, the pleasure they had taken in creating an oasis of sweets for the thirsty adults who came for a soda, or home-bound students who came to look at the candies, to watch a demonstration, to buy a nickel's worth or a dollar's worth. It really was their happy business. She remembered the little ones who would pinch a piece of nougat or a sliver of fudge when their parents were distracted. When they knew she saw them, they looked down, but she only smiled.

Later when John came upstairs, he brought her a box containing several of the items she used in the confectionery. Stainless steel and copper bowls of various sizes were in the bottom. The expensive candy thermometers that were essential for timing the sugars were carefully wrapped in the white aprons she had worn. She fingered the wooden spoons and paddles she had insisted on buying. They didn't get hot and were more comfortable in-hand. With them she was also able to detect undissolved sugar granules by feel and sound. She thanked him. *At least I have these,* she mused. She prayed that the families and children who used to frequent their establishment would not be replaced by drunks.

John had a carpenter build a twenty-four by four bar with Masonite on it for the left-hand side of the store. Taking Nadra's advice, he also had four booths built along the length of the right-hand side to accommodate women. He bought two large Coca-Cola coolers for the beer and soft drinks. Ice cooled the beverages better than Freon, so he had a fifty-pound block of ice delivered daily. Each block had a white streak in the middle. John would split each block into two with an ice pick and spread the pieces among and over the beer and soft drink bottles. He used to stay open until 9:00 p.m.; now he remained until 11:00 like the other taverns. With work, determination, and the thirsty railroaders who scaled the hill daily from the B & O, John was able to make a living.

Nadra's father, Sami Zahir, was making a very good living. His large tavern buzzed with business and he kept Lila busy in the adjacent Smoking Depot, adding the required stamps. Even though cigarettes were not rationed, name brands were hard to find because the free "butts" were sent to the GIs. Tobacco consumption was fierce during the war, so cigarette sales were at an all-time high.

Sami Zahir moved his family from the upstairs of their building to a large house shadowed by a tree-lined street. A big brick house with a front porch—a real porch where one could sit, read the paper, wave to neighbors. A living room, dining room, large kitchen with built-in cabinets, four bedrooms, enormous bath and big yard. As she toured their new home, Nadra was eaten up with envy, but she smiled and offered a benediction: "*Mahall 'amer*." ("May your home be built up forever!") The words scalded her throat like burning coffee.

On their first tour she realized that she had lost Aurelia. She found her sprawled on the tile floor in the large bathroom. Her daughter loved the cool, serene bathroom. Nadra scanned the black and white tiled bathroom, the long mirror, the large medicine cabinet.

When she pictured her bathroom compared to this one Nadra shuddered. Her bathroom had linoleum and also housed a large gray Maytag washing machine with a manual ringer. On Mondays Nadra washed clothes in the Maytag, wrung them, rinsed them in the tub, then wrung them again and carried them down the stairs to the side yard where she hung them on clotheslines.

Many summer nights when she entered her bathroom, she pondered whether to turn on the light, except for those nights when she had to go so badly that she simply bolted into the room, mindlessly switched on the light, plopped down quickly, and let loose with relief—only to be suddenly taken aback by the cockroaches that scurried away from the light into the far reaches of the corner woodwork.

She ignored John's explanation that nothing could be effective against the cockroaches. They would come into the store through the cartons that held the beer and the soft drinks. She knew this was the price of living over a tavern. But she still scrubbed, sprayed, and prayed. Yet she knew nothing would bring her comfort until the family finally had enough money to move.

For now, at least John had the fortitude to change. He had become a tavern owner and he was making a better living. But he made it clear to her that he would never suffer the indignity of having his wife serve in a beer joint. But Nadra knew a number of ways of helping and dealing with the times. She figured out how to feed her family and feed them well. She set aside her jealousy of Lila and Sami's new house and asked permission to start a victory garden in their backyard. The Zahirs' backyard, with its mature grapevine and fertile soil, was superior to the rock-laden area alongside Nadra's apartment. She knew, of course, that all the work would be hers, but the thought of saving money and having fresh vegetables for her family was worthwhile. The family liked to tease her, saying that she beat Eleanor Roosevelt to the punch. It was rumored that the Department of Agriculture had objected to Eleanor Roosevelt beginning a Victory Garden on the White House grounds. The Department was afraid that the gardens would hurt the food industry.

Nadra created her own food industry. Armed with the *Victory Home Canning Guide and Timetable*, she swung into production. She canned tomatoes, pickles, hot peppers, peaches, grape leaves, *koosa* (Syrian squash), grape juice, jellies and more. She even made her own ketchup, a dark tomato brew infused with onion, celery, dark brown sugar, allspice, cloves, celery seeds, and mace. John and the boys loved the aroma that filled the kitchen. Aurelia fled to her room. She hated ketchup as much as she hated mustard and mayonnaise, none of which had ever passed her lips. She was considered a fussy eater, but realizing that a fussy eater was a not-much-eater, Nadra did not pressure her. Being hungry-all-the-time eaters, the three boys lived up to the Syrian standard—they were "good eaters." Their "silly-skinny" sister would change.

Nadra shared her bounty with Latifa, Sonya Metrey, and Dowla. But she was careful not to take too much, lest she offend. Toting tomatoes, cucumbers, and a jar of jelly, she and Aurelia went to visit Dowla.

∾

Dowla Rahal had four daughters and two sons. The sons were the oldest children and had been drafted. Hanging in the window of her front room was a service flag with a white field and red border featuring two blue stars. Like all mothers of soldiers at that time, she lived in fear. Nadra made sure to announce their arrival loudly just before she rapped on the door so that Dowla would not even for a second fear the arrival of a telegram from the war department.

For Aurelia, Mrs. Rahal was the soft, warm-hearted grandmother that Lila Zahir didn't care to be. Dowla grabbed and hugged Aurelia and talked to her and teased her. When she and Nadra were eager to confide in each other, they sent the four-year-old to the garden or to the dining room. But Aurelia sneaked around to listen. Nadra would scold her but Dowla laughed, saying, "Let her learn so she doesn't grow up like us."

"You talk like we had choices."

"I want to have choices, Mama."

"Watch out, Nadra, this one will break your heart."

Aurelia burst into tears.

Dowla pulled Aurelia to her and rocked her back and forth. "No, no, sweetheart, never cry." But she did not take back her words.

Nadra was tired of Aurelia's crying, but she resisted telling her daughter to straighten up.

War's Perks

Women were seizing the countless opportunities in the workplace. Nadra's youngest sister, Millie, was recruited right after graduation. She was a grinder finisher at the Hardy Tool Company. She announced early on that she would be the next and most famous incarnation of Rosie the Riveter. She dressed in dungarees and a blue shirt, the sleeves of which were folded over enough to reveal her biceps. On her hair she wore a red kerchief with white polka dots. She considered herself loyal, efficient, patriotic, and pretty. She liked to hum the "Rosie the Riveter" song. For effect and, more often than not, to irritate her older sisters, she would flex her biceps and shout, "We can do it."

Tina and Eva also had jobs, money, clothes, and freedom. Eva was a clerical worker in the Union Hall of Boilermakers and Tina was a bookkeeper. Nadra liked to say that for now her work was children, Um-Hana, canning, and *Make Do and Mend*. But she looked forward to having more—a job, an opportunity to make money.

Nadra stared at Tina and Eva when they visited, taking note of their new glowing complexions. They had covered their faces and necks with a light foundation, and then highlighted it with rouge and face powder. Once Nadra asked Tina what was wrong with her lip. Tina patiently explained that she had slightly exaggerated her top lip with liner in order to make her lips look full and soft. It was the thing to do. The next thing to do was to select a shade of red that suited one's coloring or current mood. Tina had selected tomato red. Nadra wanted to say that she had been immersed in tomato red all week, but she knew Tina wouldn't be amused. Tina was still aspiring to be Ava Gardner. Eva's aspiration was Rita Hayworth.

In spite of the rationing, Nadra's sisters knew she would have something good to eat at her place. It might only be leftover grape leaves, made with more rice than meat but fragrant with lemon, or a little bit of *arishee* (cheese from leftover whey), or thick *talamee* that they could lather with her homemade jam. Once they were satisfied, they would remove their fashionable belly-full selves, swinging their handbags and tottering on their new heels. Nadra would sigh and resume her canning. One day she sashayed around the kitchen, imitating their pelvic tilt and swaying behinds. John walked in. Mistaking derision for desire, he thought that God had sent him a golden opportunity. He immediately made hopeful moves. Nadra threw him out.

❧

Delighted that other people's wages could now support gambling, 'Am-moo Ike wanted to change careers, especially since he occasionally entertained "women." So he became, in his words, a bookmaker. When Tommy asked him if that was the same as a bookie, Ike admonished him to avoid slang.

Ike decided to adopt Tommy as his summer companion. Tommy was amenable because he had nothing better to do than get into trouble. He considered Uncle Ike a soft-spoken man who liked secondhand jackets and suits with too-long pants. Smiling, he called him my 'Am-moo. Nadra was concerned when Tommy said his ambition was to be like 'Am-moo.

'Am-moo Ike took Tommy along when he made his rounds writing numbers in Hedley and Maburn, OH. To reach Maburn they boarded the streetcar in front of the confectionery. Going west on Route 50, the streetcar would pass the city hospital and take a right to Boontown where they crossed over the bridge. When they passed over, they were on Front Street in Maburn. They got off there and walked to Third Street. Their destination was simply known as Raymond's Tavern. On their way, they would stop at bars and 'Am-moo Ike would write numbers.

The numbers pad was divided into sheets of three. The top sheet was the original with the number. It went to the customer. The second sheet was the carbon tissue that stayed in the book, and the bottom or third sheet went to the numbers operator. The player played three digits. 'Am-moo started his numbers at five cents and went up in increments of one cent. Most people played a nickel or a dime. 'Am-moo got ten percent of any winnings.

Tommy's new world not only had the illegal numbers, but also the colorful gangster Moody Melrose, hot dog machines, and taverns with blue plate specials. At first he was lured by the hot dog machines, but 'Am-moo Ike quickly directed him to the blue plate specials. Their favorite was pot roast, mashed potatoes, and gravy.

On lucrative trips they dined at the Silver Moon, which was cleaner and nicer. No beer served there. The restaurant had a back room with black market suits and jackets, none of which they could yet afford.

❧

Things were looking up. They finally had some money, but Nadra still never knew exactly how much because John hustled it to the bank as soon as he could. Nadra squirreled away every penny she could, hiding the loot in the green cookie jar. Its lid was cracked years ago when the rambunctious Tommy dropped it while searching for cookies. Everyone was healthy. Um-Hana was napping in the morning *and* in the afternoon. Busy regaling his "woman friends," 'Am-moo Ike was visiting less often. Occasionally George and Billy got along. Nadra even renewed her efforts to persuade Sami to bring her sister Feheema for a visit, or at least a respite from her no-good husband.

During this period of peace John's worried frown eventually morphed into an occasional smile. Nadra was proud of his tenacity and work and let him know it. Their lovemaking, which had become more random than deliberate, increased. Taking advantage of Sunday off, Nadra fed everyone an elaborate breakfast of waffles and cream and ordered the children to take their grandmother to the park. John gave them money so they could stop at the Ice-Cream Heaven store. Um-Hana gave John and Nadra dirty looks.

❧

Nadra loved her boys, the *sebyan*, and doted on them, telling herself the whole time that she was not going to be like her mother and they were not going to turn out like her spoiled brothers, Teddy and Wasim. She insisted her boys stop calling each other names and lectured them about kindness.

Solid and sturdy, George relished each morsel she put in front of him, becoming the consummate good eater. He occupied a central pocket in her heart, being first born and most like her in intelligence and wit. The glint in his eye often signaled an outrageous but insightful comment. She understood him. George gradually took her place as John's main support in the store. He enjoyed the role of being his father's right hand.

Entertaining and charismatic, George was a magnet for people. He loved little children and could make them laugh. He knew how to tease them in that way that said I love you. He regaled young and old with stories, most of which he fabricated. His intelligence, wit, and sociability made him number one in the family. Nadra saw that he enjoyed the role. She and John had high hopes for him. He made them smile and they indulged him.

Billy, two years younger than George, was tall, lean, and disciplined. Billy occupied the tender part of Nadra's heart. She felt any pain her quiet, shy, and sweet boy felt, but doubly so. She needed to protect him—from the dentist who pooh-poohed Novocain, from the father who locked him and Tommy in the rodent-infested cellar for disobedience, from the brothers who called him Jesus, Oop, and Quality Control Man. Sensitive but resolute, Billy could not abide ignorance, his brothers, his father, and Icky Uncle Ike.

Quiet and cerebral, Billy liked all things mechanical and electronic. He took them apart then put them back together. His favorite magazines were *Popular Electronics*, *Radio-Electronics*, *Mechanix Illustrated*, and *U.S. Camera*. His interest in photography was so keen that the owner of Vecchio Photography agreed to become his mentor. Realizing that their second son was also smart and had talents, John and Nadra gave him as much as they could. They bought him a camera and listened when he said that he wanted to set up a darkroom in the horrid cellar.

Tommy, born in 1932, was the smile on Nadra's face, the joy in her heart. He was big, loud, funny, and ornery. He was usually in trouble, claiming he got all the blame because of his six-foot-four size. School was a burden for him, and the Handmaids of the Blessed Mother claimed he was a burden for them. The Sisters told John to send him to the factory.

Tommy was a worker. He was always looking for a way to earn an extra buck. His goal was to have a Schwinn bicycle, and when he earned a significant amount of money, John did all he could to come up with the remainder. When Tommy brought that balloon tire bicycle home, the whole neighborhood came to attention when he sped down the street. He kept his eyes straight ahead, fixed in concentration, like a US pilot chasing down a kamikaze. Just as he was to pass his admirers, he blessed them with a beatific smile and pressed the horn on the red tank. Tommy the Terrible soaring into the sunlight on wings of happiness. Beaming with pride, Nadra laughed out loud.

Nadra couldn't remember if Sonya said every mother deserves a daughter or every mother needs a daughter. Whatever. Five-year-old Aurelia was going to be taller than Nadra, more like John. Skinny with black ringlets crowning her brow and accentuating her big brown eyes and long eyelashes. When Nadra looked at Aurelia her heart overflowed with wonder and joy.

Aurelia wasn't what she expected, and even now she wasn't sure what she got. Quiet Aurelia was usually observing. She didn't like being called l'bint. That meant she couldn't have fun. She wanted to go out, play kick-the-can, shoot marbles, and have train sets to string around the apartment at Christmastime.

Nadra was determined to make her little girl's Christmas special. Nadra saved, carefully shopped for, and splurged on "Bundle of Charm," a twenty-four-inch baby doll with a plastic head, brown molded curls, dimpled chin, blinking eyes, and two teeth. Her fancy dress was pink and her bonnet was edged in lace.

"What shall we call her, Aurelia?"

"Baby."

The boys snickered. For a time Baby napped on Aurelia's bed, but she was nowhere to be seen after that.

"Where's Baby, Aurelia?"

"Baby sleeps better in the dark, Mama."

Nadra checked the closet, under the bed, and in the deep dresser drawers. No Baby. Nadra knew it was best not to ask again.

"I miss Baby, Aurelia."

Aurelia said nothing but went immediately to the dark room, the room at the very end of the hallway where they kept brooms, mops, rags, and old clothes. In the darkest, remotest corner they kept paraphernalia and keepsakes that they thought should be saved even though they knew they would never be used. Aurelia pried Baby out of one of the empty recesses where she had covered her with old clothes and rags. Then she put Baby on Nadra's bed.

Opportunities

Nadra's hopes began soaring again. Before her ambitions had been limited by the times and needs of her family, but her desires hadn't gone away. Now her family had money in the bank, though she didn't know how much. The desires to break free again, to look for possibilities and adventures were still there. At thirty-three she had a husband who loved her and four healthy children, the youngest of whom would go to school soon.

As she and John sat in the kitchen finishing breakfast, Nadra cautiously introduced the topic of her working.

"You know, John, they are now recruiting married women to work in the factory."

He didn't look up at her.

She poured him more coffee and spoke softly. "You can work as little or as much as you want. I could pick my own hours."

He stopped eating long enough to ask, "Do you know what it's like to work in a factory?"

"The money is good, John, very, very good. The market is tight now. They can't get enough workers, and because of the government's wage and price controls—"

"My wife is not going to work in a factory."

She poured him more coffee and spoke evenly. "They can't raise wages so they are offering health insurance now. That's the best part, even more important than the money. We've talked about it, John. We know how important it is to have health insurance."

He tapped on the table with the handle of his fork as he said, "My wife is not going to work in a factory."

"I'm not just your wife!"

"What are you talking about?"

"I'm talking about me, about what I want!"

"Nadra, the work is dirty and the noise is awful."

"Insurance is good. The money is good. We could save it for a house. When I walk in the neighborhoods, John, I study the houses carefully, thinking one day one of them could be ours. I make a game of picking out the best one."

"I'm not trying to deny you."

"The boys are getting too big for this place. And we should have a real bedroom."

He shoved his plate away. "The work is hard, dirty, and noisy."

"It's dirty and noisy here. There are several bars on this street now. I'm sick of the drunks who come out yelling at eleven o'clock, tossing their beer bottles everywhere!"

"I can't help what the drunks do. And you throwing hot water on them from the living room windows doesn't help."

"Having a business here and living here are two different things!"

Glaring at her he rose from his chair and stomped out of the room.

Watching him she thought, *Can't talk to him. Can't reason with him. What is he? Stupid? Afraid? Maybe the boozing railroaders are getting to him. Or maybe this is another way of keeping control, let-ting me know who is the boss. Another way of keeping us from having what everybody else has!*

※

John descended to the store. The day's business inched along, steady but not great. Soon Officer Cork, the policeman, would come by. The neighborhood was part of his beat and he never missed stopping to chat. John always had an ice-cold bottle of Coke for him.

Brian Cork was like the big Irishmen John worked with in the mills in Lowell. The ethnic mix of Massachusetts included the Gregos, the Polacks, the Dagos, the Micks, the Hunkies. Immigrants, working-class men who toiled well and played hard. He had worked alongside them in the mills—strong and proud of their bodies, workers, daring men who had the guts to leave the old country. They were the sweepers, bobbin-boys, mule spinners, slashers, carders, dye house workers, weavers, and loom fixers. Working amidst the gigantic looms and loud carding machines, they looked out for each other, though they were careful to mask their protectiveness with a brusque exterior. They were a rough, tough bunch, ready to defend their turf and beat the hell out of anyone who dared mess with them. And they did.

When Officer Cork finally came by the tavern, he sat enjoying his Coke for a few minutes, then said, "John, what can you tell me about this youngster called Mad Marta?"

"Marta Rahal?"

"Yes. They call her Mad Marta. She beats the hell out of the ninth-grade boys over at the high school."

"She's a nice girl, good family."

"I'm thinking to visit her good family."

Alarmed, John went upstairs as soon as Cork left to tell Nadra to warn Dowla. When she called, Dowla said, "Don't worry."

❧

While the new Catholic Middle School and High School were being built, the Syrian boys had to attend the public high school. (The girls had the option of Saint Catherine's Academy, the private Catholic school for girls.) When the boys attended the large public school, a gang of bullies picked on them. Knowing their route home, the aggressors would wait for them. What John did not tell Cork was that Dowla's youngest daughter, Marta, usually referred to as Mad Marta, decided to deal with the situation.

Unlike her quiet feminine sisters and petite gentle mother, Marta was a tall tomboy who lifted weights. A fit aggressive amalgam of crusader, warrior, and Robin Hood, she was ready to fight anytime. Her buddies the Syrian boys admired and loved her, though she herself was loathe to express such sentiments. When they told her about the bullies' mistreatment and humiliation, she took charge.

Noting that the enemies' route included a hill, she marshaled and hid her forces at the bottom. At the prime moment she led the charge with a bloodcurdling bellow. They dispatched the enemy in a wave of terror and blows. When the bullies struck a second time, her forces walloped them again. The third time she single-handedly thrashed those foolish enough to attack again. Unable to deal with, let alone fathom, a female warrior, tactician and powerhouse, the bullies made up a story and reported her to the neighborhood cop, Sergeant Cork.

When Sergeant Cork arrived at her house, Dowla greeted him with a smile and a slight limp. The only English words she used were "Hello, sir." Thereafter she spoke only in Arabic, seemingly tried her best to understand him, and nodded in apology when she did not. Maintaining her sweet smile, she ushered Cork into her kitchen for coffee and a variety of sweets. Unable to make her understand, he thanked her and retreated with a bag of sugar cookies.

Like Marta, John's best friends Joseph, Charles, and Michael were known as great fighters. One time Joseph had foiled the Micks' attempt to ambush Charles and Michael and himself behind the company store. The fight had begun when one of the Irishmen had forced Joseph off the narrow sidewalk, referring to him as a camel jockey while his companions had chimed in, yelling, "No sand niggers allowed!"

Joseph retorted with, "Right, we don't mix with smoked Irish!" It was that reference to both blacks and Irish that lit their fuses.

The five Micks chased the four Syrians around the block and behind the company store. Appearing out of nowhere with a slat that he had torn out of a fence, Joseph surprised the Irish with several whacks and then gave chase, Charles and Michael and John running close behind, howling.

Another time the Italians, sick of being called Grease Balls and Wops, joined ranks with the Syrians, sick of being called sheepherders and Muzzies, to teach the Huns and Polacks a lesson. John learned early on never to stare at a Dago and never to mess with a Mick.

Young men fearing nothing and no one. Their bravado marked them, but underneath their rough demeanor and ethnic prejudices a bond was forged during their training and the making of cloth, the carding, spinning, and weaving. Hours spent toiling next to each other and the big machines. A bond built on work and blood. When Sebastian's wife died in childbirth and when Giorgio lost his boy, they had all gone to the church and stood together outside, caps in hand, heads bowed in silent respect. In West Virginia John was just a foreigner slinging beer to hillbillies.

❦

By the time John went upstairs for dinner, Dowla had probably already phoned to tell Nadra what happened when Officer Cork went to see her. But John knew Nadra wasn't going to tell him.

After dinner he returned to the tavern.

❦

Every day was the same—stand and wait, sit and wait, hope and wait, for the customers, for the passers-by who stopped and debated whether to come in, or who simply stopped and talked but didn't drink, didn't buy. One morning after another, one day after another, one night after another. Some days one dollar more than enough. Some days one dollar less than enough. But his tavern was clean and reasonably quiet compared to the rowdy ones on the street. One could even call it a family tavern on some days. And it was his. He was a business man now. Every decision was his, every dollar or lack of a dollar was his responsibility.

The Saidnaya in which he had grown up had little for a young man of his background. His family lived among the fellaheen, the farmers who worked the land for the *effendi*, the landowners. His father, Boutros, was a camel driver. John had two older brothers. His strongest memories were being poor and being hungry. His big brothers were first to the table and John got the worst of the chores, like bagging the donkey droppings for fuel. During World War I Syria turned into a military base for the Ottoman Empire. He grew up hearing the terrible stories about the oppressive Ottoman sultans, one of whom was called Hamid the Damned. His deputy was called The Butcher. In his nightmares, John was conscripted by the Ottoman Turks.

Demons and Jesus

In September of 1943 Nadra dressed Aurelia in new tie shoes, blue skirt, white blouse, and sweater and walked her to Blessed Mother Elementary, the Catholic school run by the Handmaids of the Blessed Mother. The kids called it the BME. The Handmaids of the Blessed Mother, referred to simply as the Sisters, were a teaching order founded in Bavaria, 1895. In recognition and imitation of the Blessed Mother's love and tender care, their mission was to guide, nurture, and educate children, their goal being purity and formation of good character.

Nadra knew her daughter was shy and fearful, but she was convinced that she would adjust. Nadra carefully explained that all the things Aurelia's brothers had told her—that the Sisters were black demons from hell, that they used the knotted cords at their side for tying up little children, that some children never returned from school, that some little girls were even eaten alive—were not true. Nonetheless, she saw terror in Aurelia's eyes.

Aurelia stared at the tall creature in a little white and a lot of black. Black that flowed from the pointy peak of her head to her shoulders. Another black fold that flowed from her shoulders to her ankles.

"Aurelia, say good morning to Sister."

Aurelia's eyes had moved to the white square above the creature's eyes, and the other one below her neck that seemed to choke her.

"Aurelia!"

"Good morning," Aurelia said.

Sister patted Nadra, saying, "We will be fine."

Nadra left, telling herself the whole time not to look back.

After that it became Tommy's job to walk with Aurelia to school until she learned the way.

Other than on the occasional good days, school was an ordeal for Aurelia. It became doubly so in winter when Bridget Brown became a part of her school day. It began with Aurelia waking up in the cold dark, telling her mother she did not want to eat the oatmeal or toast. Two weeks ago her mother did not believe her when she said she didn't want to go to school because her stomach hurt; she did not believe her this morning when she explained that was why she could not eat. Nadra backed off, returning the oatmeal pan to the stove, and stood there studying her daughter, as though from that angle she could discern what made her child's stomach churn, if indeed it really did churn.

Aurelia looked straight ahead, erasing any semblance of affect from her face, as though no one and nothing could touch her. It was more effective than whining or crying. Getting sympathy from Nadra was difficult since she had never shown any sign of it herself.

Aurelia had to wear the black coat that her mother was so proud of. The supply of wool was limited during the war years, so

Nadra had cut down one of John's old coats, making a short jacket for eleven-year-old Tommy and the pocketless, trimless coat for Aurelia. The fashion could be likened to that of a perpetual funeral. She put on her mittens while Nadra tied the babushka under her chin.

"I hate that scarf!"

Nadra ignored Aurelia, handing her the cast-off from Tommy, the Smokey the Bear vinyl lunch box. Her father, John, was at the bottom of the steps, waiting to take her across the street. He all but stopped Route 50 traffic, then ordered her to run across.

Aurelia took the four blocks to Hunter then marched down the hill, shoulders hunched forward, stomach in turmoil, eyes darting from right to left in anticipation of her assailant. She yanked the maroon paisley babushka from her long black curls. She would have stuffed it into a pocket, but her mend-and-make-do did not have pockets. She continued down Hunter Street toward Blessed Mother Elementary, dread weighting her steps.

"Hey, Aw-re-lia! Were you looking for me?"

Bridget Brown was running fast behind her, jerking the babushka out of her hand, waving it back and forth. "You should wear this over your face."

Bridget Brown was a tall seven-year-old with green eyes that instantly hypnotized anyone who gazed into them. Her sly feline features revealed an imperiousness of which even an adult would be wary. Swaggering, she did not take her eyes off Aurelia.

Aurelia walked faster, ignoring her, looking straight ahead. Bridget Brown fell in line, imitating and exaggerating Aurelia's expression and posture. Suddenly she threw the babushka around

Aurelia's neck and pulled both ends hard. Losing her balance, Aurelia fell, skinning both knees as she tried to avoid rolling down the hill. The contents of her lunch box flew everywhere.

"See you at school, Aw-re-lia!"

Bridget Brown was racing down the hill, turning occasionally to look at Aurelia.

Finally, Aurelia leaned forward, spit on her scraped knees, and pressed her elbows into them to sop the speckles of blood. She put her meatloaf sandwich and thermos back into the lunch box. She found the dirty orange that had rolled to the foot of a tree. She picked it up, hesitated, then thrust it with all her strength into the trunk of the tree, watching the skin, juice, segments, and seeds slide to the ground.

Aurelia wanted to turn around and go home, home to the deep and loving topaz-brown eyes, to her mother, to Nadra.

Instead she walked on, putting on her face, putting on her mask. Within minutes she would be joining the other children, children she barely knew, children she did not know whether to trust or to fear. She could see Bridget Brown standing by the school door with her best friend, Julia. Julia had ribbons in her hair and wore a short navy coat over a fashionable plaid skirt. Bridget Brown sported a full coat, grey, double breasted with patch pockets. *Amerikan with money*, Aurelia said to herself. The girls stared at her. Focusing on the doorway, she avoided their eyes. As she readied to step inside, Bridget Brown darted forward and put out her foot, tripping Aurelia.

"Hey!" shouted the boy Aurelia almost fell on.

"I'm sorry, I'm really sorry."

"She can talk! She can talk!" screamed Julia and Bridget Brown.

Some kids snickered. Others looked away. Aurelia ignored them, marched to the cloak room, hung up her coat, tucked the mittens in the sleeves, and put her lunch box on the floor.

"Wish I had a Smokey the Bear lunch box."

"I'd rather have one of those scarves."

Aurelia walked quickly to the classroom and took her seat in the back of the room. Sister Mildred was checking off names as each pupil entered.

"Good morning, Aurelia!"

"Sorry, Sister. Good morning."

What her brothers had told her was true. She was hurled into a world of black demons preying on little children, their knotted cords used for tying up naughty youngsters. She had come out of the world of caregivers into this new world of peers, authorities, and enemies. No one prepared her. She adapted somewhat to the new geography, the new physical world of away-from-home streets. At least now she knew the way to school and could navigate on her own without Tommy. Tommy left at the same time but now, freed from the responsibility of walking his baby sister to school, he took a different route, hooking up with his buddies.

Class began with penmanship, up and down strokes and circles; her mind could wander freely with the mindless motions. As the strokes moved into cursive, she managed to focus enough to do it reasonably well. Reading, however, required more effort, concentration, and communication. In guided reading where each student in the group would read, she could not conquer her self-consciousness. Bridget Brown was watching her, smiling maliciously, or turning her head to stare until Sister told her to stop.

Then Bridget Brown turned recess into a nightmare. Aurelia joined several girls who held hands and walked in a circle singing "Ring around the rosie." Bridget Brown broke into the line next to Aurelia and grabbed her hand.

"A pocketful of posies," she sang as she dug her fingernails into the palm of Aurelia's hand. As Aurelia attempted to free her hand, Bridget's nails dug deeper. "Ashes! Ashes! We all fall down!"

Beaming at her distraught victim, her nails digging deeper, she bellowed, "Cows in the meadow, eating all the grass, husha, husha. We all stand up!"

Her hand free at last, Aurelia looked at the blood oozing down her four fingers. Bridget Brown was looking too. Their eyes met. Aurelia took off her mask. Angry, determined, she lunged at Bridget Brown. Laughing, Bridget ducked, picked up her long legs, and sprinted away. Aurelia chased her across the playground, past the jungle gym and swing sets, then all around the playground's perimeter. The school children watched, dodged, and ducked. Breathing deeply, Aurelia charged even more aggressively, lunging into Bridget Brown. Sister Mildred intercepted Aurelia at just that moment.

"What's this about, Aurelia?"

Aurelia kept her bloodied hand hidden.

"Nothing, Sister."

Her mother would be proud. For once she was strong, unafraid.

Her brothers were right. She was hurled into a world of black demons. The smaller demons were her own age but different from her—Amerikans with blue eyes, pigtails, and store-bought clothes who enjoyed preying on children who were different. Amerikans who went home to houses where everyone spoke English and

Mother made them peanut butter and jelly sandwiches. In the classroom the Sister demons often used a pointer, like the rods and bull hooks the circus men used for prodding the animals. The Sisters also directed the children's actions with the hand bells they often rang, lining up the youngsters, separating the girls from the boys.

❧

On January 14, the feast day of the Infant Jesus of Prague, the Sisters carried in the huge music box that they had brought with them from Europe. The music box consisted of a platform holding a church where the Infant Jesus of Prague hid. On the front of the platform was a slot for coins which dropped inside a drawer. Once a coin was dropped into the slot activating the mechanism, the Infant Jesus would leave the church and glide in a semicircle around the platform. The Sisters made the sign of the cross. Aurelia was mesmerized.

The Infant Jesus wore a bejeweled crown. His cape was embroidered and trimmed in gold. In his left hand he carried an orb, a small globe with a cross on top. His right hand was raised in blessing. Aurelia edged closer, fascinated by the color and richness of the scene.

Fingering the nickel her mother had given her, Aurelia got ready to insert it into the slot. The Sisters said Jesus had promised, "The more you honor me, the more I will bless you."

❧

In May Nadra received the blow she never once anticipated. She thought the principal was calling her because Tommy had once again done something wrong. But instead she called to tell Nadra that Aurelia had flunked first grade. Shocked, Nadra asked, "How?"

"Mrs. Hanoun, she hasn't made any progress in reading. She just sits there, never joining the other children in recitation, terrified that she might be called on. It wouldn't be right to pass her on."

Nadra felt a suffocating wave of heat and embarrassment. Perhaps her sisters Tina, Millie, and Eva were right after all when they said, "Aurelia is backward." She thought backward meant quiet, ill at ease. She also thought that Aurelia was rather like John, shy. But maybe backward was slow, maybe backward meant not bright.

For a brief moment she was angry, angry at this child who had wasted the precious opportunity for education.

No. No, Sister. I know my child. I knew there was something wrong, but I didn't understand at the time. Nadra's embarrassment evaporated as a dark cloud of guilt enveloped her heart.

"It's my fault, Sister. I kept her too close. Didn't see her fear, didn't even know she was having trouble. I have no education, no learning, so I didn't know and didn't help her. It's not her fault; it's mine, Sister. She is just bashful, a shy, scared little girl, Sister. Give her another chance. Do for her once more what her mother cannot do. I am glad to pay for more teaching."

"All right, Mrs. Hanoun. We will try tutoring. Beginning next week bring Aurelia to the convent at ten o'clock Monday through Friday."

∽

Ten o'clock Monday morning, Nadra and Aurelia faced a middle-aged nun with hazel eyes and a protuberant stomach. Her smile was as wide as her belly. She held out her hand to Aurelia.

"God bless you, Sister," said Nadra.

"He already has. He brought me this pretty little girl."

Waving Nadra off, Sister Agata took Aurelia by the hand and walked her to the summer house where they sat in a swing under the veranda. Sitting close, Sister kept Aurelia's hand in hers and told her stories about growing up in Germany. From her deep pocket she extracted a small worn book.

"My family, like yours, Aurelia, speaks a different language."

With great expression Sister began reading aloud, in German.

"One day you also will love your first book."

"I don't have a first book."

Sister Agata pulled another book from her pocket.

"This is called a Little Golden Book and the title is *Prayers for Children*. Perhaps this can be your first book."

Reaching in again, she pulled out a medal of the Virgin Mary, which she gave to Aurelia.

"This is your other mother."

"Sister, you sure have deep pockets."

"I do indeed. Magic pockets. Shall we read together?"

Aurelia moved closer and listened solemnly as Sister read *Prayers for Children*. Sister squeezed Aurelia's hand and reached into her pocket again, smiling mischievously.

"I have another Golden Book! *The Little Red Hen*. We can read it together."

When their session finished, one of the Sisters came from the kitchen and invited them to come sample *Weinschaum Crème*, the dessert she prepared for the evening meal. The small dish held a delicate cream with sliced grapes on the bottom and sprinkled on the top. Both nuns laughed as Aurelia's quizzical expression and tentative first taste changed to wonder and delight.

Taking her first taste, Sister Agata asked in amazement, "You used apple juice?"

"We have no more wine, Sister."

"So, it's still very good."

Aurelia would come to love the attention as much as the books she read with Sister Agata, not to mention the cakes, the puddings, and the strudels she was asked to sample. After five sessions, Sister Agata gave Nadra half her money back.

"Buy your second-grader some books, Mrs. Hanoun. She doesn't need me."

Relieved and grateful, Nadra watched her happy daughter run ahead of her, the long chain holding the Virgin medal bopping along her neck. Soon she stopped, looking back at the convent.

"Maybe one day I'll be a Sister...sitting in a beautiful garden... under a veranda...with magic pockets full of books."

Now Aurelia was confident enough to welcome school. Though still shy and wary of her schoolmates, she became an achieving second-grader. She welcomed the Sisters' attention, even when they were correcting her mispronunciations, most of which she had inherited from Um-Hana. Aurelia told the Sisters that her brothers' favorite cowboy was Hob-a-Long Cassody, that her mother liked college cheese with bitches, and that her father took Bepsi Dismol when he was sick. She lugged books home, made sturdy covers for them out of brown paper bags.

Sometimes schoolwork was laborious and tedious. She copied massive information from the blackboard, memorized times tables, struggled with lie and lay, and managed to ignore diagramming sentences. Mixed with all that were the Sisters' admonitions about purity and the difference between venial and mortal sin. Interlaced were Mass, Penance, and Communion. Stand up, kneel down, sit down.

On First Fridays of the month students attended 7:30 a.m. Mass at Saint Peter's Church. Afterward they gorged on cherry Cokes or hot chocolate and glazed donuts at Krenek's. They were allowed to be late for class. Aurelia made novenas, praying fervently for nine days for some special favor. Sometimes her petition was to escape, to live where there were exciting things to do, places to see. Other times her prayers were to live in a fine house like the one Sami bought for his family. Sometimes she prayed that her brothers might one day get along.

She adored her brothers. George smiled at her and often teased her. He took her to the parish festivals and sometimes even the carnivals. He bought all the treats; when her stomach erupted, he would guide her to the restrooms and wait. Billy bought her grown-up things, like a music box, a radio, a soldering iron. He let her join him in the cellar where he had set up a darkroom to process the many films he took. He never explained the process or tried to teach her anything. It was her company that he needed. That was okay; company was also what she needed.

In those elementary years Tommy was her buddy, especially when he had nothing better to do. She thought he was great and never once tagged him with nicknames such as Tommy Turd and

Mental Midget like George and Billy did. Being the lesser lights of the family, they were compatriots. They flourished under their parents' benign neglect, relishing the freedom to get in trouble and get away with it.

The tent revival meetings that occurred in summer intrigued Aurelia and Tommy. As they were walking along the steamy streets, they saw the posters announcing the arrival of Evangelist Booker, noted for his Bible preaching and sin-condemning. He tangled with the devil and wrestled against sin. Did he also speak in tongues, work miracles, and handle snakes?

Determined to find out, they waited until dark and sneaked into the back of the tent. What they saw was the sanctification of Sister Rebecca, a young woman with a fresh tight perm, wearing a blue-grey dress with a high neckline and elbow-length sleeves. She stood in the middle aisle, close to Brother Booker's podium. She held up her arms, perspiration staining her rayon dress.

"I commit my body, my heart, my soul to Jesus Christ. Jesus Christ who sent His son to die for a sinner like me in order to save me from hell. In order to give me eternal life in Heaven with Him." Her voice rising with volume and intensity, she continued, "I repent my sins! I accept Jesus Christ as my Lord and personal Savior!"

Turning from side to side in order to claim the attention of all, Brother Booker shouted, "Rejoice, rejoice. Sister Rebecca is born again! Sister Rebecca has received the baptism of the Holy Spirit. Will you join your sister in holiness? Will you repent your sins and be saved from hell? Will you put your trust in Jesus Christ?"

"I should have worn a dress, not shorts," Aurelia said. "All the women and girls are in dresses."

"Let's get a little closer," Tommy said.

"I think they're looking at us, Tommy."

"Just shut up and look down, Aurelia, like you're praying."

Very cautiously they inched forward. Suddenly a voice said, "Come along, I'll find you a seat."

Alarmed, they both screamed, "No, thank you!"

"Bring those young folks to a seat up front here!" Brother Booker had noticed them.

"We're Catholics!"

They bolted to the back where they had entered. Amused, an older man lifted a flap so they could make their escape.

Brother Booker dismissed them with, "Jesus also loves the Catholics!"

Deaths and Disappointments

In 1943 the Syrian community was shocked to hear that Simon Metrey had died suddenly of a heart attack. Aurelia rushed home from school after hearing the principal, Sister Alberta, on the loud speaker, extolling the virtues of "The Catholic father of nine children who passed on to the loving hands of our Lord and Savior." Nadra was busy cooking dishes for Sonya's house. Sonya lived directly across Route 50, four blocks away in a dilapidated two-story. Nadra dressed in black and Aurelia helped her carry the food to Sonya's. At the wake Sonya tore her hair, beat herself, and wailed for the loss of Simon, her dazed children clinging to her.

A month after Simon Metrey's funeral, Sonya seemed even more in the depths of despair. When the women gathered in the kitchen that Friday, Shanti asked, "Why is she still wailing?"

"It's probably shock," Nadra said.

"It should be a blessing!" Shanti said.

"Blessing!" Nadra said. "She has those nine kids to care for."

"But she's got money now!" Shanti said.

"Yes! Can we believe it! All those times she did without and the children ate only burghul and bathed in dirty water, he was banking money!" Nadra said.

"So why is she still wailing?"

Dowla said, "I'll talk to her."

Dowla went to see Sonya that evening. Sonya had already settled the younger children in their beds. She was kissing them goodnight when Dowla arrived. When the older ones saw Dowla, they seemed relieved and immediately gave her private time with their mother. Despite Dowla's protest, Sonya insisted on making tea. The usually ebullient Sonya shuffled about the kitchen, a withdrawn and haggard shell of herself. They drank their tea in silence.

Finally, Dowla asked, "Why are you still crying, Sonya?"

"*I* killed him, Dowla."

"How, sweetheart?"

"I told him, I said to him, 'I want you dead. I want you dead!'"

"You never said that before."

"No."

"What made you say that, Sonya?"

"The last time he didn't touch me. Instead he grabbed the little one and shouted, 'It's Alex's turn now!' And he hit him so hard he landed head first into the door. I thought he had killed him! I got hysterical when I couldn't revive him! When Alex finally came to, Simon said, 'First time always seems like the worst, son.' Then he laughed."

Holding her gently, Dowla wept with her. Finally, she held her at arm's length saying, "It was nothing you did or said, Sonya. Don't you see? It was God's wish to spare your son."

∞

Nadra stood at the corner, looking toward Sonya's house, waiting for Dowla. When Dowla exited from Sonya's house, she did not look Nadra's way. Nadra knew instantly she was trying to evade her. She waved her over.

"Well?"

"She feels guilty," Dowla said.

"Why?" Nadra asked.

"She told him she wished him dead."

"He did something after that?"

"Before."

"Tell me!"

"It's done. Leave it alone."

"That's what you always say, Dowla! Leaving it alone has never cured anything."

Exasperated, Dowla responded, "The man is dead. The all merciful Allah will lift Sonya's feelings of guilt."

"What did the bastard do to her before?"

Dowla told her. Stunned, Nadra cursed Simon. "How smart! How vicious! He knew there was no better way to beat Sonya than to hurt her child, especially the little one who could not leave her side."

"Alex is his child also," replied Dowla.

"That's why I hope he is rotting in hell!"

"I'm going home."

John was observing them from the front window of the store. He ran out to Nadra, asking for information.

"Why do you care now? It's too late. You did nothing when she needed help! All you jackals could say was 'what can we do, no one can interfere with another man's family, it may make things worse.'" Seething, she turned away from him.

"Obviously Simon did something else. Tell me what it was."

"Yes, I'll tell you. I want to see her pain reflected in your eyes. After he nearly killed Alex, he said the first time was the worst. Yes. He started on Alex. What better way to break a mother's heart." She left John standing on the corner.

John ran up the steps to the apartment behind her and demanded to know when it happened.

"Three days before he died."

John sat and wept. She did not comfort him.

Nadra was astounded by her own feeling, by the resentment she felt toward John and the other men. Worse yet was her satisfaction in the anguish that clouded John's face.

❧

The second man to die might have wished to live in that American community but never did.

'Am-moo Ike arrived, his long serious face even longer and more solemn than usual. He carried a letter from Saidnaya, which he read to them in his sonorous tone. Boutros Hanoun, Um-Hana's husband and John's father, was dead. John bowed his head. 'Am-moo Ike trained his eyes on his sister. She looked at him for the briefest of moments as she asked him to read the letter again. She listened attentively but said nothing.

She doesn't know what to do with the news, thought Nadra. *Is this the way it goes after years of separation? Is this the kind of numbness that sets in? Did Boutros die a long time ago, perhaps when she stopped caring about him? Or is she simply a woman who doesn't know how to embrace the day she longed for?*

Nadra didn't know what to do for her, or feel for her. The woman was herself devoid of feeling, or seemingly so. Perhaps she decided to stop feeling something for Boutros a long time ago. Perhaps that was what was happening to her mother, Lila; perhaps that was what was happening to her. These thoughts frightened Nadra, but what frightened her most of all was the realization that she was going to have the old lady forever. Hadn't she realized this before? Perhaps she had, perhaps that was part of the reason she was becoming such a shrew.

∽

In 1945 at age thirty-five, half of Nadra's family was grown. George became eligible for the draft just before the end of World War II, but he was not inducted because of his flat feet. Nadra and John were thankful, not only for his safety but also because he was now old enough to help John in the tavern. John was not literate so he had devised clever ways of keeping his accounts. Using a notebook, he kept track of the customers by drawing caricatures of them. The caricatures exaggerated a customer's dominant characteristic, such as a big nose or wire rim eyeglasses. Under the drawing were the sums charged to their accounts. Accounting and budgeting were now easier with George's help, until John discovered that George's itemization could best be described as sporadic. So he had to nag George, threatening that what he didn't write down would come out of his wages.

It was assumed, however, that upon George's graduation, he would go on to more schooling. Sometimes he talked about becoming an attorney, boasting, "Someday they will call me George Hanoun, Esquire." Other days he talked about engineering, still other days it was accounting; that made John laugh. "Office of Mr. George Hanoun, CPA."

Nadra and John were proud of George's ambitions and would have supported any one of them. Convinced of his superiority, they were determined to do all they could for him. But George never went beyond talking about his goals. He seemed content working in the tavern, listening to the railroaders' stories or regaling them with his own tall tales. Late nights he spent cruising with his buddies, devouring footlong hot dogs at the new drive-ins. When it was obvious that he was going to do nothing about his stated ambitions and set his sights no farther than the stool he occupied at the center of the tavern, John decided that he should someday leave him the tavern. Nadra was torn between disappointment and annoyance.

John seemed to have endless patience for his oldest smart boy, but Nadra did not. She loathed George's lack of industriousness and feared that he would turn out like her brothers—spoiled, indulged boys who believed they were owed all the good things of life. In fact, her second brother, who everyone now called Wicked Wasim, was George's best pal. Born in the same year, growing up together, George and Wasim became good friends. They came to be known as pranksters, jokers, and gamblers. George was chunky, smart, and hilarious. Wasim was dark and decadent, a taller version of his father, Sami. In the presence of a woman he had a kind of lisp, which would draw her attention to his mouth. He returned the attention, escalating his smoky look from the lady's mouth to her eyes. He was warm and affectionate. With his lisp, dark eyes, and long eyelashes, his ambition was to lure women to his Packard Patrician.

Wasim amused Nadra but she wasn't fond of him. He reminded her of Sami. Nor was she fond of her brother Teddy, a giant of a man, broad, and imposing. She could hear him before she saw him. He filled the room, usually her kitchen where he automatically seated himself, anticipating being served all that was in her larder. Nadra could enjoy his company but she knew his main interest in her was her good food. After Teddy left, John said, "Never once did he come with something in his hands for you!"

Giving up on George, Nadra banked her hopes on Billy. John followed her suit, though he was loathe to say much to Billy. Even though he wasn't gregarious, witty, and able to speak fluent Arabic, everyone knew that Billy had to be at least the second smartest in the family. He knew and could do things. He could repair appliances and fixtures in the tavern or apartment. When televisions first came out, it was Billy who talked John into buying a television for the beer joint. He was willing to spend time adjusting the television set for the amusement of the customers, but otherwise he refused to work there. He asked his brothers, "Other than wiping your butt, what can you do?" In retaliation George and Tommy called him the quality control man and "the Oop." They claimed that Billy's biggest problem was his virginity.

After school Billy spent much of his time working at Vecchio's Photography Studio or in his darkroom in the dank cellar. So, believing they were doing the best for their boy, Nadra and John saved their money and bought what they thought would be a spectacular gift.

In 1947, after Billy's graduation ceremony, the family gathered in the living room and waited for Billy. In the middle of the room was a professional Canon camera mounted on a tripod. When he opened door one to the living room, Billy remained glued to the entrance, his eyes taking in the camera and tripod. Looking around the room, he said, "Who told you to do this?"

Taken aback, at first no one said anything. Then Nadra said, "We wanted you to have it."

"Why?" Billy asked.

Nadra added, "Because we thought it would make you happy, Billy. We thought you wanted to be a photographer."

"It's a hobby for God's sake! Don't try to rope me into something I don't want!"

"We just wanted to give you something special," John said.

Glaring at his father, Billy said, "Since when do you know anything about photography?"

John and Nadra looked at each other and left the room.

George said, "You seem to have only two speeds, brother, pissed off and really pissed off!"

Pacing around the tripod and camera, Billy said, "I wasn't expecting it. Took me by surprise."

Acidly, Tommy said, "We noticed."

"What did everyone want? What was I supposed to say?"

Aurelia said, "Try 'thank you.'"

Billy spent his days working part time at Vecchio's and the rest of his time learning about televisions, eventually becoming an expert in television repair. He showed no interest in earning his living in photography. Nadra accepted his decision but couldn't help regretting buying the expensive camera.

She wasn't ready to concern herself with her youngest son until Tommy began quizzing 'Am-moo Ike on how much money he could make as a bookmaker.

Americans Never Had It So Good

In the turmoil of the forties, America was dominated by the preparation for World War II, by the war itself, and by the emergence of the Cold War in 1947. The positive that was born of those war years was a strong post-war economy. People had more money and more time to spend it. The theme became: "Americans never had it so good." The economic boom fueled a wave of prosperity that resulted in a feeling of expansiveness that characterized the nation. Nadra wanted to ride that wave.

The railroaders who frequented John's tavern for a quick beer at the end of their shift would now return at night with their wives. They sat in the booths. Mr. Rose, the pharmacist next door, remodeled his store. Plagued with stomach distress, John admired the changes before saying, "Please, Mr. Rose, I need a bottle of Bepsi Dismol." On the corner one block east of John's store the Greek Papadakis was building a huge confectionery crammed full of exotic confections like *Loukoumi* or Halvah in vanilla or chocolate, studded with almonds or pistachios. At Easter time candy eggs from small to gigantic were available in fillings of buttercream, coconut, fruit and nut, and peanut butter. The eggs were hand dipped in milk or dark chocolate and decorated with icing flowers. Chocolate Easter bunnies carried baskets filled with jellybeans, and one might have an errant butterfly perched atop his shoulder. Like all the other children Aurelia gazed in wonderment at the huge display, but she never asked to have any of it. Baba bought each of his children one-pound nougat eggs studded with pecans.

The Syrian immigrants were doing well. In addition to his small hotel on the south side, Andy Rahbone now owned a large hotel in the heart of downtown. Charles Mensore sold his small scrap metal yard to a wealthy Syrian entrepreneur, and then invested his sale money in sporting goods stores. Joseph Mensore owned property all over town when he hit on his most profitable strategy—he started the town's first drive-in movie theatre. Coming up with an idea that he considered as profitable as it was brilliant, he began working on his friend Farid Ferris, owner of The Oasis.

Farid was not doing well. Joseph had warned him, "You can't sell kibbe to hillbillies!"

Farid said, "I'm not after the hillbilly trade. There are people in this town with class and money—the doctors, the businessmen."

"Those folks want shrimp cocktails and steaks."

"Well maybe the Americans haven't been the big customers, but I thought at least my countrymen would support me."

"Farid, you think your cooking is as good as my wife's?"

"Well, it's not bad, Joseph. It's not bad."

"You listen, Farid. I have a good plan that can make us both some money."

Joseph's plan was to build a drive-in restaurant next door to his drive-in theatre. Farid would be manager and head cook.

"You're kidding me—footlong hot dogs and French fries!" Farid shrieked.

"That's where the loot is, you dumb donkey. They drive into you, load up on eats, then come over to me, watch a movie and neck all night."

Farid would not bend to such a proposal.

The youngest Mensore brother, Michael, was doing well with his used car lot, but he was bored and wanted to move up. Michael was illiterate but smart and bold. American consumers were on a spending spree in the 1950s and the auto industry was booming. Michael wanted to be part of the boom.

Michael's biggest help would be his wife, Jeannine. Even though she had three children at that point, she still managed her gambler brothers' wholesale grocery business and, according to gossip, was also having an affair. The ladies were sure they could also accomplish as much if they too had a full-time housekeeper (not the affair, of course).With Jeannine's help and encouragement, Michael plunged all the money they both had into an Oldsmobile dealership. Jeannine dropped her brothers' business and assumed management of the dealership (which, according to the ladies, would probably help Michael keep an eye on her).

Extolling the assets of the Rocket line of V-8 engines, Jeannine's brothers made sure all their gambling buddies went to Michael for their new cars. The well-heeled and prominent came to their gaming rooms. The police were regularly paid off. The brothers also employed bookies; 'Am-moo Ike was one of them.

With the good years, the more lucrative years, international travel had resurgence. Syrians were returning to or visiting the old country. Sometimes sons accompanied their parents and returned to the US with a Syrian bride. The Hedley women embraced the Syrian brides warmly; behind their backs they couldn't help snickering about their dark complexions, tight dresses, and thick makeup. Very few Hedley daughters accompanied their parents to the old country and even fewer returned with husbands. The women said nothing about them; however, Shanti liked to needle them, asking, "Whatsa matter, didn't you want an old country turkey?"

When a traveler returned from the old country, he or she had a world of information about all the families back in the little village of Saidnaya. Information was shared, stories told, and letters exchanged. Um-Hana's husband was dead by that time, but her sons and their wives extended invitations, telling her of their longing to see her. Tempted by the invitations and lured by the selective memory of the country she left thirty-eight years before, she told John she wanted to return. She was seventy-five years old by that time. She had the opportunity to travel with friends who were returning to Saidnaya in the spring. John was stunned and did all he could to talk her out of the journey. She insisted that she wanted to see her old home and her sons and that they wanted to see her. Exasperated and worried, John could not talk her out of it.

Already having a jaundiced view of the old country brothers who had their hands out for John's money, Nadra knew that their open arms would soon grow cold. And she was certain that their wives would not relish Um-Hana's company. She pondered the old lady's motivation, wondering if it was genuine longing or the encroachment of dementia. With all the kindness she could muster, she explained to Um-Hana that the old country would not be the same, that she was an American now and used to the ways of this country. Um-Hana reminded her, with some pride, that she was not an American, that she had never been naturalized.

"They might not let you come back," Nadra said.

"Why should I come back? What do I have here that I won't have there?" Um-Hana said.

"John is here, your brother Ike, your grandchildren." Nadra did not say "me."

"If I want to come back, I will. I want you to shop for me. I will need a present for everyone."

So Nadra shopped, filling a suitcase with souvenirs, fancy hand towels, jewelry, leak-proof Paper Mate pens, Silly Putty eggs, Matchbox cars, silver dollars, and for Um-Hana's two sons, Parker 21 pens. In the second suitcase she packed new underwear, shoes, and seven blouses and long skirts that she made herself. Remembering how cold the winters could be in the Mount Qallamoun range, she also bought sweaters, flannel nightgowns, and robes. She included a new handbag for Um-Hana's travel documents, handkerchiefs, and the money John was withdrawing from the bank.

Everyone came to kiss Um-Hana goodbye and to wish her Godspeed. Even Jeannine came with her husband, Michael. She wasn't so much interested in bidding Um-Hana goodbye. All smiles, Jeannine came to squeeze Nadra's hand. Even though the bond between them and their grandmother was more incidental than significant, the grandchildren were also present, to eat the pastries Nadra had prepared for the occasion. Nadra wondered how John would fare with the loss of his mother. Would his sense of duty and loyalty turn to worry, or would he eventually feel a sense of freedom?

❧

To their surprise, Nadra and John found each other again, as though seeing for the first time. Rekindling the curiosity, the wonder, and the flame they had first felt on their honeymoon. Reigniting tenderness, craving love. Nadra not only welcomed but hankered for John's touch. The children noticed that the sacred doors were locked more often.

Nadra felt it was a new beginning. Hope began sprouting roots again.

❦

Nadra knew that Um-Hana would never return. But she felt her presence for a long time. She was always behind her or beside her, peering from an open door, hesitating, turning her eyes away, walking the long hallway. Ironically, when the absence of Um-Hana finally turned to life-breathing freedom, Nadra began worrying. Had the old woman's sons embraced her? Had her daughters-in-law at least tolerated her? Was she well? Who would make her long skirts and blouses? Even though she had never wanted her, Nadra realized that she had lost another child.

❦

After Um-Hana's departure, the women gathered at Sonya's house for coffee. After accepting her cup of coffee from Nadra, Shanti grinned, saying, "Now he's all yours, honey!"

"You can send the kids over here," Sonya said, as she passed the cream and sugar.

"What do you mean?" Nadra asked.

"You got the best looking one in the lot and you're still trying to be a virgin!"

"Shanti, ibe alike," Dowla said.

"Ibe, *shibe*, it's time to loosen her up a little." Looking pointedly at Nadra, she said, "Or maybe it's already happening. She's walking a little looser and the frown's gone."

Shanti's remark unnerved Nadra. *Having sex shows that much? Obviously others know. They can tell.* She hoped Shanti wouldn't focus any more attention on her.

Shanti moved her chair closer to the table and looked them all in the eye conspiratorially. "Anyway, what I really want to know is what you know about Jeannine?"

"Michael's Jeannine?" said Dowla.

"No, Harry Truman's!"

Sonya proffered, "People see her with Ken Simmons, the guy she hired for her brothers' grocery business."

"Where?" Shanti demanded.

"Okay places. You know, at the bank, sometimes in restaurants."

"She's a business woman!" Nadra said.

"Oh, she's that all right," Shanti said.

Nadra started to say, "Come on, Shanti, don't be spreading—"

"I'm not spreading anything."

"Just because she's not one of us, because she's not from the old country..." Dowla said.

"Was I brought up in the old country?" Shanti asked.

"What's your point?" Nadra asked.

"If she's messing with Simmons, Michael will kill her."

"Shanti, you just want something to talk about," Sonya said.

Shanti asked, "So what else is there to do in this town?"

"You like to cause trouble!" Dowla said.

"You're getting on my nerves. Who wants to go for a ride?" Shanti asked.

"Maybe just for an hour," Sonya said as she poured more coffee.

"Sure, I'll have you back in an hour—so you can tend to your cooking and baking and cleaning," Shanti promised.

The women climbed into the car, eager for the chance to get away, yet resentful of Shanti's freedom and most of all her big car, a Buick Special four-door sedan. Like Jeannine Mensore, she was a Syrian-American, born in the US, married to a rich immigrant who dared not tell her what to do. The women considered her a big mouth troublemaker, but they were taken with her boldness and wit. Shanti said what they were often thinking.

As the years of prosperity moved on, business continued to pick up for John. More wives accompanied their husbands on the weekend, and it was not unusual for a few of the women who lived on nearby streets to come together for an afternoon Coke or beer. Those were women whom Nadra had come to know either through the neighborhood or through church. They liked her and she liked them and their houses. Picturesque frame or brick houses with front porches and roses growing on white trellises. Ever the hospitable one, she invited them upstairs. Aurelia was there, reading as usual. The ladies gushed and complimented Nadra: "You have done so much with it!" Not sure how to take the compliment, Nadra glanced at Aurelia who avoided her eyes.

Nadra's desire for a home beyond the commercial confines of an upstairs apartment on Route 50 was growing by the day. Her need was intensified when the state decided to widen Route 50, the main artery for traffic coming from Ohio to West Virginia. It was the second widening of the roadway, which narrowed the sidewalks from six to three feet. The semis, trucks, and cars were even closer to their tavern and apartment, and of course the noise was worse, particularly at night.

John had paid his loan debt to Michael and now they even had a growing savings account, so Nadra began nudging John again. Afraid of debt, certain of another Great Depression down the road, he moved hesitantly. When people asked if he had found a place, he said it was Nadra who was looking, not him. Then Jeannine Mensore paid a surprise visit.

Jeannine was on a mission to tell Nadra about the beautiful brick house that would soon be for sale on Woodland Drive. The present owner had big debts so he would be putting the house up for sale soon, probably at a low price. Her husband, Michael, had told her all that. He had also added that he was torn. He didn't know who he should tell first, his best friend John or his brother Charles, who was also looking for a house. Getting the hint, Jeannine told him not to worry about it. She went immediately to Nadra. Nadra was elated.

"I know that house. I love that house!"

Nadra began her campaign, rushing John to Woodland Drive to look at the house. They pretended they were just taking a walk around it. Nadra explained that the red brick would require little maintenance, that it was on a corner, that it had a sufficient front yard but a large back one, that it had a framed inside porch that let in a lot of sun, and on and on she talked.

"It would be a long walk to the tavern," John said.

"Not so long, John. A beautiful walk. We like to walk."

John also figured it was a bad omen that the present owner had to give up the house because of debt, and that the same might well happen to them. The thought of borrowing money again horrified him. He wanted to wait until they had more saved. Nadra tried to quell his fears and explained the value of this house and this opportunity. Finally, she pleaded.

"I want out of this hell, John! I spent four years growing up here as a teenager and now a lifetime as a wife and mother. I want to live in a neighborhood. I want my children to breathe clean air, not the fumes of cars and trucks. I don't want to share my bathroom with cockroaches. I want to look out on a yard, plant flowers, grow mint and tomatoes for my tabouli. I want to *shum al hawa* (smell the air), feel the sun on my face..." But she could not move him.

Michael's brother Charles bought the house.

Nadra felt helpless and depressed, again the discounted child who could not have what she wanted most. She was the twelve-year-old pounding the massive ball of dough in the khalkeen to please an angry mother, the sixteen-year-old pleading with a father who would betray her, stunned by the iron mother who gave her to a man before she was ready. Helpless. Betrayed. Humiliated.

John made promises for the future, but she did not hear him nor would she look at him. Finally she was rid of his mother; now she wished to be rid of him.

Mahrajans

In the spring and summer, Syrian folk from the neighborhood gathered on the corner of the Hanouns' tavern. Most of the men stood as they talked about the news and bantered in English and Arabic while the women sat on the Hanouns' apartment steps. Aurelia sat halfway up the steps, taking in the characters and drama below her. After so many years of hearing her relatives' stories and reminiscences about the old country, it was comforting to hear them talk about the here and the future. They decided to resurrect their Syrian club, elected officers, rented a building and began having the picnics and *mahrajans* (assemblies) they had enjoyed in previous years.

At the mahrajans, nothing delighted Aurelia more than watching her godmother, Dowla Rahal, play the *darabuka*, the goblet-shaped Arabic drum. Most of the darabukas were ceramic with goatskin heads. Dowla Rahal was the drummer par excellence. She moved both hands gracefully around the head of the drum, sometimes with them working independently and other times together. The intricate interplay of her hands produced deeper flat pops from the drum's center, interwoven with higher pitch metallic sounds from the rim. As the rapid rhythmic sounds of the darabuka rang out, one person would start the dancing and then would extend a hand in invitation to another. The dancer's demure steps and undulating arms beckoned other women and men to the dance. Responding to the seduction, the men insinuated themselves slowly but boldly into the erotic circle. All who were not dancing were clapping and encouraging the female dancers by shouting "*huzzie, huzzie.*" The dancers would respond by shaking their shoulders and bosoms.

Nadra's dancing was more commanding than sensuous. Her motions were staccato, her face a blank tablet. She was dressed in unhappiness. Serious rather than lighthearted. Her sister Eva was the reverse. Happy with her body and luxuriating in the music, she moved sensuously across the dance floor, her energy invigorating her audience. Aurelia watched from the sidelines. Nadra had not taught her how to dance. Perhaps she assumed she would learn on her own. Perhaps they all learned on their own.

The most popular of the dances was the line dance called the *dubkee.* A leader waving a handkerchief or some kind of a baton would guide the dancers around the center of the hall. Eager participants would break into the line. Dowla began the beat slowly, gradually increasing it, prodding the dancers to go faster and faster. Everyone danced. Even Aurelia tried and Shanti, who was next to her, coached her, saying, "You have to stomp, Aurelia, stomp." Buoyed by the music and the enthusiasm, even Nadra broke into the line, laughing, hopping, and stomping to the rapid beat. John broke in next to her. She did not acknowledge him.

Huge, grander mahrajans were held in the big cities like Cleveland, Detroit, and Grand Rapids. Those places were exotic to Aurelia and so were her sexy aunts. Petite with full busts and brown smoldering eyes, the aunts were witty and engaging. Millie, tall and athletic, did not attend the big city mahrajans. She preferred sporting events.

Aurelia realized that her heritage was about more than exotic food and sexy music. She began to see the old country as colorful and fascinating. Eventually her interest embraced the language as well. She was eager to learn Arabic. George was able to teach her some of the rudiments, like the alphabet and writing from right to left, but she needed more instruction. So she asked her grandfather. A friendlier person than her austere grandmother Lila, Sami agreed to teach her.

∾

Their meeting took place on his back porch. Sami was sitting on the glider. He greeted her with a broad appreciative smile that showed his teeth, and patted the seat next to him. He put an arm around her, and with his other hand opened his old textbook, *Al-Bookoorat Al-Gharbeyat*, to Lesson 1, "The Different Forms of the Arabic Alphabet Pronounced in English." He pronounced each letter carefully, "*Alef, Ba, Ta, Sheem, Hha, Kha, Dal, Thal, Ra…*" and had Aurelia say each one after him. When he reached the consonant "*Zine*," his fingers feathered her breast. The instant before she could react, he began fingering her breast more aggressively. Stunned, she stood up immediately and faced him. His response was a demented chuckle. He was still cackling when she ran off the porch.

She told her oldest brother about the encounter. "If you tell Baba, he will kill him," was all George said. She never told anyone else.

∾

Meanwhile, Sami continued neglecting his wife, Lila. When he was not after local women, he was traveling to Florida or California in search of "life-giving sun." His friends and associates loved to use that tagline. They thought Sami might be getting a little unhinged. But he never forgot to bring Lila a crate of figs from California.

In his frequent absences Lila not only took care of the tavern, properties, and cigarette business, but also parlayed knowledge and participation to her advantage. She sought legal counsel and took over the enterprises that Sami was neglecting. She hired a young manager for the tavern. Property, money, and decisions she controlled.

The only endeavor Lila left Sami was a tiny part of his wholesale distribution of cigarettes. He sold the cigarettes to the various retail establishments in his end of town. The government sold stamps to the wholesalers. The tiny—usually just a quarter of an inch—stamps came in long sheets or webs, which were formed into rolls. The wholesaler had to affix the decals on each pack.

In the small alcove adjacent to his tavern, Sami sat alone, fingering the sheets just enough to release the tax stickers, which he glued to each pack. When his fingers turned numb, he left for the streets, to distribute his wares.

Lila stopped peering around doorways and hiding in corners. She walked taller. Sometimes she even smiled.

The Good Years

John was making more money than he ever had. The tavern business continued to grow. It picked up even more when George convinced his father to bring in punchboards. The punchboards, self-contained games of chance, were an incredibly popular form of gambling in the 1950s. The boards were made of pressed paper containing holes; marked tickets were inside each hole. For as little as a nickel or as much as a dollar, the player could punch out the ticket of his or her choice to win the prize.

John didn't like the "girlie" boards, but at first he did allow George to bring in NO LOSER, Double Jackpot, and Pabst Win A Can of Beer. In the Hanoun tavern eventually the prizes were always cash. Though punchboards were a form of gambling, the authorities usually ignored them or pretended not to see. The money was easy, everyone was doing it, and no one was watching.

Then one night a police officer came to the tavern, asked for Mr. John Hanoun, and escorted John (with George trailing alongside of him) to the police station. An hour and a small fine later, he was released.

John was relieved when Sergeant Cork arrived on schedule the next day. The policeman didn't know what had happened. When he heard, he was not surprised.

When John handed Cork the cold Coke, John said, "I thought everyone was doing it."

"Everyone is," Cork said.

"So who turned me in?"

"Maybe someone jealous. Maybe someone who doesn't like foreigners."

John didn't say much after that, but Nadra could tell that his anger was as intense as his embarrassment and anxiety. What she regretted was the loss of that extra punchboard money.

When the parish middle school was being constructed Aurelia was transferred to Saint Catherine's Academy for sixth grade, a private school for girls run by the Sisters of the Holy Grail, a semi-cloistered order. The school was dedicated to nurturing girls to become educated, confident, and articulate women of faith. Sending Aurelia to Saint Catherine's was expensive, but Nadra had insisted on it, and John acquiesced readily when he learned it was an all-girls school. Sami and Lila had sent Tina, Eva, and Millie to Saint Catherine's.

Lunch bag in hand the twelve-year-old walked to the hillside school in the north end of Hedley. When the weather was bitter Nadra gave her money for the bus. Aurelia was nervous but excited for the change.

Sister Agnes, Aurelia's homeroom teacher, greeted her warmly and allowed her to choose her own seat. Aurelia chose the last row. She was soon to learn that the Sisters were intent on teaching, her first exposure to women who concentrated on education rather than religion and deportment. Reading comprehension and composition were stressed as well as proficiency in basic math. Students also had to memorize lists of facts related to grammar, science, and history. The first weeks of school were challenging.

Friday was the occasional day when the cooks made cream puffs, which they sold to the students. Aurelia knew that Susan Humphreys, the daughter of Aurelia's family doctor, always had money. When Aurelia leaned close to Susan, Sister Agnes said, "To who are you speaking, Aurelia?"

Aurelia hesitated before responding. "The girl *to whom* I am speaking is Susan."

"And what, in the middle of math, is your subject?"

"I want to borrow a quarter to buy a cream puff, Sister."

"If Susan says yes but insists you pay her back three times as much, how much will that be?"

"Seventy-five cents, Sister."

"And what percentage of your allowance is seventy-five cents?"

Since she never received an allowance, Aurelia was stumped and embarrassed. Everybody was looking at her.

Immediately Sister said, "Let's just say your parents give you seven dollars and fifty cents."

"I wish," Aurelia said. Everyone laughed.

"Ten percent, Sister."

"And if they give you three dollars and seventy-five cents?"

"Twenty percent, Sister."

"Now, Aurelia, what fraction—"

Aurelia interrupted with, "Blessed are those who show mercy!" from the day's Bible text.

Aurelia's classmates turned and stared. Sister Agnes laughed.

"There is frequently more than one way to solve a problem. But you should focus on the process, not the solution."

∽

The following year, when Aurelia was thirteen and to be in the seventh grade, she returned to the newly-built Catholic school, still run by the Handmaids of the Blessed Mother. There she and Mary Margaret Janson were given a double promotion to the eighth grade. When Aurelia told her mother, Nadra asked, "Why?"

"Maybe they think we're smart."

Nadra merely nodded and didn't bring up the subject again.

Aurelia and Mary Margaret didn't know their new eighth grade classmates who seemed more suspicious than friendly. They referred to Aurelia and Mary Margaret as "the brains."

"They don't much like us but I don't care," Mary Margaret said.

"Me neither."

"We could be best friends."

Aurelia liked being best friends with Mary Margaret. She was cute and smart and sarcastic and lived in a regular house. She also had a cocker spaniel named JJ, and she knew how to roller skate. She was Amerikan.

Mary Margaret got a lot of attention, mainly for her sensational body. She walked proudly, flaunting her full pointy breasts. She wore nice pullover sweaters. Aurelia walked with her books in front of her and wore cardigans.

"We have an hour for lunch. Let's walk downtown. If we hang around here, Sister will make us do a trip around the beads with her."

"You talked me into it," Aurelia said.

They went to the bakery for pastries. Instead of returning to school in time for the 1:00 bell, they wandered around looking in shops. The first time they skipped school Mary Margaret told Aurelia about Randy. He was handsome, a little older, and was waiting at his nearby house for Mary Margaret. Aurelia walked Mary Margaret there then spent the rest of her time where she liked best—the public library—until it was safe to go home. She was frightened, but she felt a little freer being in a world that was outside the scrutiny and judgment of John Hanoun and the Handmaids of the Blessed Mother.

Mary Margaret and Aurelia skipped school three times; the third time the ship sailed! The Sisters called the girls' parents. Somehow, some way, Mary Margaret's parents also learned about Randy. The girls were not allowed to be friends and Mary Margaret was carefully monitored. The Jansons were forward thinking people, so they sent Mary Margaret to a psychologist.

Aurelia's punishment was simple and swift. When she entered the apartment, Nadra came out of the kitchen immediately. She and Aurelia locked eyes. Nadra wasn't sure what she saw in her teenager's eyes, but she wasn't going to put up with it. They could hear John running up the stairs and into the long hallway. Nadra reared back, straightened her shoulders like a weary queen awaiting the tardy executioner, and backed into the kitchen.

Once inside the door, John approached Aurelia slowly, and looked into her eyes as he said, "The Sisters called us." He slapped Aurelia on the face three times and made her kneel with her arms raised. Then he stormed back down to the tavern. When Aurelia looked up she saw Nadra watching.

They left her there. Gradually she made her way to her room. She cried for a long time then slept. When she awoke she went to the bathroom, dressed, and walked quietly down the hall to the front door.

Nadra came out of the kitchen. "Where are you going?"

"To hell, Mama! Is that all right with you?"

"I'm going to tell Baba."

Opening the door for her mother, Aurelia said, "Tell him! Go! Tell him right now! I'll wait."

Nadra hardened her face and her eyes but said nothing.

Aurelia left her standing there.

Nadra's boys had never spoken to her like that. Never. She wondered if she had another problem on her hands. Well, she decided, she wasn't going to be defied by a thirteen-year-old. She would wait it out for now.

Aurelia walked to the park then meandered back toward the apartment through the side streets. Counting the coins in her pocket, she found that she had enough for a hot chocolate and a doughnut. She headed for Krenek's. She returned to the apartment after supper.

Nadra knocked on Aurelia's bedroom door. "Aren't you hungry?"

"Not today," Aurelia said.

Nadra wore her angry face for two more days. Aurelia opted for the blank face. Everything continued as before except that they only talked when necessary. Aurelia continued helping in the kitchen: chopping vegetables, setting the table, washing dishes. Nadra missed the conversations most of all. Their lighthearted banter about Latifa across the street, howling, "Yo-hoo, Mrs. Hanoun!" Aurelia's imitation of George's hulking walk behind Billy. Billy's caustic reply to both his brothers: "Other than scratch your ass, what the hell can you do!" Her father's: "You made *two* pineapple pies!"

Causally one day, a Friday, Nadra said, "We haven't been shopping for a long time." Aurelia reached into the Hoosier for a large bowl.

"Tomorrow is supposed to be a nice day," Nadra said. "Let's go tomorrow."

Aurelia nodded as she said, "The rice is done." Then she ladled the rice into the large bowl.

⁂

Saturday mother and daughter got up early, had coffee, toast, and headed for downtown. But first they had to deal with John's game. Descending the apartment stairs, they stood at the corner of the store where he immediately spotted them. He came out, looking surprised to see them.

"We're going downtown, John."

"Again?"

Nadra just looked at him. He reached into his pocket for his billfold and handed her five dollars.

"Enough?"

Nadra said nothing. Acting the good-natured tease, he laughed and handed her more money, one bill at a time.

They headed to all their favorite stores, noting the styles, comparing the costs, and foraging for bargains. Nadra often spoke to

Aurelia in Arabic when making a point about quality and price. Aurelia pretended not to hear or moved away. When they found a good deal, especially at one of the better stores, they snapped it up. Nadra was usually willing to indulge Aurelia in a new dress or blouse, especially if it was in red or made of linen. But she counseled Aurelia before they went home. If the dress cost fifteen dollars, she would say, "We will tell Baba we paid ten dollars." If a blouse cost eight dollars, she would say, "We will tell Baba we paid five dollars."

"Mom, Baba will go to his grave thinking nothing cost more than twenty dollars."

"Aurelia, that is just one of many things Baba will go to the grave not knowing."

"Why do we have to tell Baba anything?"

Nadra didn't reply.

Aurelia said, "I'm hungry."

"So am I."

Lunch began with a hot dog, which they relished. They ended with cherry pie, their favorite dessert. They stayed too long downtown and didn't have sufficient time to make a regular meal for the boys, so they put together what they secretly called hurry-up tuna. Aurelia smashed a tube of biscuits into a pan and Nadra sprinkled the dough with tuna. On top of that went American cheese, followed by another tin of smashed biscuits. Only the boys ate it. Nadra and Aurelia preferred to forage in the refrigerator for leftovers, like kibbe or chicken, which they stuffed into the pockets of pita, loading on tomatoes, black olives, and yogurt.

After incurring the wrath of the Handmaidens, her mother, and her father, Aurelia decided to make other friends and fit in.

She wore bobbysox, pedal pushers, poodle skirts, and listened to The Hit Parade. She blended into the "nice" kids group in her class. Those kids were the quiet inconspicuous ones who came from good families, obeyed the nuns, and were capable of learning about half of what the Sisters were attempting to teach. One of the not-so-nice girls disappeared. But no one said anything.

Aurelia was one of the nice kids, but she wasn't one of the really with-it kids. She knew that she was better looking than her friend Mary Ann, but she didn't have what Mary Ann had. Mary Ann was cute and chirpy. When boys talked to her, she giggled at all the right times. Deborah was athletic, tall, and confident. Always smiling. Even Elizabeth, intense and talking with her hands, commanded attention. Aurelia was quiet, didn't have a boyfriend, and her father owned a beer joint. Because she felt different, Aurelia knew she was different. Where that fell on a continuum of good and bad, she wasn't sure. Then Annie Lee Douglas, cheerleader, ponytail, tall, thin, and perky, asked, "What kind of a name is Aurelia?"

"It's French."

"Really? And are you French?"

"No."

"What are you?"

"Syrian."

Annie Lee Douglas' nose twitched as she said, "I'm going to call you the Serious Syrian."

When Aurelia got home she asked George if she looked like a serious Syrian.

"Well, you're not a laugh a minute." When he saw her dejected face, he asked, "So who called you a serious Syrian?"

"Annie Lee Douglas."

"You tell Annie Lee Douglas to shove it up her ass!"

Aurelia went into the kitchen where Nadra was chopping lettuce and slicing tomatoes. "Why am I called Aurelia?" she asked Nadra.

"I named you after a beautiful French girl I met in Marseille. Aurelia."

"Is Aurelia a French name?" she asked as she picked up a piece of tomato.

"Wash your hands! The girl was French."

"But was her name French?"

"What else would it be?" Nadra said.

"You live in this country but Nadra isn't an American name."

"I don't care, Aurelia," Nadra said as she sprinkled green onions on the lettuce and tomatoes.

"The boys have American names," Aurelia said.

As she poured olive oil on the salad Nadra said, "They are also Syrian names. George is Jeryos, Tommy is Tou-ma, and Billy..."

"And Billy?" Aurelia asked.

"Is short for William!" Nadra barked.

"Mama, was there a saint named Aurelia?"

"I imagine."

"Catholics have to be named after saints."

"I told the priest Aurelia was a Syrian saint."

"He didn't check it out?" Aurelia asked.

"He was a nice priest."

Smiling at her mother, Aurelia asked, "Did you make him baklawa or something?"

"I had a small tray for him."

"There anything you can't finesse?"

When Nadra raised an eyebrow, Aurelia explained, "Finesse means handle in a nice...sneaky way. Do you know what Aurelia means?"

"Do you know how too many questions make a woman's head hurt?"

"I'll look it up," Aurelia said as she went in search of the dictionary. When she returned her brothers were at the table passing around a platter of stuffed cabbage rolls and the bowl of chopped salad.

"In Latin Aurelia means 'golden,'" she announced.

"Lord, how did we miss it!" exclaimed George.

"It was the glow; she was missing the glow until now," Tommy added.

Billy said, "You really *are* our golden girl."

As Aurelia seated herself among them, she said, "I know. And I intend to wear the title with panache!"

Aurelia, like Nadra, had to ask for money. Her parents never thought to give her a regular allowance and she never thought to ask for one. If she wanted to go to the movies, she usually asked her brothers, prefacing her request with, "Can I borrow..." If they were not around, she had to ask Baba. He never denied her and thankfully he never played the money game as he did with her mother. He usually peeled out a dollar bill and whatever coins he had in his pocket.

When Aurelia realized that her mother was taking the ironing, a bushel basket full of clothes, to the lady across the street, Aurelia asked her mother how much she paid. When Nadra said one dollar and a quarter, Aurelia asked if she could do the ironing. Nadra was more than happy to keep the revenue in the family. That was Aurelia's first paid job, and that dollar and a quarter were like gold.

Aurelia spent most of her money on basketball games and movies. Hedley had six movie theatres and at least two of them had have-to-see movies, especially musicals like *Kiss Me Kate*, *The King and I*, and *Singin' in the Rain*. On her own Aurelia went to see the condemned movies like *The Moon Is Blue* or other hidden delights like *A Streetcar Named Desire* and *Baby Doll*.

In spring she and her friends hiked across the Sixth Street Bridge to Ohio. In summer they walked to the City Park to swim. Still, a summer day could be endless. While it was still cool Aurelia would help Nadra with the day's chores. After they ran the week's laundry through the Maytag that sat in the bathroom, Aurelia carried the wash baskets down the stairs and around the building to the clothes lines. Once a week they swept with the broom and vacuum and wiped the ever present soot off the furniture.

Nadra and Aurelia also cooked together. Working closely, mostly in silence, there was a rapport, a harmony that bound them in the creation of delicious meals, the smells of which wafted down the stairs, luring her forever hungry brothers and making her father smile in anticipation. Tabouli loaded with mint, parsley, tomatoes, and bulgur; cucumbers languishing in laban flavored with garlic and mint. The juice of kebabs with sweet onions soaking into the pockets of pita. Ground lamb, rice, and toasted pine nuts simmering in chicken broth flavored with a hint of cinnamon. For the weekend there were desserts. When there had been dessert during the hard times, it was a simple pudding made from junket tablets.

Now there were cakes, chocolate, angel food, and spice. Pies, apple, lemon meringue, and pineapple.

Being in the kitchen with Nadra was a quiet, intimate experience. Duty gave way to pleasure. Nadra's creative and sensual nature was even more apparent when she prepared Syrian pastries. For the baklawa, she ground walnuts or pistachio nuts which she flavored with sugar and rose water. She made her own phyllo dough, rich and smooth with eggs and butter. She kneaded it in a huge khalkeen until it was satiny smooth. In order to extend the dough to paper thinness, she would stretch it over her arm and throw it from one arm to another. Next, Aurelia would grab one end of the phyllo and together they would stretch it over several pans.

Nadra's aerial motions were graceful compared to her staccato moves on the dance floor. Maybe it was the difference between being happy and pretending to be happy.

Aurelia used her free time to go to the library, returning with a new stash of books. Nadra inquired several times why Aurelia stopped studying Arabic with her grandfather Sami. She evaded the question. When pressed, she told Nadra that she had lost interest. Nadra gave her that look, that look that said, I don't believe you, and Aurelia retorted with her blank tablet face, the one she had learned from Nadra. Her nibby mother wasn't as bad as her repressive father, but she was certainly an irritation.

Outside of required school reading, one of Aurelia's first books was *The Sheik*, which her friend Mary Ann found in her grandmother's attic. Aurelia searched for *Lady Chatterley's Lover*, which was not available, and other books she thought might have large doses of love and lust. Eventually she gravitated to Hemingway and Faulkner. The title of Faulkner's book *Absalom, Absalom,* piqued her interest in the Old Testament so she also checked out a Bible.

It was on a torrid day in July that Aunt Tina came to visit and discovered Aurelia in the living room, leafing her way through the Old Testament.

"Whatever are you doing?" Tina asked.

"I'm trying to find Absalom in the Old Testament."

"You're reading the Old Testament?"

"Well, not exactly reading it, just trying to find the..."

Aurelia recognized the look. It was the same as Bridget Brown's in first grade, only Tina's wasn't mean. She was just horrified. The look, however, was the same—oddball, freak, misfit.

Tina headed to the kitchen where she found Nadra. Gasping and alarmed, Tina said, "On a day like this why is a girl her age sitting there reading the Bible?"

"I don't know."

"For heaven's sake, Nadra, she's reading the Old Testament! Young girls her age should be..."

Aurelia couldn't hear any more. She retreated to her bedroom with the Bible.

When Tina left, Nadra came to her room and looked at her. Aurelia tossed the Bible aside and asked, "What are we making for supper?"

"Lamb and green beans over *shiriah*. And, Aurelia, I'd like you to make a raisin pound cake, the one with orange juice and zest. Mrs. Rathbone's aunt in Buffalo died, so we should go visit her tomorrow."

"Yes," said Aurelia, "better I go along rather than sit here reading."

Haves and Have Nots

Nadra was quiet on the way to Mrs. Rathbone's house. She was reflecting on how all the Syrians had houses, except for the bachelors. They were considered poor souls; they had neither money nor women to care for them. 'Am-moo Ike and Farid Ferris were poor souls. Perhaps the rest of the world thought the Hanouns were just poor.

Nadra wasn't looking forward to Mrs. Rathbone's large brick house. It was more than nice; it was grand. Hardwood floors, dining room, huge kitchen with a bay window overlooking the big yard. The bay window had a worn padded seat where the cat liked to nap. Had it been her home, Nadra would have upholstered the worn seat, but she had to admire the rose bushes, cosmos, and marigolds thriving in the well-kept yard. And of course there was the perennial grape vine. The Syrians manicured their vines carefully in the spring, and with the onset of summer, happily watched the emerging leaves and fruit. Good cooks would roll the leaves with meat and rice, simmer them over lamb bones, and flavor them with lemon juice.

Nadra had only been there a couple of times. Mrs. Rathbone was not one of her close friends. Actually Nadra couldn't stand her.

Rose was a short, dark, stocky woman who looked like she could have been Quasimodo's mother. She had a loud, rapid fire way of speaking. Behind her back she was called "machine gun mouth." When she sat down, her legs were spread-eagle, scandalizing the other women. It was rumored that she didn't wear underpants, but no one stared long enough to really determine whether or not that was true. Her husband wasn't much taller. He owned a thriving market and a busy hotel downtown. Prosperity had rendered him good-hearted and amiable. He surrendered to his wife long ago, leaving home happily in the morning for his walk downtown to his business.

When Nadra and Aurelia arrived, Rose greeted them, playing queen of the castle, careful to move as slowly as a docent conducting a tour so they could appreciate all that lay before them. When she came to the first of the two side rooms, she gestured slightly, "My sewing room."

Another gesture and, "…the library."

Nadra caught Aurelia's eye and smiled, thinking, *That's where she puts up her feet, shelling pistachio nuts and popping them into her big mouth.*

Aurelia asked about Molly, Rose's youngest daughter. Rose apologized, saying that her girls were out. When they reached the kitchen Aurelia gave Rose the raisin pound cake. Rose gave it an appraising sniff and announced that "her Andy" would like it. Nadra expressed her sympathy on the loss of the aunt and made the usual polite inquiries about the rest of Rose's family. Rose served lemonade and store-bought cookies. They each had one, to be polite. Nadra knew Aurelia would have liked two. She loved American cookies, but she obviously wasn't going to risk her mother's disapproval. When conversation mired on the weather, a certainty before the real stuff, Rose suggested that Nadra pick some grape leaves before she leave. "Thank you, Rose, but I don't care for the sun."

"I'll do it, Mama, I love the sun!" Beaming at Rose, she added, "That way you and Mama can gossip all you want."

Whisking Aurelia out the back door, Rose turned abruptly to Nadra, demanding, "Do you think Jeannine Mensore is sleeping with her business partner?" Nadra didn't indulge her. Taking the hint, Rose probably remembered that Jeannine was Nadra's maid of honor, so she tapped her mouth, tsk-tsking herself quiet. But Nadra thawed out her righteous attitude; she couldn't resist the other gossip, plus she wanted to give Aurelia enough time to pick plenty of grape leaves. She hoped that she would remember to add a few grapes.

Aurelia picked a huge stack of grape leaves and a handful of green grapes for flavoring. She walked about the yard for a while then pulled the chaise under the maple tree and lay in it, waiting for her mother. When her mother and Rose came for her, Nadra reprimanded her for picking the grapes and so many grape leaves.

As they were walking home, Nadra said, "I wouldn't want to live so close to downtown."

∽

Only people with money had houses like the Rathbones. Shanti's house was almost as grand as Rose Rathbone's. Aurelia's American classmates lived in all kinds of houses. Her friend Elizabeth, one of eight children, lived in that small frame house off Route 50, about a mile from the Hanouns' apartment. Aurelia never questioned why she was never invited in. Years later she would learn that there was only an outhouse.

Her friend Mary Ann's house was old and unusual and full of antiques. Carved rockers with needlepoint seats, straight back settees, a heavy oak table with enormous legs. When the family first moved to that old house, Mary Ann's mother allowed her to invite friends for a birthday dinner—what she called a Sunday supper or a company meal. Fricasseed chicken with mashed potatoes, green beans, biscuits and chocolate cake. When Aurelia described the meal to Nadra, she wasn't impressed. She made all of those dishes, but she couldn't get a handle on the fricassee part. Sick of the conversation, Billy yelled, "Chicken with gravy!"

"No, it wasn't that simple; it was white," Aurelia insisted.

"What was white?"

"The gravy, the sauce."

"Maybe she put milk in it or flour or both."

"It was delicious."

Aurelia looked up fricassee in the dictionary and Nadra went in search of the Betty Crocker cookbook.

Billy grumbled, "See what you did! Now she's gonna start experimenting and we'll have to eat chicken fricassee eighty times."

Her friend Deborah lived in a Cape Cod close to the City Park. The two-story was neat and spotless with a row of family portraits on the living room wall. Deborah's father was a Polish-American, a foreman in one of the plants and a benign taskmaster who related to his children. He had an education so he could help Deborah with her math homework. Her mother was a round-figured, good-natured lady who always wore a bib apron. A religious family, they took up a whole pew at Sunday Mass.

∽

Aurelia was beginning to resent that they lived in an apartment with old country tapestries hanging on the walls. The big-eyed camels and their turbaned drivers were forever staring. When they were in the living room together she groused about it to Tommy and he immediately took up the mantle, informing her that the camels were not staring at her but at her parents. The camels were peeping toms.

"Could they possibly have a sex life?"

"Obviously they did at one time," Tommy said as he sat on the sofa.

"The sacred doors are seldom closed," she said.

"They have nothing to hide," Tommy said as he put his feet up on the coffee table.

Aurelia came and sat next to him and brushed his feet off the table. "What does that mean?"

"Jeeze, I have to tell you about the birds and bees, Aurelia?"

"Don't be a smart ass."

"You think I'm capable of that?"

"Hey," Aurelia said as she poked Tommy good-naturedly in the arm. "I'm not one of your mean brothers."

Tommy ruffled her hair.

"You going to answer my question?" she said.

"Mom's not been happy, Aurelia. Everybody's moved up, except us."

"Why is that?" she asked.

"Because he's calling the shots."

"He's so old country!" Aurelia said.

Turning to her, he emphasized, "And he's not about to change. When it comes to taking a chance and moving up, he's going to keep those nickels in his pocket in case there's another Great Depression."

"Rigid," Aurelia said. "Like George always says, 'We're not even allowed to fart in a corn field.'"

"Nags me about going to Mass, but he never goes," Tommy said.

Aurelia mocked, "When people come here, he's always on Mama to 'Make coffee!'"

Tommy added, "'And serve sweets!'"

Korea: The War that Never Ended

June 25, 1950–July 27, 1953

"I have never seen such devastation," General Douglas MacArthur told Congress after President Truman fired him as leader of the United States and United Nations forces in Korea. "I have seen, I guess, as much blood and disaster as any living man," he added, "and it just curdled my stomach." Those were the words Nadra and John heard just after Billy and Tommy received their draft notice to report to duty in 1951. George was also called, but once again he was rejected because he had flat feet.

Two other boys in the neighborhood had also received their notice. When the families gathered together at the depot, everyone was friendly and cheerful, as though the boys were going to summer camp together. One couple, assuming the inductees would always be together, suggested they exchange names, addresses, and phone numbers. Tommy wrote the information for his parents.

Each father shook his boy's hand, hugged him, then turned away slowly, perhaps fearing that this might be the last time he would see the youngster alive. The mothers embraced and kissed their boys, smiled bravely, and held back their tears until the boys were out of sight.

After boot camp Tommy was sent to Fort Belvoir in Virginia where he was to be an engineer supply specialist. His work site was a huge depot with mile-long lines of jeeps, bulldozers, cranes, and other earth-moving equipment. During the Korean War, and even when it wound down in 1953, civilians ran almost everything on the bases since the military men were needed overseas. When the war wound down and ended in 1953, nothing changed. The work was still entrusted to civilians. Consequently, Tommy had time on his hands, which he spent swimming, working out, and running. When he returned he was lean and handsome and looking to spend his discharge pay on a pretty girl.

After boot camp, Billy became a member of the Signal Corp and was sent to Nuremberg, Germany where he became a radar specialist. Happy to be working with smart people who were familiar with mathematics, science, and electronics, he forgot to be homesick. In his spare time he toured the country and visited little shops where he found wonderful gifts for the family. Even though he was shy, he enjoyed the Germanic blondes' compliments on his dark hair and eyes.

Both sons returned home two months earlier than their two-year deployment. When the boys first returned, Nadra was ecstatic. Her boys were home. Her boys were safe. She cooked the meals they loved. She baked apple pies and pineapple upside-down cakes. She picked up their socks. She did their laundry and ironing. She begged them to go to church and thank God for their safe return.

They stayed out late with their friends and slept in all day. They pooled their money to buy a used car and then fought over it daily. Tommy went to the bars to ogle the girls. Billy complained about

George's smelly feet. George tormented Billy, asking him if he got any when he was in Germany. They fought and Billy hit George with his ammo box.

Nadra asked John if they were going to get jobs.

"Let them rest awhile, Nadra."

And so she did and so they did. When she tired of the status quo, she said, "You know, John, maybe they're not going to fly."

"What do you mean?"

"*Bee-ran-khou!*" ("They're just making themselves at home forever.")

"They're smart boys!"

"They're not going to win any prizes, John. They are not doing anything."

"Give them a little time."

"We're six adults in a walk-up apartment!"

"You're always complaining."

Coming Out of It

While Nadra was quarreling with John and praying that her sons would make something of themselves, Aurelia at age fourteen and fifteen was reaping the rewards of ninth and tenth grade in the new high school. The Handmaids of the Blessed Mother brought in two American Sisters to teach sciences. Sister Rose and Sister Maria were young, could teach, and even liked students. Sister Rose, the biology teacher, was a small, quiet woman with warm eyes, a kind soul who could instill love of nature in anyone. Sister Rose asked her students to make a pressed leaf collection. Aurelia corrected her posture and began looking up at the trees. With Billy's help she made a leaf book consisting of pressed leaves and photos of the trees from which they came. Sister Rose praised Aurelia and asked her to pass the book around. When Aurelia showed her leaf book to her mother, Nadra said, "So Billy took these photographs?"

Sister Maria, a tall mountain of a woman with a perpetually amused expression, taught chemistry. Aurelia considered chemistry difficult and was especially wary of the lab experiments. Not only did she have to understand what she was doing, but also she had to write it up. Once she spilled hydrochloric acid on herself.

Another time she singed her hair in a Bunsen burner. The boys laughed and teased her. Sister Maria declared that a mistake was a learning experience.

The old country Sisters seldom smiled. Their mission was to subdue the unruly and teach a little on the side. Aurelia was fond of the short robust one, Sister Agata, her former tutor when she almost flunked first grade. Sister Agata did smile. Another was Sister Joanna who taught music and choir. Tall and flamboyant, her long arms in sweeping black folds gliding over the air. An eagle of a woman with a powerful build and a broad wing span. When the school prepared to stage its first musical, Sister Joanna had tryouts. After Aurelia had no more than opened her mouth, Sister relegated her to the straight actors' pool. Nonetheless, Aurelia loved to sing so she attended when students were needed to sing the funeral Masses. To her and Sister Joanna's horror, she was the only one who came for one of the Masses. Sister Joanna sang loud enough for ten students while Aurelia merely mouthed the words. Afterward, embarrassed and awkward, she said goodbye, telling Sister Joanna, "You sing like an angel, Sister."

She replied, "So do you, Aurelia, with your heart."

Sister Mary Alberta, pale and proud, walked with her hands folded under her long black sleeves. She was both English teacher and principal. One of her distinctions was that she liked Syrian people, having lived among them in Cleveland, Ohio. She had trained to be a nurse, but after she joined the convent, the Order insisted she become a teacher. Teachers were needed. She never forgot her nursing training. She was forever reminding the girls of the dangers of smoking and drinking during pregnancy, adding descriptions of babies whose mothers had not heeded those warnings. In sopho-more year, tenth grade, one of the girls mysteriously disappeared from class. Though no one ever explained, it was assumed that Terry Ann had gotten pregnant. Though quiet and nice enough in class, Terry Ann was no longer considered a "good girl." Aurelia responded to the critics, saying, "Terry Ann is still a good girl!"

"Well," the girls said, "we hope she doesn't smoke or drink!"

Though nursing may have been her preference, at this point in her life Sister Alberta embraced education. But it was students' be-havior that sent her over the edge. Raised in an upper-class English environment with gentle brothers who went to Oxford, the imper-tinence of teenage males from working-class families was too much for her. After a number of incidents in which Sister Alberta made a series of threats only to have the teenagers call her bluff, disci-pline of unruly boys was left to the assistant principal, Sister Mary Geertruida. Wiry, black eyes, steel heart, Sister Mary Geertruida was rumored to have been in Hitler's SS. She systematically elimi-nated opposition. Thereafter Sister Mary Alberta devoted her time to health issues and English literature.

Although Sister Alberta's ability to teach grammar never came close to her nursing skills, she made up for it in her enthusiasm for English literature. Richard Mills and Aurelia were her best stu-dents. Sister Alberta would occasionally call Aurelia and Richard to her desk for more advanced assignments, to comment on their work, or to deliver an imperative such as: "Good nutrition will aid a vibrant mind." She would end each at-her-desk session with a nod to Richard and the comment, "You're active." For Aurelia, the nod would end with, "You're passive." Aurelia never understood exactly what that meant, but she did discern a pecking order. In everything Richard was considered number one and she number two.

One day Sister Alberta received a call from a savings and loan office. The manager needed someone to work a couple of hours a day, filing and stuffing envelopes. Such jobs were permissible for students ages thirteen to seventeen as long as they worked after-school hours and for no more than eighteen hours per week. Sister Alberta sent fifteen-year-old Aurelia. It was her first real job. She raced home. She couldn't wait to tell her mother!

"How much will they pay you?" Nadra asked as she washed dishes.

"Don't know. Probably won't be much, but it's a real job, Mom."

"Good." Nadra handed Aurelia a dish towel. "How about drying these pans."

Well, this is a bonus, Nadra thought. *She's doing well in school and now will make a little money. Such a nice surprise. But why am I surprised? It's the women who best understand the value of money. Men think women can live on love.*

On payday Aurelia and Nadra shopped and had lunch at a café. It amused Nadra to watch Aurelia count and recount her money. She was like her father.

Eventually, Aurelia's boss had her work the counter, collecting payments from customers during busy hours. Soon after she was given that assignment she was terminated with no explanation. Was she no longer needed? Had she made some kind of fatal error? She remembered only the sympathetic glances of the women employees as she was leaving.

Nadra's disappointment was as keen as Aurelia's, but she said nothing.

❧

In summer when Aurelia turned sixteen, her friends surprised her with a party. At first she was shocked and self-conscious, but happy, loving the attention and surprised by the gifts. Included among them was a red dachshund autograph hound. Each friend signed the fabric dog, adding endearing and funny words and sometimes pictures. She had never received so much attention. The red dachshund occupied a special place in her small bedroom.

Why does she love that stupid dog, Nadra wondered. *She has Baby, Bundle of Charm.*

That was also the summer Aurelia started an intense search for a summer job but could not find one. She considered babysitting.

"But you have never taken care of a baby," Nadra said.

"I can learn. How hard can it be?"

"No, no," John said. "It could be dangerous."

"What?" Aurelia said.

"Something could happen," he said.

She dropped the idea. Actually she didn't know any family who could afford babysitting.

In desperation she went to Koorshaks, the factory that manufactured clothing for infants and small children. It was a three-story buff brick building on the south end of town, the undesirable end. The hiring officer did the usual interrogation, which ended with his asking her age. She lied.

"Be here Monday; you work seven o'clock to three o'clock on the second floor," he said in a monotone without even looking at her.

∼

Monday morning Aurelia merely said she was going to work. After the first two days John asked Nadra where Aurelia was working. When she told him, he bellowed, "That's a factory!"

"So?" Nadra said.

"I won't have my girl in a factory!"

"I'm sure she will be okay," Nadra said. "They employ a lot of women. Women take care of other women."

"So what! She's working in a factory!"

"In the office, John, in the office."

When Aurelia came home, the first thing Nadra said to her was, "Tell Baba about your office work."

"Oh, you know, lots of typing, invoices, some filing, keeping the plants watered..."

Nadra didn't ask Aurelia what she really did at Koorshaks.

Aurelia was a floor worker assigned to Margo, a middle-aged woman with weary brown eyes who was in charge of Section 4.

"My, my," Margo said as she appraised Aurelia from head to foot. Looking over at the sewing operators who were packed side-by-side in long rows, she shouted, "Look what they sent this time!"

The women looked up but clearly were only interested in sewing as many pieces as possible.

Margo told Aurelia what she was supposed to do and insisted that she was "never, never!" to let the sewing operators run out of work.

Section 4 employed thirty sewing operators, all women, many of them Italian, Polish, and Irish immigrants who did piece work. Aurelia's job was to remove the completed bundles and replenish them with bundles ready to be sewn. The women's pay was determined by the number of pieces they completed. They never wanted to leave their machines. Women who got their periods unexpectedly even had Aurelia fetch their sanitary pads in advance of leaving their work to go to the restroom. Aurelia spent her time running from one sewing operator to another and from one end of the floor to the other.

There was no camaraderie. Other than giving orders, Margo said little to Aurelia and the same was true of the sewing operators. The floor overseer, a sallow-faced man with dirty brown hair and too tight pants, liked to leer at her. He trained his eyes on her chest or pelvis whenever he saw her. She had to walk by him because he often stood imperiously in the middle of her path. She suspected his eyes were glued to her behind once she passed him, but she wasn't about to look back to check. She knew the "girls" were watching him watch her. She pretended he wasn't even there. At first she assumed Margo would be a kind of protector. But the ambience of factory work soon disabused Aurelia of that notion. She was careful never to be alone or in an enclosed space.

When she first began her long walk to work at 6:15 she was aware of a tall newspaper boy who was delivering along that route. After the first three days he crossed the street and walked alongside her. Then he grasped her hand. She pulled away and walked faster. He did it again. What alarmed her was not so much his touch, as his eerie tunnel-vision expression.

She couldn't risk telling anyone at home about it. Instead she asked her Uncle Teddy to help her. "Sure, kid," was his instant response. He agreed to meet her in the morning, two blocks south of the apartment, to walk with her the rest of the way. When the paper boy approached on the other side of the street, Uncle Teddy vaulted across the street, blocked his path, put his fists on his hips, and stared malevolently. Terrified, the boy sprinted away. Uncle Teddy's parting remark was, "Remind me to show you how to kick a guy like that in the nuts."

In Koorshaks, Section 4 was making fancy baby buntings, or, more accurately, a piece of the baby buntings. The bunting had a zippered front with raglan sleeves and mitts. The hood ended in three contrasting hat peaks and tassels, a kind of fools cap. The sewing operators were sewing the multicolored hat peaks and tassels to the top of the hood, eight hours, five days a week. When they first saw the completed product, in a glass case at the end of the room, some sniped, "Looks just like the ones my babies wore!"

Smiling bitterly, others snorted, "Yeah, mine too!"

Aurelia's pay was good, for a girl, but the summer work ended prematurely for her.

Holding her last paycheck and crying, she raced home and told her mother.

"Well, there's plenty of work for you here."

At that point Nadra was relieved that all three of her sons were working. Of course, George was working in the tavern, but he was also keen on a new enterprise. He bought vending machines—nickel ones dispensing candy, quarter ones dispersing nuts. He lugged them around to other establishments. Billy thought the enterprise hilarious. George retaliated by declaring that his venture was a noble one going back centuries. He explained that the Greek mathematician Hero of Alexandria invented a device that dispensed holy water inside Egyptian temples.[*]

Billy had discovered that television repair was increasingly in demand. Tommy had steady work in the rayon plant.

[*] Bellis, Mary. "The Incredible Reason the Vending Machine Was Created." ThoughtCo. Accessed February 21, 2017. https://www.thoughtco.com/the-history-of-vending-machines-1992599

Aurelia's Junior and Senior Year

In her junior year Aurelia's classmates elected her May Queen, the girl chosen to crown the statue of the Blessed Virgin during the May procession. After the election her classmates carried her on their shoulders and made a fuss. Noting her astonishment, her friends and classmates teased her.

Nadra was happy making Aurelia a beautiful tea-length dress in white organza. She laboriously trimmed the V-neck with tiny handmade ribbon roses. But Sister Geertruida would not allow such a neckline. She insisted that Nadra add a Peter Pan collar. Lovely gave way to ludicrous. Incensed with the change she was forced to make, Nadra cried, "Is a mother to take no pride in the event?" Aurelia cursed. Nadra told Aurelia it was not fitting for a May Queen to curse.

The procession would be in early evening. The aunts, Tina, Eva, and Millie, were ecstatic. They were going to wear their best dresses and heels. Tina splurged on a cherry red fascinator hat that sat side tilted on her head, creating a flattering line across one eye. Eva opted for a pillbox with a bow attached to the edge and crowned with a veil. Millie wanted to wear a scarf, but they screamed at her so she borrowed a mantilla.

"Maybe I should close the tavern," John said.

"What? And lose all that revenue?" George responded. "You go. I'll watch the store."

John raced upstairs to change. He said to Nadra, "I'm going. Wait for me, Nadra!"

Edging past him, she said, "I'm leaving now. I have to help Aurelia with her dress."

As John left he saw Billy organizing his photography equipment, the Canon included.

❧

The May procession was an elaborate affair. The youngsters who made their Holy Communion processed around the main and side aisles. The boys were dressed in suits, the girls in white dresses and veils. The high school girls wore white or pastel dresses, carried bouquets, and had wreaths on their hair. The May Queen, Aurelia, was the last person in the procession. She wore a long train that was carried by two little girls.

Sister Joanna blasted out the melody while waving her arms to keep the company of compliant children singing at the top of their voices "Bring Flowers of the Fairest" with its refrain: "O Mary, we crown thee with blossoms today, Queen of the Angels, Queen of the May." When the participants reached the center aisle, the high school girls formed an arch with their bouquets for Aurelia to pass through.

Aurelia took the role humbly and seriously. Several times she had practiced the prayer she was to say before the crowning. When she said it, she felt it, and all who heard it also felt it. Booming voices declaimed, "Hail, holy queen enthroned above... Hail,

Mother of mercy and of love…" Aurelia rode the wave of emotion.

Nadra looked at her daughter and felt proud. *She does look like kind of a queen, wearing that crown, walking around the aisles, little girls carrying her train, everybody singing.*

Nadra hoped Billy wasn't too obvious in his picture taking. She didn't want to be embarrassed, have people thinking they were bragging. *Aurelia is certainly the emotional Catholic, talking to the Blessed Mother as though she were in their kitchen.*

◈

The next year, her senior year, Aurelia joined the debate team and the drama group. Though quiet and still shy, she was not afraid to take part in controversy and express her views. She had an objectivity that allowed her to see both sides of an issue. This objectivity made her immensely effective. She could anticipate and deal with arguments in a cool and detached manner.

She began remedying her bad voice habits. She learned to breathe deeply and to avoid directing the sound of her voice through her nose. She practiced speaking by reading aloud, putting feeling into her voice that reflected the words she was speaking. All that helped her when she joined the drama club.

She played the role of a Jewish matron in their high school play. She fell into the role naturally, having been nurtured in a world of family, food, and feuds. Her rendition of the character was hilarious. The play was part of a statewide competition and she won the award for best actress. There was an article and pictures in the Hedley newspaper. People were saying, "That's that shy little Hanoun girl. She's certainly come out of it."

At home there was no recognition of Aurelia having "come out of it." Her parents never said anything about her accomplishments. It would be unseemly to boast about a child. That was not the Syrian way. No, wrong! That was not the Hanoun way.

Growing Discontent

The liberators were visiting, helping themselves to leftover grape leaves, olives, and bread before they mounted their latest assault on John, parental protector and tyrant. John had begun another grand inquisition because Richard Mills invited Aurelia to the senior prom. John told Aurelia that she could not go. Aunts Tina, Eva, and Millie were there to make him bend. They had a ready arsenal.

Tina began with a demand. "You've got to be a little more American, John."

Eva followed with a gentler, "This isn't the old country, John."

Millie closed with, "*This* is your world now, and look how good it's been to you."

They knew how to reason with him and how to appeal to him, but what made the sale was their teasing and flirting.

Nadra used to find their performances amusing. If charm was a gift, she knew she hadn't received it. If it could be learned, nobody had taught her, certainly not Lila with her sharp tongue and imperious manner. At one time it hadn't much mattered what her sisters said or did. She was only concerned with her painful feet and throbbing varicose veins.

This day, however, she was starting to resent her sisters. She hadn't forgotten their hurtful remarks when Aurelia was little, implying she was backward and referring to her as "The Cry Baby." *Well, now look at them,* she thought. Now Aurelia was someone to brag about, especially since she made the newspaper. Last year in her junior year, their niece was the May Queen, now in her senior year their niece was voted best actress.

They worked on John for Aurelia's sake, but they never did anything for her. As she watched them she was convinced they could charm a rattlesnake. But why was she surprised? They loved John. Maybe they thought he was an old country fart, maybe they talked about him behind his back, but they had always loved him.

She wasn't sure she loved him.

"Now don't go making her dress," Tina said.

"What?"

"Nadra, the prom isn't an occasion for a homemade dress," Tina answered.

Agreeable and smiling, John said, "Nadra will buy Aurelia something nice."

"Something nice is going to require a lot more than the usual amount you peel out of your wallet," Nadra said.

Tina laughed. "She's just punishing you a little, John."

Eva added, "It's what wives do."

"Without the Peter Pan collar, maybe the May Queen dress could work," Millie said.

"Never!" Tina and Eva screamed.

Embarrassed, John said he had to return to the tavern.

Turning to Nadra, Tina said, "It would also do *you* good to get away from the old country."

"Easy for you to say once you have eaten your fill!" Nadra said.

Embarrassed, Tina turned away. "Let's go!"

Eva and Millie waved an embarrassed goodbye as they exited behind Tina.

❧

Aurelia wouldn't have to be the only girl in the senior class sitting home alone. Even though she was his superior female counterpart, Richard Mills hadn't shown any particular interest in her before. But maybe the match was inevitable. After all, they were the reigning king and queen of the class, at least as far as Sister Alberta was concerned. He was nice looking.

Nadra and Aurelia spent an entire Saturday downtown looking for the perfect prom dress. The one they loved had a sweetheart neckline and a V waistline that emphasized Aurelia's hourglass figure. The gown was white and flowed into gently tiered tulle ruffles. Aurelia wasn't sure that she would feel comfortable in such a showy dress, but Nadra nodded her approval readily while remarking, "It's beautiful."

"But am I beautiful, Mama?"

"Aurelia, do you want it or not?"

"Oh yes, I want it," she replied.

They bought white satin pumps and pearl earrings to match the dress. Richard Mills brought her a corsage of red roses.

The prom, her first date, went well. Smiling and attentive, Richard Mills told her she looked beautiful. She didn't know how to dance, but she managed to follow. The occasion went well until Richard brought her home. The second they reached the top stair Nadra opened the door. Richard jumped back, dropping his hand from Aurelia's waist. Blushing he said goodnight and rushed down the stairs.

Aurelia took off the beautiful gown and hung it carefully on the padded hanger. Hearing a sound by her door, she saw that it was slightly open. She shut it with her foot, taking note of her mother's shadow. So began their dance, the inside partner step, one stepping into the other's space only to have the other step backward.

Before Richard Mills there was no one. After prom night there was no one. Did Mama scare him off or did he only ask her in the first place because they were the senior class big deal? She hadn't been particularly attracted to anyone before, not that there were many possibilities given the insularity of her life and environment. No boyfriend, no love, certainly no sex.

∽

In the Zahir house sex was everywhere—on the front porch, sometimes right in the living room, other times smoldering behind the white painted woodwork in the kitchen. Certainly in the eyes of Sami. Never did Aurelia meet his eyes except for the time he caught her unawares. She saw his smirk.

The last time Aurelia was in the Zahir house Aunt Eva announced her plans to marry Barry Koch. He was not a Syrian; worse yet he was a Protestant. When Eva came down the stairs, her unusually ample breasts bounced. She was glowing. All the other women were frowning. Eva was obviously happy and exuberant. She was pregnant. Hoping to erase the women's frowns and lighten the mood, Uncle Wasim announced, "She's in love!" Wasim would have known. He had innumerable such experiences, though none were held against him. His preferences were young, nubile women who were impressed with his smoldering eyes and 1955 Packard Patrician. Packard's advertising slogan was "Let the Ride Decide," which also became Wasim's slogan. By then his older brother Teddy was into divorced women, two of whom he eventually married. His mother, Lila, referred to them as "used" women.

Aunt Tina finally married, to her and everyone's relief, but the chosen one was an American and, to everyone's dismay, a hillbilly. But Tina tried to make it right by insisting he marry her in the church; besides, it suited her sanctimonious side. Oran Ryan was as good-natured as he was handsome, so everyone liked him, in spite of themselves. (George liked to mispronounce his name in front of Tina, calling him "Oral.")

Oran never refused an invitation to eat at Nadra's, and his charm and wit never failed to entertain her. They loved to banter, he regaling her with stories about the "billhillies down in the holler," and she trying to upstage him with stories about the language gaffes Syrians made, such as Sami having "Gandies" inscribed on his store window. Oran's fatherly attention to and appreciation of Aurelia made her glow. He was the first to notice that she had started wearing cologne, remarking, "You smell so 'licious, Aurelia," as he sniffed the air. To Nadra he often said, "You have got to market this wonderful food. You could make a fortune, instead of slaving away feeding all of us ingrates, like me."

On one such occasion, unfortunately the last for Oran, John came upstairs and took note of the happy scene. "You know, Oran, you can get all of this wonderful food down at The Oasis."

Aunt Tina and Uncle Oran had a house. It was a rental, but it was a *house*, in a neighborhood with a small front yard and a respectable backyard. Nadra liked to call it Tina's "shrine." Tina never invited anybody to visit, except Aurelia. After those three events, Aurelia had to give Nadra details about the rooms, the furniture, the level of cleanliness and anything else she might have observed. Nadra was most annoyed when she learned that Aurelia had seen no more than the living and dining rooms and the bathroom. Thank God she had enough sense to go to the bathroom, but she had seen nothing of the bedrooms on the way there. But knowing that Tina had a dining room was the most niggling information of all. Why would someone who can't cook and entertain have a dining room?

After her distinguished career as a Rosie the Riveter double, Aunt Millie used her money to leave home. She hoped to become a designer in New York. She made it as far as Cincinnati where she became a seamstress and spoke knowledgeably about fashion and politics. She never married and, according to her, never wanted to marry. According to her sisters no man wanted her. She was too independent, contrary, and humorless. Worst of all, she was a Democrat. Tina verbally abused her, Eva tolerated her, and Nadra asked for details about the location and size of her apartment.

∽

At the Hanouns, sex seemed not to surface; it was never acknowledged or talked about. The sacred doors were always open. Unlike her sexy sisters, Nadra was matronly. Their hair was short and wavy. Nadra wore hers in a bun. They wore sheath dresses with boleros. Nadra wore wrap dresses in size 16.5. Now that she was an accomplished seamstress, she often sewed for Aurelia. The shorts and tops were usually big enough for two girls, but the dresses and suits were expertly tailored, emphasizing her daughter's figure.

John frequently gave Nadra gifts. On one occasion he insisted on taking her to buy a fur-trimmed winter coat, popular apparel that winter. On a Sunday afternoon when the family and aunts were gathered together, John insisted she model the coat. All smiled as they eyed Nadra engulfed in blue wool and fox. To cap off the show John brought out his surprise, a large hatbox which contained, according to him, what Nadra insisted was much too expensive—a hat with a blue wool top and a wide fox band. The fur was long, lush, and silky. Nadra frowned as John fitted it on her head.

"My God, she looks like an angry Mongol warrior!" Tommy whispered to Aurelia as he tried not to laugh.

George asked, "Is that raccoon or beaver?"

"It's whatever you want it to be," Nadra said as she tossed the hat to George. She tried to laugh but all she felt was frustration and humiliation.

She took off the coat and Aurelia took it from her. "I'll hang it for you."

"So who wants coffee and cake?" Nadra asked.

Sitting there amongst them, quietly watching them sip coffee and fork chocolate cake into their mouths, Nadra wondered if this was the way her life was always going to be.

She hadn't wanted the hat, which was why she told John it was too expensive. Now she was probably stuck with it. Bad enough the coat, which she hadn't wanted either. What she wanted—change, satisfaction, opportunity, a little excitement—was not to be had.

She felt like she was floating through life, without hope, unmoored in a time when everyone had more than she. So she did the only thing she could do. She retreated to the world of her youth, to the world where possibilities were still ahead of her. To the world of the loving grandmother, Sitto, who had given her the amulet and told her that she had golden hands.

Sitto was gone now. She died in 1948 at age seventy-six.

Being the traditional housewife, Nadra made mostly Syrian food, but now she did more than that. She began recreating the old country in their walk-up. Energetic, creative, determined, Nadra relived Saidnaya in that railroad apartment. In her kitchen she now often labored over talamee that she used to bring home from the khubbaze's tannour when she was a little girl. The mothers of brides-to-be implored her to bake baklawa and *aribee* (butter cookies) for the wedding reception. To her repertoire of sweets Nadra added the *knafee* (stuffed shredded wheat) and *halawa cake* her mother used to buy in the old country bakeries. Nadra got sentimental when she prepared the *roz ib haleeb* (rice pudding) that her Sitto made for her.

In summer Nadra put cloths on the overhanging roof outside the small bedroom and covered them with a combination of yogurt and bulgur, which she sun-dried for several days. She ran the mixture through a sieve until it became a fine dry powder. That mixture, called *kishik*, she made into a winter soup.

Aurelia waved the grocery order sheet for Middle Eastern products in front of Nadra, saying, "Look, you can order a ton of kishik for ten dollars!"

"It's not the same," Nadra said as she painstakingly boned a leg of lamb into small pieces, using lean and fat in equal portions. She would salt and cook it slowly until done. She stored it in a large earthen crock, taking out spoonfuls to flavor the kishik or any other dish that benefited from the addition of lamb. The meat in the crock was called *awarme*. The boys called it Mama's beef jerky.

Nadra also understood all the skin and medicinal benefits of olive oil and she knew various home remedies. When a friend came to her with a large painful carbuncle, Nadra gently inserted a dry chickpea and applied a bandage, explaining how to change it without aggravating the infection. She also knew everyone's genealogy, and no one ever disputed the accuracy of her facts about the old country.

Nadra was consumed with a methodical frenzy that kept her body working, creating, so that her mind could find rest in weariness. When she was not cooking, baking, sharing, ministering, and advising, she was sad and listless.

∽

Both Nadra and Aurelia were caught in a trajectory of frustration hurtling toward depression.

∽

The reality of Aurelia's life was also imploding daily. The chief pleasure of life was food. Only a mad woman like her mother would unwrap a piece of beef and ask, "Isn't this the prettiest piece of meat you ever saw?" Only men like her brothers spent their nights cruising the drive-ins, stuffing themselves with footlong hot dogs and French fries.

And her father! Always looking her over when she went out, his eyes scanning her body, her clothing.

If it were not for her aunts she would never have been permitted to wear jeans or shorts. If a male classmate happened to pass them on the street and said hi to her, Baba would turn to stare and demand, "Who is that?" Her father was obsessed with correct behavior, avoiding shame. "*Ibe alakun*" were the catchwords of the household.

Were it not for her new interests and accomplishments in debate and acting, the dreariness, monotony, and dullness of her surroundings would have overwhelmed her.

Her Catholic faith and its ritual helped, especially the solemn Masses that began with the censer leading the way with the incense. The vestments were costumes. Catholicism was drama, color, and music.

Aurelia had asked Sister Mary Alberta about the vestments and Sister, pleased with her curiosity, had given her one of her own books that explained both the Mass and the vestments. Aurelia had read it cover to cover. When she returned it, she couldn't help commenting that it was too bad that the priests got to wear the beautiful colors while the Sisters were relegated to black and white. Surprised, Sister had merely said, "It's not for us to question." Sister Mary Geertruida labeled the comment "impertinent," while Sister Joanna found it "hilarious" and Sister Maria said it was "true."

It was a frantic year for Aurelia, but at least it was senior year.

An Oasis

Nadra sat at the top of the apartment steps, looking down on the street's morning activities. The distributors were wheeling cases of beer into the tavern, housewives in dresses and hats were making the trek downtown, and railroad engineers were coming off the morning shift. Watching the activities she fought the everlasting frustration that often overwhelmed her. Today she was determined to avoid it. Today she would count the money in the green ceramic jar and deposit it in her interest-bearing savings account. She had always saved money. After John denied her the house on Woodland Drive, she was even more careful to salt away the extra dollar, the extra few cents. Weekly she poked into the cushions on the horsehair sofa and chairs, hoping to find loose change. She even stole money from the till in the store. She figured John would just send it to the old country.

She did not give up her dream of having a house. She just decided to go underground with it.

She only counted the money when she was sure she was alone in the house. Today she tucked it carefully into her handbag and descended. Entering the tavern she indicated to John that she was leaving. He ran after her, asking, "Where are you going?"

"Downtown."

"Downtown?"

"Yes, John."

"You want some money?"

Exasperated, holding her breath, she looked down and turned on her heel.

"Wait!"

John reached into his pocket and handed her all the bills he found.

"Thank you."

"You're welcome."

When John turned around he saw the Kettle Brand man smiling at him. He was hanging bags of potato chips on the stands. Embarrassed but returning the smile, John said, "What is it they say about women?"

"Can't live with them, can't live without them, John."

While Nadra squirreled away money for a house and hoped for a brighter future, John remembered the happy past. When Nadra smiled at him, teased him about his insistence on white shirts, and adjusted his tie. When she looked up at him and, catching the longing in his eyes, moved eagerly into his arms. When they played together—he undressing and spreading himself on the horsehair sofa—she, pretending surprise then coyly fitting herself on him. When she arched her body against his, accepting each thrust as they moved to mutual orgasm.

Those embraces lit the warm nights and ignited the cold days when they made love ever so quietly, making sure they wouldn't awaken Um-Hana or the children. Behind the sacred doors. From those quiet encounters they learned that it was the soft breath and the gentlest touch that spoke love.

Leaving the store, he stood on the corner to watch her, her figure fading away as quickly as the good times.

He did not want to live without her.

Nadra went to the bank, but instead of shopping she spent the rest of the morning visiting friends. She wanted to save the money. When she returned, George was tending the tavern. He told her that Michael Mensore was upstairs with John. When she went upstairs, she realized that they were in the living room, but both the sacred doors were closed.

She went into the kitchen and waited, sure that John would eventually come out and look for her, wanting to make his usual demand for sweets! Coffee!

But he did not. Not this time. So she stood carefully outside the closed door, as she learned to do when she followed Lila around to spy on Sami. Michael was speaking of "a deal...making a change... taking a chance," and insisting that he "would take the fall if it didn't work out." John thanked him and said he would give it some thought. Michael admonished him saying, "You don't want to wait too long, end up like Farid Ferris wishing you had taken the chance."

She waited three days for him to tell her about it. Finally, one night when they sat alone together in the living room, she asked. He replied that Michael had offered him the chance to be part of a deal and that he had turned it down.

"You turned it down and you didn't even tell me about it."

"I was afraid to risk it, Nadra."

"Afraid to risk what? An opportunity?"

"You could call it that," he said as he reared back into the horse-hair chair.

Shifting closer in her seat, she asked, "You don't trust Michael?"

"I trust Michael, but I'm not going to take a chance with our money."

"He said he would take the fall if it doesn't work out."

He looked her in the face, amusement playing on his lips. "If you know, why are you asking?"

She was caught and she didn't care. "I am your wife! Why are you keeping secrets?"

His voice and his expression were hard. "There's nothing to talk about, Nadra." He rose to leave.

"You just don't want to talk about it. You don't want *me* to know about it. That's it, isn't it?"

"There's nothing you have to know."

"There's nothing I *have* to know!" she screamed.

He stood and turned away from her, his hand brushing away the knickknacks on the table beside him.

"Look at me!" Mocking him, she said, "I don't *have* to know?"

She wanted to throw something at him. Had she been able, she would have strangled him in the leering camels tapestries. "Haugh!" she cried, splaying the fingers and palm of her left hand toward him. (An insulting gesture: the hell with you.)

There's nothing to talk about, she thought. *Years I spent working with him, making suggestions, weighing alternatives, taking measured risks, prodding, succeeding, now he throws away an opportunity without even telling me about it. There's nothing to talk about? There's nothing to talk about! Obviously I'm no longer his partner. I'm just his wife.*

The next day she noticed that he avoided her, like a puppy caught urinating in the corner. She put his clean clothes in the drawers, put food in front of him, went to bed without saying goodnight, and never once met his eyes. After a week of shame but no explanation, no apology, he entered their bedroom just after she had undressed and gotten into bed. She watched him lock the sacred doors behind him. He carried a small box embossed with the name Papadakis. Hesitantly he put the box next to her. She looked at him for a long time, partly as amusement, partly as punishment, enjoying his discomfort. He was contrite. She could see that. His childlike stance, pleading eyes. Had he shifted from one foot to another, the picture would have been complete. Finally she opened the box, finding pistachio-laden halvah.

The child thinks I'm a child, bringing me candy to make it up.

Laughing, she said, "Do I look like I need a piece of candy, John?"

"I don't care what you look like, Nadra, as long…as long as you always need me."

You will always need me more than I will need you, she thought. She opened her arms to him and finally let herself go, probably more out of need than love, but what difference did it make now? She accepted his embrace, and when she lay back, spent, satisfied, he wiped away the wet curls on her forehead and whispered, "Habibee."

Yes, she was his beloved, but she wasn't so sure that he was hers. She was moved by his word of love, but looking at his closed eyes and smile of pleasure, she realized it was also relief, relief to be back in her good graces.

"Tomorrow let's go to Farid Ferris's place for supper," she said.

"What?"

"Let's go to Farid Ferris's for supper."

"We never eat out."

"We never make love before the children are asleep."

She was amused when she saw that he didn't know what to do with that.

"You want to eat at Farid's?"

"You don't understand English? We should support him. He's our friend."

"Of course."

∽

In the three days of silence, in the three days she had waited for John to tell her about the deal that Michael had offered, in the three days she had anticipated discussing it with him, Nadra ruminated over her situation. All right, she was no longer a partner, she was a wife, a loving dependent whose job it was to rear the children and manage the home. But why did he stop looking to her for guidance? Why could she no longer motivate him? And most important of all, why was it so difficult for John to take a chance, to be strong? Why had he become even more reticent? Yes, she had complained. Yes, she had made demands.

The situation is crazy, she thought. *My Lord, after all these years all I want is a house, a home of our own. Could my need be more modest? Is it wrong to want windows that look out on trees rather than telephone poles, and grass rather than concrete? Is it wrong to crave the quiet of a neighborhood rather than the noise of trains and a highway?*

I want to shum al hawa. Why am I trying to figure it out? Why am I trying to understand my husband? Why can't I be like Dowla?

Dowla gave up trying to figure out David a long time ago. She had the grace to accept him like he is, to live with it. I either have to live with it or have the strength to do something about it.

Finally, those three days of silence and John's gift of pistachio-laden halvah moved her to a life-altering decision—since she could no longer work with John, she would work around him.

∽

Farid's restaurant was on a side street in the heart of the courthouse district, next to an alley. The red brick building's first floor housed the restaurant, the second floor housed Farid. The Oasis sign hung high above a series of three windows. A green and white awning edged in red shaded the windows.

For Nadra, going to Farid's restaurant was an adventure. She had heard a lot about it. Now she could see and taste for herself. John took her hand as the small entry gave way to a softly lit informal dining room. Wooden tables with ladder back chairs occupied the center of the room and sand-colored vinyl booths flanked the two side walls. *The place looks good*, she thought. She feared that it might look cheap or dirty. The walls were maroon. Centered on each table was a maroon candle under a glass globe. Nadra smiled. A man who cared about looks and atmosphere. Along the back wall, near the kitchen door, stood a deli case holding salads and desserts. Now she would find out if he could cook.

Repetitive Arabic music played in the background. Farid Ferris sat in a corner smoking a hookah. When John and Nadra entered, he bolted out of his chair.

Farid was overwhelmed with delight. The Hanouns were his

only customers. He escorted them to the front booth, the best table in the house. "*Ahlan wa sahlan!*" ("Welcome!")

"Thank you, Farid, thank you," John said.

"Mrs. Hanoun, it is my pleasure to have you."

"My pleasure to be here, Farid. Probably John has already been here."

"Never, Mrs., never."

Feigning disapproval, Nadra replied, "Shame on him."

"My poor offering cannot compare with what comes from your hands, Mrs. Hanoun."

"I'm sure your menu will tempt him," Nadra responded.

"Inshallah." Farid gave them a two-sided laminated menu. He pointed to certain items as he named them. Nadra was at once taken aback by the ambitiousness of the menu.

"Your cook can do all of this?"

John laughed. "Farid is the cook!"

"I should have known," Nadra said, smiling at Farid.

Farid was quick to bring drinks and meze, cheese, hummus, olives, and pickled turnips. Nadra ordered the tabouli and the baked kibbe. She figured those items would already be made. John wanted the kebabs, *fatayers* (meat pies), and the yogurt sauce.

Farid was quick to serve the main courses. Nadra found the tabouli adequate but the kibbe dry. She knew the kibbe must have lingered in its pan more than one day and had been reheated several times. She took some of John's yogurt sauce to moisten the kibbe. She complimented Farid on its nice mint and garlic flavor, adding, "You know, Farid, you could serve a little cup of this on the side, with the kibbe."

John's kebabs with sweet onions were nicely charbroiled, served on top of a loaf of pita. The bread was thick and dry. John realized it did not have the requisite pocket when he tried to stuff it with the meat and onion. Instead he tore it into fourths and folded pieces of meat and onion into it. Some of the pieces he used as scoops for the cucumber salad. *Mint and garlic are cheap,* Nadra reflected. *Good bread takes patience and time.*

Realizing that the smell of meat being grilled did not waft through the restaurant, Nadra asked, "Where do you grill, Farid?"

"I have a secret."

"Where is your secret?"

"When you're finished, I'll show you."

Nadra noticed a look of irritation on John's face so she decided to feed it. She finished her meal quickly and followed Farid to the secret. Inside Farid's enclosed preparation area was a side door that led to the outside. Outside that door was a roof-covered patio that housed a large brick fireplace.

"A tannour!"

"No, no, Mrs., just a large fireplace grill, but it could easily be a tannour."

"How easily?"

"Well, you would need money and the right person to build it, a brick layer of course."

"When I was little, I used to prepare the dough and take it to the tannour for baking."

"The tannour is not used so much anymore. Now they use a furn. It's like a pizza oven fired by either gas or wood. Something like the oven you use at home for your bread."

"But probably bigger and faster."

"Oh yes."

"You should build a furn, Farid."

"Funny you should say that. Everyone thought I should take Charles's deal and sell footlong hot dogs and French fries."

"Money isn't everything, Farid," she said, but she was thinking, *It may not be everything, but Farid and I could sure use a bit more of it.*

Farid wanted them to end their meal with Turkish coffee and baklawa. Nadra tried to refuse the baklawa. She feared it would have absorbed the flavors of the three salads that sat beside it in the deli case. She finally relented, fearing that she would hurt his feelings. The baklawa was sodden with too much syrup and too few nuts.

Farid would not accept payment for their meal, but John was insistent, saying that they would not come again unless he took the money. Farid gave him back half his money, remarking that he had fed them well but not like royalty.

All the way home, John talked about "poor Farid" and his failing enterprise.

❧

Once home, John went into the store to make sure that George was tabulating all of the sales. He found him with Wasim, planning their nightly fling to Maburn in the Packard Patrician. When John asked what they were doing in Maburn, Wasim winked at George and said, "Rolling the dice, John, rolling the dice."

"You mean gambling?"

"No, no, John," he said as he pushed George toward the door.

Nadra went upstairs to find Tommy flexing his muscles as he eyeballed his physique in the mirror. He smiled, dousing himself with aftershave. Catching her watching him, he turned and picked her up, effortlessly.

"I'm going out to celebrate. Guess who is going to college, Mama?"

"Who?"

Tommy broke up laughing. "Who do you think?"

Flustered, Nadra picked up a towel Tommy had left on the floor. "I didn't realize you were interested."

"Well, surprise, miracle of miracles!"

Nadra folded and hung the towel on the rack and then picked up another.

"No one should pass up an opportunity," Tommy said laughing. "Me, Tommy the Turd, Tommy the mental midget in college."

"I hate that kind of talk, Tommy."

"I know you do, Mom. Listen, I can go on the GI Bill; the government will pay for it. My reward for wearing a uniform and eating swill for two years."

"Thank God the war ended before you could be thrown into battle."

"Yes, and thank God for the GI Bill. I might have Billy talked into going with me. We can commute to Growley College. So don't you worry, we will still be here."

"You talked Billy into it?"

"Yeah, I have to have someone help me cheat. It hasn't been easy. He may be bright but he's a blockhead."

"Be nice to your brother, Tommy."

"Yeah, I love him, but I'm not so sure I like him."

"I'm so happy, Tommy, my boys in college!"

"Yeah, well, you pray we pass. Billy is a sure thing, but I will need all the angels and saints at my side. Don't wait up!" he said as he bounded for the stairs.

Nadra was elated. Her boys in college, and paid for. She began wondering if the GI Bill paid for other things, but she put it out of her mind. Her boys were going to college, that's what counted. They would have all the things she never even dreamed of having.

She was feeling hopeful again. She would call Farid and make an appointment. First she would have to stop at Lila and Sami's "mansion."

Propositions

First thing in the morning Nadra went to her parents' home. She went straight to her garden. She hoped Lila and Sami wouldn't see her; she didn't want to take the time to talk to them. Even though victory gardens were way past their time, Nadra had kept up hers. As soon as the frost left the ground and the soil was warm and dry enough to work, she had planted cool weather vegetables, which she would replace with summer's variety. Kneeling on a pad, she pulled leaf lettuce, spinach, carrots, onions, and radishes and arranged them carefully in a market basket.

Just as she moved across the yard, ready to leave, she saw the kitchen curtain part. Lila spotted her and tapped on the window. Nadra tried to avoid her by waving and moving on. But Lila opened the door before she could get away.

"What are you up to, Nadra?"

"Just picking vegetables, Mama."

"You need so many?"

"There are many more left. Just help yourself."

"How nicely you have arranged them in that basket. Where are you taking it?"

Nadra hesitated, trying to curb her irritation. "I'm going to sell them."

"I can give you work."

"What kind of work?"

"You can clean, run the house, cook for your father."

"No, thank you."

"You do for so many others for nothing. I will pay you."

"How much will you pay me?"

"A just wage."

"I remember when you paid me nothing."

"We had no money then."

"Thank you anyway."

"Go on, go sell vegetables." Lila slammed the door.

Lila returned to the house and Nadra left, relieved.

❧

When she arrived at The Oasis, Farid was scooping coffee into the coffee machine.

"Good morning, Farid."

"Good morning to you, Mrs. Hanoun." He poured water into the machine. "I'll have coffee for you soon."

"Thank you."

Using the white towel he carried, he carefully whisked errant coffee grains off the counter and into the hidden trash hamper.

Thank God he's clean, she said to herself.

He smiled at her, wiped down the table in the nearest booth and invited her to sit.

She remained standing, saying, "I'll wait until the coffee is done." She handed him the basket. "I brought you some vegetables, from my garden."

"Thank you. You are too kind, Mrs. Hanoun."

"Oh, not so kind, Farid. I am hoping to make a deal with you."

"How so, Mrs.?"

"I want to buy your place, Farid."

Astonished, he hesitated before replying. "Mrs. Hanoun what do you want with this poor place?"

"I want to turn that fireplace oven into an old country furn and sell Syrian breads—the big thin loaves, pita, and talamee. I'll top the talamee with *sumsum* (sesame) or *jeben* (cheese) or *zahtar* (savory). Hot off the oven! The hot bread in brown bags, the cool bread in plastic bags with a tie."

Taken aback, Farid said, "Mrs. Hanoun, I've been struggling and I still barely manage to keep this place open."

"That's because you're attempting too much. I only want to offer one product, one unique product, and a simple way of making and delivering it."

"Just bread?"

"Just three kinds of bread. Plain Syrian flat bread, pocket bread, and talamee with different toppings."

"You would have to sell a lot of bread."

She inched closer to him, smiling, holding his eyes with hers. "What happens when the smell of hot bread fills the air, good hot bread flavored with subtle mahleb, bread smeared with zahtar or sumsum and honey? The Amerikans might like it with butter or preserves."

Farid directed her to a table where they both sat down so he could better study her and her proposition.

"The secret, Farid, the secret is concentrating on one product that everyone likes and making it well. People will pay. Hot Syrian bread isn't something they can go home and make readily, nor would they want to."

"Let me get you a cup of coffee while we talk about it." He went to the coffee machine and returned with two cups of coffee, sugar, and cream.

"May I serve you a piece of baklawa?"

"No, thank you. People will like my bread, Farid."

"Of course, everybody likes your bread! But you will have to stop giving it away! Everybody knows what a fine cook and baker you are!"

"Made in a real wood-fired furn, my bread will be even better!"

"You would have to have a real assembly line."

"With a large furn you can make many loaves at once."

Farid got up again. "Are you sure you wouldn't like some—"

"What I would like is your price."

Farid sat across from her again and studied her closely before he spoke.

"I don't want to sell. I want to partner with you."

Nadra quietly breathed a sigh of relief; that was what she had hoped to hear. She knew she didn't have enough money to do it on her own.

"I don't want to sell anything but bread, Farid."

"That's okay, that's good. But you have to be willing to take half the risk. You know, you can't just start selling bread to the public. You have to deal with the health department and you must have a business license. All that costs money."

Nadra said, "But haven't you already done that? You *have* already done that?"

"Of course. But you must remember, with any business there is risk and you have to be prepared to take big risks if you want to make money."

"Risk I am not afraid of, Farid. I know what I want and I know that people make their own fortune. Now tell me how much so I know if I can afford you."

Farid got up for a minute, paced, then turned and faced Nadra.

"Mrs. Hanoun, John knows about this idea?"

"Of course."

Farid explained that he would have to go over his records and do a variety of other tasks, like seek out a brick layer to determine the cost of revamping the fireplace into a furn or making a separate one. They agreed to talk again in a week. So she left, thinking she would tell John in a week if the deal went through. But she had not anticipated nor wanted the phone call from Sister Mary Alberta.

In the new Catholic school, the first class was looking forward to graduation. Aurelia was one of the seniors. As Sister Mary Alberta described them, the seniors consisted of "the boys," "the rude boys," and "her girls." On that bright morning when tulips pushed their way toward the sun, next to the crocuses, Sister took out her stash of silver medals of the Blessed Mother and asked "her girls" to line up in alphabetical order outside the closed door of her office. She called them in one-by-one. She stood in front of her oak desk, facing the portrait of the order's foundress, Mother Siegfreda. She smiled, held the girl's hand and made the following speech: "I want you to know that after your graduation the door of our convent, The

Handmaids of the Blessed Mother, is open to you, should you then or ever feel the call." Finally, she pressed the medal of the Virgin into the girl's other hand.

They all responded with a polite, "Thank you very much, Sister," then once outside they laughed and compared stories.

When it was Aurelia's turn, Sister smiled, held Aurelia's hand and said, "I wish you all the best, Aurelia." She pressed the medal of the Virgin into her hand.

Outside, picking up on Aurelia's bewilderment, the other girls asked, "Well?"

"I didn't get the invitation!"

"You didn't!" they exclaimed in unison.

"She must have heard you say 'shit' that day in the cloak room."

"What about the medal?"

"Yeah, I got that."

Sympathetically they said, "Well, I wouldn't think anything of it if I were you."

Aurelia talked of nothing else when she walked home with Elizabeth. "I guess she figures I'm not good enough."

"Don't be silly, Aurelia. You're as good if not better than all the rest of us."

"But I'm not Anglo-Saxon or Irish or whatever the hell. Supposedly Mary Alberta likes Syrian people because she lived among them and all that malarkey. Maybe she's just as prejudiced as that hard-assed German, Sister Geertruida."

Entering the apartment, she had no more than slammed her books on the floor before Nadra came into the hallway to say, "Sister Alberta called me."

"I didn't do anything."

"She said she wants to see me tomorrow."

"She didn't say why?"

"No. Should I take her something?"

"Christ, Mom."

"Watch your mouth, Aurelia."

❧

The next day, when Nadra returned from her meeting with Sister Mary Alberta, at first she said nothing until Aurelia said, "So tell me, what's going on?"

Shaken and agitated, Nadra looked as though someone had kicked her legs from under her. "She said I should send you to college."

Aurelia smiled like a child who had just received a wonderful but totally unexpected gift. But Nadra's response was shock. Sister Alberta's suggestion was an unexpected blow, weakening and confusing her. Everything turned black from the outside in, like a lens closing. She had not factored in Aurelia's needs. College for Aurelia was not on her radar; indeed, it had never been on her radar.

"She says that to everybody, Mom."

"Do you want to go to college?"

"I never saw college in my future."

"Why not?"

"Criminey, Mom, for all the obvious reasons."

"Like what?"

"Brains, money."

"Sister says you are smart; 'bright' is how she put it."

"Sure, I'm no dummy."

Of course, thought Nadra. *Aurelia has not been the cry baby and the backward little girl for a long time.* She stopped worrying about her. She could already cook and bake better than Eva and Tina. Aurelia was hard-working and capable. She had worked a couple of jobs—the savings and loan, the baby clothes factory. In her junior year she was May Queen. And she was in the newspaper.

No, she hadn't given any thought to her daughter's future other than assuming that someday she would marry and have children. "Aurelia, have you ever considered nursing? I wanted to be a nurse."

"Sorry, Mama."

"I thought Mary Ann, Elizabeth, and Deborah—"

"They're going to nursing school. But that's not my trip, Mama."

Finally, Nadra asked the big question. "What do you want?"

"You know me. I've never been sure what I want. What's for supper?" Aurelia asked as she reached for the green cookie jar on the table.

Nadra shoved the jar away from Aurelia. "You're trying to avoid the subject."

Grabbing it back, Aurelia looked inside and said, "Your boys were already here."

"Talk to me!"

"What I want doesn't have to be your worry, Mama, so let's drop it."

Nadra put the cookie jar on the Hoosier's sliding countertop.

"Do you think I don't care about you?"

"I never said that, Mama."

"Then why don't you talk to me?"

"I talk to you all the time."

"You don't tell me what's in your heart."

Leaning across the table to look directly at her mother, Aurelia said, "This from the lady who says, 'listen to the words but hear the heart.'"

Nadra was taken aback, then persisted, "I'm asking you what you want, I'm asking about, about your...future."

"Who told you to do that? Sister Alberta?"

"Don't play with me, Aurelia."

Aurelia said sharply, "This is the first time *my future* has ever come up!"

"You think I did not want you to have opportunities, these chances?"

"It's not that you did not want me to have them."

"What then?"

"It's that *you* did not have them!"

Nadra stared at Aurelia in disbelief. As the recognition penetrated her heart, she sat down and quietly replied, "I'm sorry, and ashamed."

"Don't be," Aurelia said angrily. "*My future* is not your responsibility."

Aurelia turned away from her mother.

"Billy and Tommy are going to college," Nadra said.

Turning back to her mother, Aurelia said, "Good for them!"

"You could go, Aurelia."

"They're on the GI Bill."

"We can figure it out, Aurelia."

"You don't have to figure it out. It's my future."

"Talk to me! What do you want?"

"I want out! I want to get away from here!"

Stunned, Nadra didn't know what to say. It was as though she were seeing her daughter for the first time. Looking at Aurelia now,

Nadra finally saw herself thirty years removed. But that did not keep Aurelia's words from breaking her heart, nor did it ward off the mother guilt that rides on the wings of each child's hopes, or disappointments. She watched Aurelia's expression change from anger to frustration to appeasement.

Smiling, Aurelia said, "I just meant that I'd like to get out of Hedley for a while—shum al hawa and all that stuff."

Dowla had been right. This child would break her heart.

Farid Ferris called a week later, just as he had promised. He had an itemized list of all the start-up expenses, starting with hiring a brick layer to build a large furn. Fortunately he knew an Arab living nearby who knew about furns and how to build them. The other expenses included rent, utilities, licenses, flour, yeast, spices and seasonings, all added and divided by two. They would buy the spices and seasonings from Mr. Amour, the traveling salesman who filled orders for Middle Eastern foods and goods. Nadra gulped when she saw the bottom line on Farid's itemized list. It met but did not exceed her savings.

Nadra waited until she was sure all the children were out. She locked sacred doors one and two. Then she told John. He acted like it was all a bad dream. After she brought him back to reality three times, he began shouting and cursing.

"God dammit, my woman is not going to sling Syrian bread with Farid Ferris!"

"Don't worry, he will be slinging but I'll be baking."

"People will talk!"

"People will buy, John, they will buy!"

Moving right up to her, he said, "They will say I can't take care of my family. Ibe alike!"

"Stop shouting!"

He grabbed her by the arm and swung her around.

"I forbid it, Nadra!"

Frightened, she felt the same shock she felt when her mother, Lila, had asked, "Where will you go?" and the same despair engulfed her as when Sami had left the room, abandoning her. But fear and despair gave way to desperation and fury as she broke away. She reared back from him and glared into his dark angry eyes.

She spoke quietly but malevolently. "Don't ever touch me like that again, John!"

"Listen to reason, Nadra!"

"No! You listen to me! Give me grief, John, and I leave."

"You're not going anywhere!" he screamed as he swept his hand across the table holding the ceramic animal figures. The sound of the crashing objects stopped their yelling, temporarily.

She drew closer to him, her small frame intruding on his space and stature.

"No! You just watch me! You think people will talk about your wife selling bread, wait and see what they say when she marches down the street with her bags in her hands." Then she paused and said as quietly and deliberately as she could, "And I will do it, John, and you know that as surely as you stand there!"

"You're crazy; I think you have turned crazy."

"Maybe, but I'm not afraid. Do you hear? I'm not afraid of you,

John, or anyone or anything. I'm not going to let being afraid stop me from getting what I want."

"Like me."

"Yes, John, like you." She bent down to pick up the ceramic figures.

Infuriated, John paced the room, turning at times to glare at her.

As she lined up the fallen knickknacks on the table, she said, "It would be best if you tell the children."

"Why!" he screamed.

"So they don't have to ask, 'Does Baba know?'"

&

When the brick mason came to build the furn, Nadra was right there to watch. As he made his measurements, she suggested he increase them.

"This is not Saidnaya, Mrs. Hanoun. We are not expecting to bake for a whole village," said Farid.

"More than a whole village, Farid. We will sell a lot of bread. And maybe someday we will want to sell fatayers also."

"Maybe, Mrs. Hanoun, but now—"

"Measure again, please," she said to the brick mason. "Since you are already here, you will give us a good price."

After glancing at Farid for approval first, the brick mason said, "Of course." He smiled at Nadra and asked, "And you will give me some of your good bread?"

"Of course."

The next task at hand was figuring out the arrangement of what was still a restaurant. They would need less furniture, a clear pathway, and a counter and register.

"You know, Farid, we ought to just knock out the left wall."

"Mrs. Hanoun we are not going to knock out any wall!"

"What we need is a direct access to the furn where customers can—"

"Mrs. Hanoun!"

"Take it easy, Farid."

"You take it easy, Mrs. Hanoun. Let's make some money first."

"We will, I promise you."

Business

Before she did anything for the business, Nadra set her house in order, washing clothes, making meals in advance, cleaning. She knew she would have to leave early, but she would make sure that John's coffee and breakfast were ready. And she would return in time to make supper. Aurelia helped her as much as she could, but she peppered her with questions about the business, Farid, and her plans. Nadra ignored most of her questions and concentrated instead on taking advantage of her help.

Aurelia's "future" never left Nadra's heart, but Nadra knew she had to secure her own first.

She prepared a small bag in which she inserted the long white aprons she had worn when she made candy in the confectionery. Included also were several hairnets and kerchiefs. She pulled her hair back in a bun, put on her best housedress, and hung the amulet around her neck, tucking it under her collar.

On the patio Farid placed three large tables and a sturdy work-bench next to the furn, as she instructed. She asked a local wood-worker to make two baking peels for her—the big flat wooden boards used to slide the dough in and out of the oven. Nadra put on a hairnet and assembled her ingredients—twenty-pound bags of flour, cakes of yeast, canisters of salt, sugar, and spices plus large jugs of water and a hot plate on which to warm the water. She made the sign of the cross and, touching Kef Miryam, invoked the Virgin's help. "Mother of God who nourishes us all with love and care, bless these hands. May the bread satisfy and please everyone."

She lined up three large khalkeens, and beginning with the first one, she dissolved cakes of yeast in lukewarm water, added sugar, and let it proof for five minutes. After that she mixed in salt and several cups of flour, removing lumps. She continued adding flour, kneading as she went along, scraping flour from the sides of the bowl with her hands. She added more water as needed. When the dough was thoroughly mixed and had a smooth moist consistency that did not stick to her hands, she divided it into many small balls which she rolled in flour and placed on a cloth-covered surface. She left space between them, allowing them room to double in size. She covered the balls with a damp cloth and left them to rise. While that was happening, she moved to the second khalkeen and mixed another batch. Then to the third, ending with three large batches of dough that would become many flat loaves of bread.

For the occasion Farid wore black trousers, a white shirt, a red tie, and a long white apron that accentuated his lean six-foot-four frame. His jet-black hair glistened and a wide smile beckoned welcome.

He began firing the furn. When it was hot enough and the balls of dough had risen, she flattened the rolls. Then began Nadra's bread dance. She passed the flattened rolls from hand-to-hand or arm-to-arm, sometimes even tossing them into the air and catching them. Sometimes she held the dough circles at one end and draped them over her hand, gravity stretching them as she rounded the circle. She flipped the loaves onto the large baking peel and Farid pushed it into the furn. As they were browning, the loaves formed air bubbles and puffed up. Farid pulled the peel out of the oven quickly, tossing the loaves into a huge container. Nadra and Farid continued this routine for about an hour before they realized that a row of spectators was forming in the alley. From that point on Farid threw the hot loaves into the row where the watchers caught them and began eating.

"Tasty, Farid, real tasty!"

"You gonna do this every day?"

Laughing, Farid said, "Sure, sure, but every day it's not going to be free!"

Flipping more loaves to the crowd, he shouted, "*Sah-tine, sahtine!*" (Enjoy, enjoy!)

Meanwhile, Nadra worked as quickly as she could, watching her hands, not the crowd, as her heart beat wildly. When the children started arriving, she cut the risen dough balls in half and patted the halves into smaller loaves that would fit perfectly into their hands. Perspiration was starting down her face and neck; she was beaming with pride and pleasure.

Farid bellowed, "See! See! A mother always smiles as her golden hands make bread for the children."

I've got to tell Farid to shut up, Nadra thought as she continued her labors. *He's embarrassing, but he sure knows how to work the crowd. Hope he's this good tomorrow when they have to pay.*

"This mother learned to make bread in the old country. In the old country bread is the staff of life!"

"And what is it here, Farid?" asked Sonya.

Nadra looked up to see Shanti and Dowla staring at her.

Responding to Nadra's surprised look, Dowla embraced her, saying, "We're the Three Magi, sweetheart. We saw your rising star and followed it."

Her eyes scanning the environment, Shanti demanded, "So what's going on, Nadra?"

"Just trying to make a living, Shanti."

"Looks more like a show to me."

Farid flipped Shanti a loaf of bread, which shut her up. Sonya and Dowla, however, were still dumfounded, but eventually they were eating bread like the rest of the crowd.

"It is not good to keep secrets," Sonya teased as she walked away with Dowla.

Dowla turned around and threw Nadra a kiss. Shanti laughed and shouted, "Ibe alikee!"

Farid did a triumphant march around the trestle table and furn.

"Did you count them, Mrs. Hanoun, did you count them?"

"I tried to but I lost count between patting out the dough and listening to you."

"When they come back tomorrow, they will have a couple of nickels in their jeans!"

"Inshallah, Farid, inshallah."

And they did come, some out of pure curiosity, but many were friends and acquaintances to whom she had given bread and pastries for years before. Now they were all quick and eager to buy what she had once given them. Acknowledging her, they paid their money, and promised to return. Their goodwill bolstered her weary spirit, renewing the hope she feared she had lost. Many others came, the comforting, homey aroma of baking bread beckoning them.

Farid handed customers their bread in plastic bags. Each bag was secured with a bread clip, a notched plastic piece through which the bag was threaded. He was proud to tell them that bread clips were the new thing, just invented by a Mr. Floyd G. Paxton.

Waving his arms, Farid said, "Mr. Paxton was on an airplane, coming home. The stewardess gave him a bag of peanuts. He ate some then realized he had no way to close the bag."

Farid screwed his face into chagrin and frustration.

"He searched his pockets and found nothing to close the bag with. He searched his billfold and found an expired credit card and carved his first bread clip with his pen knife. Eureka!"

Nadra hoped Farid would skip the "eureka!" the next time he told the story.

"Now you can open your bag of bread a hundred times and close it a hundred times and the bread will stay fresh. Eureka! I bought a thousand bags and a thousand clips!"

When the curious children asked for the bread clips, he reddened and said he would need them all.

Each succeeding day, Nadra and Farid introduced a different topping for some of the bread, particularly the thicker loaves. In hopes of appealing to the Amerikan, they used sweet butter or sesame seed and honey. For the Arabs there was a savory topping called zahtar. Fearing that the dark zahtar mixture would scare the Amerikan, Nadra cut it into small pieces so they could sample it first. She had more converts to zahtar than she expected.

Farid explained that zahtar was the name of savory herbs grown in the Middle East, and usually referred to a mix of thyme, oregano, and sesame. He went on to add that the zahtar mixtures were different in each village, and sometimes even in each family. He boasted that Nadra's recipe for zahtar was the authentic version still made in her native village of Saidnaya, and that she wished to share it with everyone. Like a whirling dervish transfused with enthusiasm, he placed slices of talamee with zahtar on the extended hands. Nadra wondered if there would be a history lesson every day.

On more than one day, a specter seemed to be trolling the edges of the establishment. When she turned to see who it was, however, no one appeared. She asked Farid if he saw anyone. Looking at her quizzically, he said no, smiled, and offered that it might be the good-luck ghost.

For the next two weeks business ebbed and flowed, sometimes brisk, other times slow, but they were making money.

"It's time to make another addition, Farid."

"I agree, Mrs. Hanoun. Let's do *manaqish*. We'll fill a talamee with tomatoes, cucumbers, green onions, and cheese and call it a breakfast sandwich. We'll stuff it, roll it up, and hand it to them in newspaper. And for lunch, spinach pies, meat pies—fatayers."

"Let's just start with the manaqish; that will be enough work for now."

"God bless you. You work so hard, Mrs. Next week I will have a surprise for you."

"Tell me."

"No, no. It will make you happy."

"We're partners, Farid."

"I know and each day I thank God."

Now Nadra worried about the garden she had started in spring at Sami and Lila's house. She needed to tend to it and add the tomato plants and make sure the mint was coming up. She would need the tomatoes and mint for the manaqish. She debated asking Billy and Tommy to tend to the gardening.

❧

First of the week Farid greeted her at the door and led her to the kitchen. Standing before her was a steel monster on four rollers. Four controls stared at her from its curved dome.

"These controls are for the various speeds and actions," Farid said. One ear sat on the left side of its head. "This is the on/off switch."

In the center was its huge bowl of a stomach, wearing a wire hat.

"I'm afraid of it!"

"It's a Hobart, the best dough mixer money can buy!"

He ran his hand over the wire cover. "Don't worry. It will operate only when the wire cover is lowered. No chance to catch anyone's fingers."

"Hobart won't eat me?"

"Hobart is going to be your best friend, after me of course. He can mix up to one hundred eighty pounds of flour."

"Where did we get the money?"

"Don't worry, Mrs. Hanoun. I took out a small loan, in my name. We can't go on mixing dough by hand. Takes too long and it's exhausting. We're a business, not a home."

"And we're partners so I pay half."

"Of course."

"How much?"

"I'll tell you later, after we make some more money."

Farid operated Hobart as Nadra handed him the amounts of flour, yeast, water, mahleb, and sometimes margarine to feed it.

"That mahleb is expensive," Farid said.

"It's one of my secrets. You keep it quiet."

With Hobart's help they produced large quantities of various breads and toppings. For those customers looking for breakfast or a quick snack, they prepared talamee with zahtar, talamee with sesame, or manaqish. By lunchtime they had produced several trays of fatayers, meat pies and spinach pies. In addition, they accumulated stacks of pocket bread, which they dispensed in plastic bags sealed with bread clips.

Sami and Lila came one day to observe. Farid introduced Sami to the crowd as Saidnaya's scholar, but they weren't interested. Lila kept her eyes riveted on her daughter, taking in the kerchief Nadra wore on her hair to keep it in place, the long white apron, and the beads of sweat that gathered on her brow. When Nadra took a break, Lila sidled up to her and said, "So John let you do this?"

"I told him I was going to do it."

"He didn't object?"

Nadra ignored the question.

Lila laughed. "John's a lamb. You can do whatever you want with him."

"I have to go back to work," Nadra said.

"Marriage is war and whoever is in power wins," Lila said.

"I'm not in a war."

Lila laughed at her before she said, "Didn't I tell you? You only have to decide what you want to do."

She walked away, Sami following her, carrying a bundle—one of everything and a dozen pocket bread, none of which he paid for.

❧

The friends returned together, Shanti, Dowla, and Sonya, on the hottest day of summer, wearing hairnets or kerchiefs, and aprons. They asked Nadra to assign them a task.

"I appreciate your help, but you don't have to do this."

"Yes, we do," Shanti said. "People are comparing you to Jeannine."

Dowla was already cutting up balls of dough that she tossed to Sonya, who automatically took the rolling pin to them.

"What do you mean?"

Looking closely at Nadra, Shanti whispered, "You know, with Farid."

"You're kidding."

"Nope, but we're going to stop the gossip."

"*You* are going to stop the gossip?"

"Hilarious, isn't it!" Shanti said as she laughed uproariously. Dowla and Sonya tried but didn't succeed in stifling their laughter.

Shanti whispered to Nadra, "There isn't really anything going on, is there?"

"Of course not!"

Dowla and Sonya couldn't stand it any longer and came over to join them.

Nadra asked, "You're all not here to play 'does she or doesn't she,' are you?"

"We know you are a good wife, sweetheart," said Dowla.

Sonya added, "Shanti says you already have the best looking man, Nadra."

"Yes," said Shanti, "but none of them are worth fidelity."

"Ladies, the furn is blazing!" Farid shouted.

"We're on it, Farid!"

Farid had never seen so much bread turned out so fast. Watching him, Nadra knew what he was thinking—if only they could afford to hire them. For three weeks the women came on the two busiest days, Monday and Friday. Nadra could see that they liked the energy, the goodwill, and the humor that the bustling business generated in the neighborhood. And she knew it would go beyond the neighborhood. Mr. Amour, the salesman of Middle Eastern goods, came and roared with delight when he saw what Nadra and Farid had done. He would carry news of their enterprise everywhere he went.

Farid offered to pay the women something, but they brushed him off, saying, "Nadra gave us bread for years. When she was baking, our kids sat in her kitchen spreading jam on hot bread, and on holidays we feasted on her baklawa and aribee."

"God bless her, God bless her! But may I make a suggestion?" Farid said.

Standing by the bowls of sesame seeds, zahtar, oil, and butter, as well as the cheese and chopped vegetables, he motioned for them to come closer.

He whispered, "You might want to be a little less generous with the toppings and fillings."

They said nothing.

"I'm not saying be stingy, ladies. I'm saying be a little more controlled with the portions. You're selling, not feeding your family." He scooped a large handful of ingredients and said, "Not this." Then he used his thumb and two fingers to pick up a smaller portion. "But this."

Nadra, who was tending the furn, said, "What's going on over there? Why has the action stopped?"

"Mr. Rockefeller is showing us how to make you more money."

One increasingly warm morning, Nadra again felt the presence of the specter, someone outside the range of her vision, watching her. She turned abruptly to discover that it was not the good-luck ghost. It was her sisters: Tina, horror etched on her face, and Eva, grinning with delight. Tina was dressed in a spring suit, a fitted short-sleeved jacket with a flared peplum and a flared skirt. Nadra wondered if she was going to a wedding. Eva was jaunty in narrow ankle-length pants and a loose printed top.

Tina said, "What the hell are you doing?"

"Making bread," Nadra said.

"Jesus Christ, in public!" Tina said.

"Are you making money?"

"Yes, Eva, I am."

"How much?"

"Why do you want to know, Tina?"

"Because I hope it's enough to make this disgrace worthwhile."

Nadra's eyes lingered on Tina's flared silhouette as she said, "You sure look swell today, Tina."

"Don't try to change the subject." Tina walked along the three large work tables and lifted the canister lids to sniff the spices, her peplum fluttering.

Nadra thought Tina looked like a one-tailed peacock. "What's disgraceful about making bread?"

"Might as well clean houses, other people's toilets!"

"Give her a break, Tina!" Eva insisted.

"She's an embarrassment," Tina said.

Nadra knew that Tina had been a holy roller, but she wondered when she made the transition to dictator. Maybe it was after she married Oran.

"This is no different than the confectionery," Eva said. "We used to love watching her make candy." Eva reached for the samples of talamee with zahtar and began munching.

"She was helping out then, working alongside her husband," Tina said.

"This happens to be my business, Tina—me and Ferris."

"I can see that. You and your tall impresario, Mr. Farid Ferris, proprietor and head dishwasher of The Oasis. Hawking bread for Christ's sake!"

"It's honest work, a good business."

"If I had known you were so needy, maybe I could have found something for you," Tina said.

"They didn't send *me to* school, Mrs. Bookkeeper. I'm doing what I know and proud of it. And if you don't like it, you can turn your fancy ass around and go home!"

Tina yanked again on her peplum, seemingly trying to calm herself. She lowered her voice. "You're this desperate, Nadra?"

Nadra spoke quietly. "In the beginning I was, but now I'm proud."

Eva stopped eating long enough to say, "I think you look beautiful, Nadra. You lost your big belly, your eyes are sparkling and—"

"Get yourself some new clothes for Pete's sake!" Tina interrupted.

"I'm thinking to cut my hair, Eva. My bun comes loose and I worry about getting hair in the dough."

"Do that! Then you can ditch that rag on your head!" Tina barked.

Her eyes lingering again on the too-tight jacket and peplum, Nadra asked, "What did I do to deserve a sister like you?"

"You started slinging bread in public."

"She's just jealous, Nadra," Eva said as she put two talamee into a plastic bag.

"Let's get outta here before somebody sees us," Tina hissed as she walked away.

Eva winked and threw Nadra a kiss.

John never went to see Nadra and Farid's enterprise. From the very beginning he had been prepared to be offended, jealous, embarrassed, or angry. It was difficult for him to accept that Nadra was not always where she used to be. Upstairs, washing, cooking, baking, or at least in the neighborhood visiting, stopping in the store to talk, to tell him the gossip, to bring him two freshly baked cookies. Or at least to look in the window, to catch his eye, to smile.

George went to The Oasis for his lunchtime fix, and most days he was late in getting back for his shift. He was enjoying himself so much he lost track of time. John wanted to ask him how it was going over there, but instead he made remarks like, "Lots of Amerikans over there." Once John forgot himself and asked, "What about Syrian people?"

"Hell, Baba, they have been there from the start."

Eventually Officer Cork came in for his usual visit and free Coca-Cola. He was carrying a fatayer.

"Grabbed this just before they ran out. That place is jumping, John."

Officer Cork carefully unwrapped the fatayer, making sure the steaming meat, onions, pine nuts, and lemon juice didn't stain his uniform. He inhaled the aromas greedily while John opened the free Coke.

"I expect you get plenty of this good stuff," Cork said.

"Sure. At home," John said.

Surprised by John's reaction, Cork gave him a long curious look.

As Cork savored his fatayer, their meandering conversation touched on the weather, the news, politics, changes on the street, etc.

"Looks like your boy is finally here to relieve you," Cork said as George entered.

"Top of the day to you, Officer," George said as he did a mock tip of the hat to Cork.

"We'll let George tell us a few lies and then we can walk over there, John. I forgot to get a couple of those talamees for my wife."

"Yeah, now's a good time. Give you a chance to see their operation in motion," George said.

John said, "No, they will be busy now."

"There will be a lull now," Cork said. "Let's go, John."

"Yeah, go now," George urged.

"I'll take them a couple of cold Cokes," John said.

Grinning, George reached into the cooler and extracted two Cokes, which he handed to his father. John took them and reluctantly joined Cork for the walk to Nadra and Farid's business.

John and Cork arrived just as Nadra was doing the last of her bread dance. She flattened the risen rolls of dough, stretched them along her arms, then flipped them onto the long-handled baking peel. Farid slid the peel into the fiery furn.

Nadra caught John's eyes immediately. Farid saw him also as he retracted the long peel. Farid tossed the finished loaves into the container and strode straight to John, his hand extended. "Welcome, welcome!"

John managed a "Thank you" then thrust a Coke into Farid's hand. Slowly Nadra came forward and worked at putting a smile on her face. John handed her a Coke.

Farid showed John around, introducing him as "Mrs. Hanoun's Mr. Hanoun" to the remaining customers.

Nadra would always remember the surprise visit and John's astonishment. Hopefully now it was only astonishment about the business, not jealousy of Farid.

❧

John watched from the front window for Nadra's return home. She was carrying the bag in which she tucked her kerchief and long white apron. She held her head high and maintained her ramrod posture. She looked strong but thinner. Her dress hung on her. Her feet had to be aching, her varicose veins throbbing. She saw him pretending not to be watching her and offered a small wave. Forgetting his pretense, he waved back.

When he went upstairs for supper a delicious meal was awaiting him, as usual, but without dessert. He almost said, "Where is my dessert," then he remembered that they only had desserts on weekends. It was her rule; desserts were special, only for weekends. So he just sat there eating, needing something to criticize, something for which to blame her.

Billy and Tommy had already eaten. The last time they were there, Tommy had teased Nadra about being an entrepreneur, asking what she would be buying John when she made her fortune. Tommy recommended a Chevy Bel Air, perhaps a Buick Roadmaster, or better yet a Porsche Silver Bullet. All his good-natured comments went *splat!* like an overturned gravy bowl. Tommy shut up when John glared at him and when he saw Billy's enlarged pupils register alarm.

"Where is Aurelia?" John asked.

"She's at a friend's house tonight," Nadra said.

Before he could say anything else, Nadra added, "I told her it was okay."

Because Nadra was obviously tired there was little additional conversation. So John sneaked peeks at her as he passed a bowl, forked a vegetable, lifted a glass. Her simplicity, earthiness, black curly hair, naturally pink lips, cheeks that glowed with sunlight and exertion—all that he dearly loved. But did she still love him?

The ladies were ending their volunteer work for Nadra and Farid, but Nadra asked them if they would help one more day.

"Will you take my place on Wednesday?" Nadra asked.

"Of course," said Shanti, "but where are you going?" With a mischievous wink, she said, "Second honeymoon with John?"

"Shanti! Stop it!" Dowla said.

"No, Dowla!"

"I have to talk to Sister Alberta," Nadra said.

Shanti said, "I could think of better things to do with a day off."

Sister Alberta

Nadra was hoping that she wouldn't run into Aurelia when she went to see Sister Alberta. Perhaps sensing that, Sister was waiting in the corridor and ushered her into the office immediately. She pulled two oak bankers chairs together under the portrait of Mother Siegfreda, and sat next to Nadra, waiting.

"I'm sorry I wasn't able to come back sooner, Sister."

"I understand, Mrs. Hanoun."

"I tried to talk to Aurelia about college, Sister. But I didn't get anywhere. She said she can take care of her own future."

Sister did not say anything so Nadra added, "All she said was she wants to get out, to get away!"

"Well, that's no surprise. That's what they all want, Mrs. Hanoun. They don't want to stay home with their mommy."

Nadra stared at her, speechless, then she began laughing. "I can't move my boys farther than the kitchen table, and my only girl can't wait to say bye-bye."

"She's young. Curious, bright. Do you want her to go to college, Mrs. Hanoun?"

"If she wants it, I want it. But I have to know how much college will cost so I can plan."

"She's looking for a job?"

"Yes."

"You're working outside the home, Mrs. Hanoun?"

Nadra wasn't sure if that was a question or a challenge, so she ignored it. She figured Sister Alberta already knew everything.

"Her grades are good so there may be some scholarships she can apply for. With the added help of some prayers perhaps we can get a few dollars for our Aurelia."

"Praying I'm good at, Sister, but not the other things."

"I'll handle the other things."

"And Aurelia?"

"And Aurelia."

To Nadra's surprise, and chagrin, Sister Alberta decided to handle Aurelia immediately. She had her summoned to the office. When Aurelia entered, Sister dragged a side chair opposite the two that she and Nadra occupied, and said, "Sit."

Aurelia sat, facing the triumvirate—Sister Alberta, Nadra, and Mother Siegfreda.

"Your mother and I have determined that you should have, and deserve, the privilege of attending college. If that is what you want. But you need to know that in order to do that you will have to take the SAT exam. That stands for the Scholastic Aptitude Test. It is difficult and time is short. But you are bright and you have been a good student. You would have to begin studying immediately and study hard. Do you understand?"

"Thank you for the opportunity, Sister, but I've decided to become a secretary. There's a shortage of women willing to do secretarial work. I aced typing and shorthand, you know. Later I might move on to other goals."

Frowning, Sister said, "Why not move on now?"

"I beg your pardon."

"The world doesn't need another secretary," Sister said.

Flustered, Aurelia began, "College would be a hardship, Sister. My family doesn't—" but she was suddenly cut short by Nadra's glare.

Nadra's pale face reddened, her eyes watered as her discomfort advanced from embarrassment to anger. "We will manage," she said.

Sister said, "This is your chance to seize an opportunity, to be active, Aurelia," as she looked to Nadra for affirmation.

Nadra nodded and said curtly, "Be honest and answer Sister's question."

"I understand."

"And?"

"I would like to go to college."

Nadra rose from her chair and shook Sister Alberta's hand. "We thank you for your help, Sister."

She left without speaking or looking at Aurelia.

After school Aurelia went right home, washed her hands, put a chicken in the oven, peeled potatoes, chopped vegetables, and waited for Nadra. The minute Nadra stepped into the kitchen, Aurelia asked, "Why are you so damn mad?"

Nadra dropped her bag and turned on her immediately. "How dare you tell the world that we are hard up!"

"I didn't say that, I just—"

Mocking her, Nadra said, "College would be a hardship, Sister... my family..."

"I'm sorry, I didn't mean—"

"You know what's worse than a rich person bragging about his money?"

"No, you better tell me."

Edging closer, Nadra said, "A poor person belly aching to the world."

"I was just stating a fact."

"You keep your facts to yourself, Aurelia."

"I was just trying to say that I don't want you to sacrifice for me, Mama. I don't want you to give up more. I see how you're working and I want you to have what you want."

"What are you afraid of, Aurelia? We asked you a question and you answered it, now stand behind it! Don't be spineless!"

Aurelia burst into tears.

Nadra picked up her bag and fished in it for a handkerchief, which she then gave to Aurelia. She pulled out another one for herself, sat at the table, and said in a soft voice, "What kind of a mother would I be if I didn't want the freedom for you that I never had?"

As principal, Sister Alberta had acquired a wealth of nursing school catalogs as well as college catalogs for West Virginia and Ohio colleges and universities. Of course, she was mostly interested in the Catholic ones, so she would use the best source—the Catholic Sisters underground. After a few days and a few telephone calls of, "I think of you often, Sister," "With the grace of God and your goodwill, perhaps you can help me, Sister," and, "Bless you for all you do, Sister," she had leads and opportunities. In addition to studying for the SAT, Aurelia would be writing essays for Sister Alberta's connections.

A week after graduation Aurelia had a tuition scholarship to Mary Ward College in Columbus, Ohio, a respected school for girls. Sister Alberta was beyond elated. She crowed to Aurelia and Nadra that the college was named for an English woman dedicated to education. That pleased Nadra, though she wasn't sure what to make of Sister's delight that the order followed the Spirituality of Ignatius of Loyola, the founder of the Society of Jesus, the Jesuits.

Aurelia had also secured a summer job doing billing at Saint Anthony's Hospital. She doubted that the modest pay would be sufficient to cover board and books. Nadra did the math and knew instantly that it would not; she said nothing. When Aurelia worried out loud, her mother brushed her off.

"But you have to think about the house too!"

"You don't have to worry, Aurelia. I'm not going to give up what I want just so you can have what you want."

"You're already giving me what I need."

"And what is that?"

"A good example."

Nadra laughed out loud. "You talk like a nun."

"Sometimes I think I would like to be a nun."

Nadra looked her up and down before deciding to ignore the comment. "I want you to make a couple of pineapple pies."

"What's the occasion?"

"There has to be an occasion?"

"It's not the weekend."

"Go!"

⸎

George was minding the tavern so John came upstairs to share new information and have a second slice of pineapple pie.

As he sat at the table, John said, "'Am-moo Ike finally bought a new raincoat."

"Why? His girlfriend didn't like the old one?" Nadra asked as she cut a big wedge of the pie.

"No. He took it to the cleaners," John said as he dug into the pie.

"Good! Finally!" Nadra said.

Laughing, John said, "It fell apart there."

"I'm surprised they even accepted it."

"He complained they charged him double then wouldn't even refund his money," John said.

"Would you have?" Nadra asked.

"I never argue with 'Am-moo," John replied.

I've noticed, Nadra thought to herself.

"Do you want more coffee?" she asked.

"Maybe half a cup," he said.

She put a teaspoon of Instant Sanka Decaf and half a cup of water from the kettle into his cup. "I heard Joseph Mensore is making a fortune from his drive-ins."

"I'll say. He bought two new Oldsmobiles from his brother Michael."

As she sat across from him she sipped her coffee and said, "Aurelia is going to college."

John put his cup down and stared at her.

"Who decided that?" he asked.

Speaking matter-of-factly, Nadra said, "Aurelia wants to go to college. She has a scholarship to pay for the tuition. Her job and my new job will help pay for the room and board."

"And did anyone think of asking her father?"

"I knew the only answer would be 'No' or 'You can't.'"

John looked at her for a long moment before he spoke again. "Why does she want to go to college?"

Trying to act nonchalant Nadra said, "To get an education."

"What for?" John said.

"Because she wants one," Nadra said.

"But she's a beautiful girl."

"Every time you get a year older, John, I pray that you will also get a day smarter." Nadra cut him a second piece of pie, which he shoved away.

"I was joking, John."

"No you weren't."

"It's what she wants; it is her life."

Raising his voice, he said, "I agreed to let her go to Saint Catherine's! I paid the money for that!"

"Yes. Yes, you did."

"She's our only daughter. Do you really want her to leave home?"

"No, John, missing her will break my heart."

"Everything is breaking my heart!"

Complications

In order to meet the growing demands at work, Nadra knew that she had to simplify her tasks at home. When she was the one cooking dinner in the evenings, she made a large quantity so there would be leftovers to reheat the next day. She could usually count on Billy to do that properly, and sometimes Tommy, if he was hungry enough. Eventually she assigned Tommy gardening duties at the victory garden at her parents' home. She also decided to teach John how to fry eggs when he wanted them in the morning.

"I know how to fry eggs!" he said.

"Since when?"

"You think I don't have eyes?"

"So. Tomorrow you fry your own eggs. I want to get out of here early."

"Why don't you just move to The Oasis?"

"Why don't you just make life harder, John?"

In the morning he was already in the kitchen, pouring lots of olive oil in a small cast iron skillet.

"You don't have to French fry them, John."

"You don't have to boss me!"

While the eggs sizzled, grease splattering all over the stove top,

John put bread in the toaster and grabbed the ketchup from the refrigerator.

"You want eggs?"

"No, thank you, John."

When he slid the eggs onto his plate with a spoon, the yolks broke. He used a couple of napkins to swab the excess oil on his plate, doused the eggs with ketchup, and began eating with gusto.

Disgusted, she finished her coffee and rose to leave.

"You never eat."

"I'll have a talamee with sumsum at work," she said.

"You never bring me talamee with sumsum. You never bring me anything!"

"Gonna cost you two dollars."

As his mouth dropped open, Nadra said, "That was a joke, John."

Nadra and Farid's enterprise had only begun in spring, but by early summer it was thriving. Business was so brisk that Nadra began leaving earlier in the morning to make sure there were sufficient mounds of dough ready for baking, and that the fillings for the fatayers were prepared. When it was still dark in the mornings she left, John got up also, to walk her to work. She protested, saying there was nothing to fear. He could not be deterred. Bolting down his coffee, he stood at the door waiting for her. She thanked him when they arrived at The Oasis. He merely nodded. She felt a pang when she turned to watch him, shoulders slumped, head bent, trudging back home. Guilt? Pity? Whatever, she had no time to speculate.

Mr. Amour was making an extra and unexpected visit to Hedley. His routine was to come by only every four to six months to take orders from the Syrian households. He came this time to offer Nadra and Farid a deal. If they could furnish him enough loaves of bread, he could sell them to the places he visited in Clarksburg, Huntington, and Charleston. He would come for the bread once a month, on the last Thursday of the month. They said yes before they thought it through. After he left, they asked each other how they could do it.

They decided to make a study of the *what* and *when* of their sales. They hired Sonya's teenage daughters, one to bag and dispense the products, the other to keep track of what was sold and when. From that inventory they worked out a strategy. They would make the breakfast and lunch items only on Mondays, Wednesdays, and Fridays, though they would also make bread. That way they could concentrate on making nothing but bread on Tuesdays and Thursdays in anticipation of having large quantities for Mr. Amour. That strategy worked well. A fluctuating flow of traffic for breakfast and lunch became instead a steady and growing demand. The locals' orders for bread were steady. Nadra was happy. Farid was ecstatic.

The work bonded them, just as it had bonded her and John in the confectionery. Farid minded the boundaries, as did she. In the quieter moments and less frequent idle times, however, she wondered what it might have been like if there were no boundaries. She knew he respected her, not only because she worked hard, not only because she was a woman, but most of all because she had the skills, the talent, the creative spirit that said let's go, we can do this. She knew he was as eager as she to succeed. He had not succeeded in his business before, so perhaps that was why he was willing to bank everything on her idea. No matter. Their enterprise was hard work, but it was also a joy to toil with someone who wanted the same thing. Farid was like those barkers who led the circus into town, extolling the pleasure of hot bread, zesty zahtar, and sweet sumsum. He was bold, brassy, and funny. He made her laugh.

Once when she was watching him, laughing at his antics, their eyes met, and that second of communion held a world of desires and regrets for what could not be. They turned away quickly.

But not quickly enough. George, who was there as usual just before lunch, had caught the exchange.

∽

Nadra didn't feel nearly the stress she had felt when they first began their business. Even though the physical demands were enormous, she was exhilarated. She had made a decision and a plan for herself and carried it through successfully, so far. Finally she was in charge of her life, or at least in charge of a significant part of it—her desire to be her own boss, to make decisions that were good for her, to strive and work for what she wanted. Hope blossomed.

As their business grew, the work accelerated. She had to begin work earlier and stay later. She was expecting John to complain, but Aurelia stepped in to calm the waters. Aurelia worked in the hospital billing office until 4:00, and then walked home promptly to deal with supper and the laundry. Seeing that her brothers were doing very little—Billy occasionally heating the leftovers and Tommy leaving dirty clumps of vegetables on the drain board—she lit into them with all the power and menace of an experienced harridan.

Billy and Tommy were working, but only part time so she assigned them tasks. They were reluctant to take orders, however, so she listed the tasks and let them decide. Billy chose to do the laundry. He claimed he was the only one capable of dealing with the Maytag when it broke down. Tommy said he would sweep, with a broom and the vacuum, but he would never dust. George claimed he had his duties in the store, but Aurelia insisted he do the shopping. She knew he could borrow Wasim's car.

That arrangement worked reasonably well. Between the two of them, Nadra and Aurelia had earned enough money to pay the first installments on Aurelia's room and board at Mary Ward College. Aurelia would have a work study job at the college. To calm her daughter's concern about accepting money for college, Nadra assured her that the savings account for the house was growing steadily, while in reality the money into that account was still more of a trickle. Consequently, when Mr. Amour said he could sell as much bread as they could provide, they took on more orders. Their customers were asking for them so they also reinstituted the lunch items on Tuesdays and Thursdays.

Nadra had begun going to bed early soon after the business began, but now she was retiring even earlier. She would need to leave the apartment at 4:00 a.m., and so Farid insisted he could come pick her up in his car. She told John, thinking he would be glad that he wouldn't have to walk with her at that hour. Nadra had expected relief but what she got was rage.

"What the hell do you mean? That man is pulling up to my place at four o'clock in the morning and my wife is sneaking into his car!"

"That man is your friend and my partner and I'm not sneaking into his car."

"We only need one person to see and the whole east end will be talking!"

"Hell, John, the whole east end could care less."

"People will talk!"

"People are sleeping, not talking, at four o'clock in the morning."

"I won't have it!"

"I don't give a damn!"

"You have gotten coarse, Nadra, very coarse. You never talked that way before. You talk like an American with a big mouth."

"That's better than being a Syrian slave who jumps when her husband makes a demand."

"*I* treat *you* like a slave? You don't even respect me!"

"I respect you and I also respect me!"

When they heard footsteps in the hallway, they turned abruptly. Aurelia was returning after an evening at the movies. She avoided looking at them and went immediately to her room.

Ashamed, they stopped talking and went to bed, as far away from each other as possible, each hugging a side of the bed.

John awakened before Nadra and acted as though nothing had happened, but when she descended the stairs, so did he. When Farid pulled alongside the curb, John approached the car first, thanked Farid profusely, and told him to go ahead because he enjoyed walking his wife to work. Readily taking the hint, Farid pulled away.

John turned toward Nadra, expecting her to fall in next to him. Her throat tightened, her face flushed red and hot, and her heart beat rapidly as her hands automatically clenched into fists. She took her place alongside him, saying nothing. Lila's comments formed a refrain in her thundering heart: "Marriage is war. Whoever is in power wins."

When they arrived, she faced him, smiled, and said, "Thank you, John."

"Sure, sure," John said.

Once inside, Nadra assured the very apprehensive Farid that "John was just being John," and he would "get over it." She had seen Farid peeking at them from the side of the window.

❦

Like a heavy winter coat, the early morning's darkness weighed John down. The twenty-one apartment steps were a mountain to the hallway cave. Once inside sacred door two, he crawled onto the middle of their bed. Several hours later he heard activity in the kitchen.

Speaking softly, Aurelia said to Tommy, "I told you to hose off the vegetables when you picked them at Sitto Zahir's, or at least to rinse them in the sink here."

"Why do you keep making a big deal of that?" Tommy asked as he ate his last bowl of Corn Flakes.

"Because of the soil that gets on the floor and all over the kitchen."

"Okay, okay, you made your point." He put two slices of bread in the toaster.

"And you don't have to change your clothes every day," said Billy as he poured himself a cup of coffee.

"Says who?"

"Says me! Now that I'm the laundry slave, I'm not processing all your precious duds through the Maytag," said Billy.

"Mom never complained."

"Funny *you* didn't hear her," Billy said.

As he tucked his new shirt into his pants, Tommy asked, "Sis, do you think I look like Dean Martin?"

Stepping back to look him over and ponder his question, Aurelia said, "Maybe a little more like Jerry Lewis."

He said, "Thanks a lot" as he buttered his toast.

Indicating the shared bedroom, Billy asked Aurelia, "How come you don't wake King Farouk and nag him?" He finished his cup of coffee.

"Don't worry about George, I gave him a job." Aurelia put another cup and saucer on the table and took out the marmalade.

"Bet it's easier than ours," said Tommy.

"Don't you two have to be somewhere?"

"Yeah, yeah, we're going," Billy said.

Tommy grabbed the last slice of toast and began singing "That's Amore" as they left.

Once he heard the main door close, John went to the kitchen.

"Did Thomas Edison and Dean Martin wake you, Papa?"

Shaking his head no, John asked, "Who was Thomas Edison?"

"A very famous inventor. He gave us the light bulb and the phonograph."

Indicating the closed door to the other bedroom, he said, "I know who King Farouk is."

Aurelia laughed. "That one isn't worth his weight in gold."

John took his usual seat at the head of the table.

"What would you like for breakfast, Baba?"

"Maybe a couple of eggs, three, and toast, Vienna bread toasted."

"You've got it."

She melted a little butter in the frying pan and once it began sizzling, she added four eggs. Once the whites of the eggs turned crispy and the yolks modestly runny, she served him and herself. Eggs just like he loved them. They didn't even need ketchup.

Aurelia sat across from him, reading the paper and telling him the news. Her eyes were as dazzling as her mother's, but they were soft and kind.

Aurelia was smiling at him, the coffee pot in her hand.

"One more cup, Baba?"

"Please."

She told him she was going to the hospital, to her work, and as usual he told her to be careful.

She smiled. "Dear Baba, I am *always* careful."

Dear Baba, she said *dear* Baba. How that calmed his troubled heart. He finished his coffee and descended to his work.

Another day of waiting for customers in his beer joint. Another day of greeting the railroaders with lunch buckets swinging by their sides. He had once carried his lunch, before he became a businessman, when he was happy, before he became a sad husband. For the most part the railroaders were fine in the late afternoon, cheerful, full of life, eager to have a couple of beers and relax before going home. When they came in with their wives in the evening, they were playful, their wives happy to be with them, sometimes accompanied by their children who loved having Coca-Cola and potato chips. On those nights he was happy to kid around with them and share in their jokes and good moods.

The last hours of the night, however, could be awful. Those were the hours when the bad-tempered husbands and the lonely bachelors would want to drink themselves blue. Despising their grouchiness and slurred speech, John would send them home. When George began working the late hours, he let them stay, treating them to salty snacks that would encourage them to drink more quart bottles of Budweiser.

The most troublesome of the railroaders were those who began drinking early in the day. They would come to his tavern to get beer and then gather around the potbelly stove in the red caboose to drink, smoke, and play cards. On the way home they would stop for more beer and their wives would begin calling John on the phone. Before he even answered, the men would shout, "Tell her I'm not here!" Those wives needed money to feed the children. Particularly on Friday nights, some of those railroaders looked forward to going home and slapping their wives around.

The Secret

Nadra was sick of Farid eyeballing her when she wasn't looking. Obviously there was something on his mind.

"Out with it, Farid."

"You know that guy who comes in at closing time?"

"Sure, the one you give all the leftovers to."

"He has a big family!"

"I know, I know. I'm not complaining."

"He wants to do us a favor."

"And?"

"He's a house painter. On the side he paints signs and he will do one for us for free."

"You don't like The Oasis?"

"It should read Nadra's *Khubz*."

"For crying out loud, Farid, nobody but the Arabs knows that khubz means bread, let alone knows how to pronounce it."

"They can learn!"

"It seems to me, Farid, that the first rule of advertising should be using the native language."

"All right, then it can just be Nadra's. Everybody knows that's your name."

"What about your name?"

"No need, no need."

"You don't want to name the place Farid and Nadra's?"

"No, Mrs. Hanoun."

She understood. He felt it would be unseemly.

"Farid, I want it to stand as it is—The Oasis."

"Okay, okay."

She wanted to laugh. How would he feel if he knew that "Mrs. Hanoun" wanted to leave Mr. Hanoun. That last bit of humiliation—"I will take *my* wife to work."—did it. She could leave once she had more money, but where would she go?

She would need time and money to deal with it. The thought of leaving was foreign and confusing. More than money it was the embarrassment. Syrian women did not leave their husbands, their families. There was nothing more sacred than family.

People would talk. They would think she had something going with Farid. She remembered all the gossip about Jeannine and her partner. Gossip that probably wasn't true. She didn't know if she could stand that. The thought of leaving made her cold, weighed her down, stabbed her heart.

"Mom? Mom!"

George was fanning his hands in front of her in an effort to get her attention.

"You in some kind of daze?"

"What's the matter?"

"Baba has bad news. His mother died."

"Go, Mrs. Hanoun, go!" Farid said.

✧

She found John in the tavern with 'Am-moo Ike. George indicated he would take over the tavern. The three of them went upstairs to the apartment. In the living room John nodded at 'Am-moo Ike who began reading the letter again, pausing at certain parts: "Your mother spoke of you often, telling us she wished to return to America, eager to see you once more, but unfortunately she was stricken, grew weaker and died quietly on the first day of May, the priest and her family at her side."

John bowed his head and wept.

Good Lord, thought Nadra. *It took them months to tell us.*

John's friends gathered around him, coming in the evening to offer their sympathy and sit with him. Farid shuttered The Oasis for three days and maintained the establishment for the rest of the time on his own. The women dressed in black and brought food for the family. Even though it had been more than forty days since Um-Hana's death, Nadra booked a Mass for the Forty Days Observance.

The Forty Day ritual occurred two weeks later. Nadra had ordered five pounds of the whole wheat from Mr. Amour and took great pains to prepare it properly. She soaked the wheat overnight and cooked it for hours until tender. She added walnuts, raisins, and cinnamon. The last addition was sugar to signify the sweetness of everlasting life. She mounded the mixture on serving trays and made an impression of a cross with powdered sugar on top. The trays were bordered with Jordan almonds.

After the Mass, Nadra served lunch and the cooked wheat, *kilbee*, to close friends and family. She wished she had more space for the occasion. She borrowed card tables and folding chairs and set them up in the living room. 'Am-moo Ike was touched by Nadra's efforts to memorialize his sister. In the kitchen the helpers gossiped.

Shanti said, "I heard they were not good to her over there."

"Don't say it in front of John," Benny said.

"He knew. And he would have brought her back if she could have made the journey," Michael said.

Nadra let Aurelia know that she was to take charge. Then she went to corner Dowla.

∽

"Surely, you can tell me now," Nadra said to Dowla.

They went outside to the small landing at the top of the stairs. They watched closely and spoke softly.

Dowla began, "While he was still working in the caravan, John's father, Boutros, started collecting goods that he could eventually sell on his own. When he quit the caravan, he began selling and making a little money. One of his neighbors, known to be a jealous troublemaker, accused him of stealing the items. Furious, Boutros denied the charge.

"Many of Boutros' buyers believed, or chose to believe, the accuser and demanded that Boutros give back their money. He lost all that he earned. Worse, he was shamed."

Nadra said, "Had he stolen the goods?"

"No, but it was some time before the caravan chief was back and came to Boutros' defense, explaining that Boutros had made good trade deals and swaps."

Nadra held her breath, fearing the rest.

"Just before that the accuser was brutally assaulted."

"By Boutros?"

"He was one of the suspects. His alibi was his wife, Um-Hana. He claimed he was with her at the time of the crime. Meanwhile, Boutros, Um-Hana, and John rushed to set sail for America."

Nadra interrupted to say, "John said they had to work a long time to have enough money."

"I know only what she told me and I know only that they only had enough to come steerage class."

"So you think there are missing pieces."

"There are always missing pieces, Nadra."

Nadra bristled. "Don't get philosophical on me now, Dowla."

"I said I would tell you what I know, Nadra. The rest you will have to figure out."

"Just tell me what you know."

"When Boutros was not allowed to enter because of trachoma, he had to return to Syria."

"He was probably out of his mind with disappointment and anger," Nadra said.

"He wanted Um-Hana to return also."

Nadra said, "He didn't want to be alone."

"He wanted her there, in Saidnaya, to help clear him in case he was indicted."

"And?"

"She refused. Syrian police jailed Boutros. His accuser had died of his injuries."

"Did Boutros commit the crime, Dowla?"

"I don't know, Nadra."

"Was Um-Hana with him at the time, Dowla?"

"Yes."

"How do you know?"

"She told me. It was the day he beat her, the day John tried to help her. The day he almost killed John."

Once their life returned to its usual and predictable pace, Nadra asked John, "Why didn't you tell me why your mother never returned to your father and what he did to you?"

"Why do you think!"

"You could have told me, John!"

"We chose to keep it to ourselves."

"And you chose to keep it from me. Had I known, I would have understood many things better."

"Maybe, or perhaps you would have pitied me, as you pity me now. I don't need your pity, Nadra! Go back! Go back to your furn and bake your goddamn bread! I know you want to leave me! I saw the same look in my mother's eyes a hundred times—the desire to go, the need for freedom. You think I don't see it in you?

"Boutros beat her often so she had cause. My father deserved her leaving and she made sure he spent the rest of his life regretting it.

"You women always want us to be brave. We are not brave. We're scared boys. We are always expected to come through, especially for our mothers, for our wives. I was a child, barely knew my left from my right when he began slamming me into the wall, for no good reason, for no good reason other than he hated the world and his place in it! He wanted to come to America.

Not because it was his dream, but because he could not make it in the old country. So we left the old country, my father, my mother and I. But the new world didn't want my father so he had to go back. He was afraid to go back. He knew the police would come after him. But my mother and I were glad."

"And you carried that burden all this time."

"We carried his shame and our guilt."

"You did what you had to do."

John stared at her, his look lingering and hard, as he said, "That's right, and so should we all."

Realizing what he was telling her, she felt herself torn between panic and relief, like the discovered child being told to go ahead and run away from home. She didn't know what to say, and it was obvious that he had no more to say. They sat in silence for a long time.

Softly, with great compassion and sincerity, she said, "You are a good man, John. That was the first thing Jeannine said to me."

He did not respond.

She could not bear the silence.

She was glad to go to work the next day, which would be busy. Mr. Amour would be coming to pick up the bread. She said little to Farid, and picking up on her mood, he left her alone. She did her work mechanically and quietly, but her mind was racing.

The Smiling Lion

Mr. Amour came early, all smiles and goodwill. He sat next to the coffee maker and took out samples of halvah and sesame candy that he brought for them, making it obvious that he was eager to talk. They took the hint and joined him, Farid pouring coffee for the three of them.

Smiling broadly, Mr. Amour said, "Friends, your good bread is very popular in Charleston, actually everywhere, Clarksburg and Huntington too, but especially in Charleston." Then he frowned, eyes downcast, his brow furrowed. "So I am worried."

"Why should you worry?" Nadra asked.

"In time, some savvy Syrian down there will copy your idea," Mr. Amour said.

Farid shook his head. "You really think someone can make bread as good as Nadra's?"

"It's the idea they will try to copy, not the recipe."

"So let them," Farid said.

"You don't understand what I am trying to tell you," Mr. Amour replied.

To Farid, Nadra said, "He's telling you we should beat them to it."

"That's not possible. Mrs. Hanoun's family is here and..."

Grinning, Mr. Amour asked, "You have somebody here I don't know about, Farid?"

"No, but I have you and you are still making us money in other places like Charleston."

"Not nearly what you could make if you had a bakery in Charleston. It's an ideal place to open up another business. It's bigger, cosmopolitan."

"Cosmopolitan in West Virginia?" Farid asked.

"It's a big, growing city, full of Middle Easterners and other foreigners. You could make a lot of money."

"We're just starting to make money here," Farid said.

"There's so much more to be made. You have to be bold." Smiling as he nodded toward Nadra, Mr. Amour said, "Mrs. Hanoun could buy you out so you could make your move. Of course I would continue to work with both of you." He offered Nadra the halvah. "The best, with pistachio."

Nadra passed up the halvah but returned his smile while thinking, *You son-of-a-bitch.*

Farid said nothing.

Opening his arms as though to bless the establishment, Mr. Amour said, "Look how successful you are! You have to expand before your idea spreads to others. Now they think it's just foreigners making strange bread. Eventually they will see it's Arabs making money!"

No one responded. They continued sipping their coffee in awkward silence. Mr. Amour couldn't interest them in the sesame candies.

Finally Farid said, "Let's start loading your van."

It never took them long to load Mr. Amour's van, but it was some time before Farid came back. Ever polite, Mr. Amour ducked in the door long enough to say goodbye to Nadra.

Farid sat down, flushed and irritated. "Glad to get him out."

Leaning toward him, Nadra asked earnestly, "Do you want to move to Charleston, Farid?"

"Of course not!"

"You're a businessman; you should do what's best for you."

"I would miss Hedley..."

Nadra raised an eyebrow and laughed.

"...and working with you, Mrs. Hanoun."

"Thank you, Farid."

"How did you know?"

"I can read the man," she replied.

"You are a very smart lady, Mrs. Hanoun."

"And you are a very ambitious man, Farid."

"Enough, Mrs. Hanoun. We need to get started on the lunch items."

"Of course."

Nadra was heartsick and angry. She knew there was some self-interest in Mr. Amour's "worry." She just didn't know what it was at this point. If Farid changed his mind about moving to Charleston, she didn't have enough money to buy him out. She hadn't even paid her full share of Hobart, and she would have to buy Farid's building or at least rent it from him. Maybe she could go to Charleston by herself.

The Syrian Gospel

At 4:30 Aurelia came to The Oasis instead of going directly home. "You're going to have company so bring some fatayers plus some extra bread."

"Who is coming?"

"'Am-moo Ike."

"Your father invited him?"

"He invited himself. He's in a hell of a mood."

"That means trouble."

"I don't think so. He's all perky. Well, as perky as someone like 'Am-moo can be."

All the way home Nadra tried to determine the meaning of perky in relation to 'Am-moo Ike. When she reached the apartment she saw that John was irritated about 'Am-moo's coming, but she knew that he was much too polite to complain. He paced the floor as Aurelia and Nadra prepared the table for company. Billy didn't verbally complain, but showed his annoyance in other ways. Tommy, however, was pleased to see 'Am-moo Ike even though he no longer idealized him and no longer had dreams of becoming a bookmaker.

When 'Am-moo Ike arrived, John greeted him with the usual "Ahlan wa sahlan, 'Am-moo."

'Am-moo responded with "Shukran" (Thank you), and went directly to Nadra who was dishing cucumber-yogurt salad into a bowl. Standing in front of her, 'Am-moo Ike patted his right hand over his heart to express his affection.

"I have come to applaud you and to thank you for what you have done."

Assuming he meant dinner, Nadra said, "You are always welcome, 'Am-moo."

When he reached for her hands, Nadra, confused, handed him the cucumber-yogurt salad. He stuck his finger in the bowl, took a taste, and handed the bowl to Billy. Aware of Billy's propensity for good hygiene, Aurelia grabbed the bowl from Billy and pushed him away, fearing that he might toss the bowl at 'Am-moo.

"*Yisslamou eydayki!* (God bless your hands!) I have come to praise you and to thank you for what you have done."

They all wondered what she had done. John slipped and asked.

"What has she done, what has she done! She has brought the Levant to West Virginia! Yisslamou eydayki! Here in Hedley West-by-God Virginia, American people line up waiting for bread—just as they do in the Syrian Christian town of Saidnaya. It brings tears to my eyes. The Amerikan of Hedley now crave talamee and manaqish. They love sumsum and zahtar. Ferris teaches them our history and has them say, '*Ma'koul il hana!*' (Good eating!) What has she done? What has she done? The Amerikan know us, they appreciate us. To love our food is to love our country. I congratulate you, John."

Knowing what his answer would be, Nadra said, "Why him?"

"He is your husband!"

"He didn't do the baking."

"This isn't just about bread, Nadra. You have brought the Arabic tradition of breaking bread from the Land of Promise, Syria, to the New World. Through the tradition of bread you are spreading the gospel. You are our patron saint, our Syrian patron saint. And Mr. Amour is spreading your gospel throughout West Virginia."

"'Am-moo, are you the good-luck ghost?" Nadra asked.

"What?"

"Never mind."

Happy and unusually exuberant, 'Am-moo Ike kept clapping John on the back. Bewildered, John didn't know what to do with his face, let alone what to say. Nadra arranged her face into a blank tablet and went about serving food. After a hearty meal and leftovers to go, 'Am-moo made his way home, saying tomorrow he would go to congratulate Farid Ferris.

Nadra was still in shock. *God bless your hands! He must have said it a thousand times! That stuck up old fart is bragging about me! He sees me now. He appreciates me. No one else in the family ever bragged about me like that...except Sitto. When she gave me the amulet she said, "It will protect you and it will bless these golden hands."*

After wiping away the tears with her apron, she reflected, *Of course there's something in it for him. After all, I'm making the Hanouns look good. I'm also bringing in some dollars. But he doesn't know how much these hands hurt and this back aches.*

"Did you know you were spreading the Syrian gospel, Mom?" said Tommy.

Aurelia shot him a look as she cast a quick glance at her father.

John rose abruptly and said, "I'll send George for his supper." He went down to the tavern.

Tommy left. George did not come immediately, but when he did, it was obvious he had heard the news. Amusement burnished his face.

"Baba's pride will heal, Mama," George said, as he took his place at the table.

Nadra served him a plate of food and ignored his remark.

"Just fork over some of the profits and he will get over it."

"And you can just mind your own business, George."

"Better yet, you know what you should do, Mama? Buy out Farid and let me take over his half of the business."

"What are you talking about?"

"I know Baba's been planning on it, but I'm not interested in the tavern. You could continue the baking, of course, but I would manage—"

"You would what?"

"I would be your managing partner."

"Why would I want to do that?"

"To avoid the possibility of scandal. Don't look so shocked, Mama. Ibe alakun could apply to you as much as anyone."

Nadra felt that little moment of happiness, that temporary triumph, slip away.

She took away his plate and slapped him as hard as she could. George's hands flew to his face and his eyes popped open.

Aurelia was so taken aback she dropped the plate she was holding.

Billy shouted, "You are such a jackass!"

"I was just talking about people's perceptions," George said.

"That is what people think?" Nadra asked.

"No, that is not what people think!" Billy said. "If it was, do you think 'Am-moo Ike would have congratulated you and praised you as he did?"

Aurelia took Nadra's hands. "Billy's right, Mama."

"I was only talking about what people *could* think. I'm sorry, Mama."

"I'm sorry too." She gave back his plate. "You are right, George, people *could* think that."

Offering the salad bowl, Billy said, "Have some of the cucumber-yogurt salad. 'Am-moo put his finger in it."

George stood up abruptly and moved menacingly toward Billy. Aurelia intervened.

"Now my family's going to hell!" Nadra screamed.

Aurelia untied Nadra's apron as she said, "Go downstairs, Mama. Sit with Baba and have a Coke. I'll take care of things here."

Nadra did what she was told. When she entered the tavern she nodded to the customers and made her way to the back booth. After serving beers to the customers at the bar, John took Nadra a Coke.

"What's the matter?" he asked.

Nadra wouldn't talk, just shook her head. After a few minutes John returned to his clientele.

This was the tavern's early evening crowd. Singles wanting to horse around, drink a little, maybe watch some TV. Married men staying out while the wife did the dishes and bedded the children. Noisy friends who liked to banter, tell jokes, make bets and tease.

And the single men.

Always the first to arrive, Jake never once greeted John. "Quart of Budweiser" was all he said before he retreated to a side booth.

Tim always tipped his cap, took it off, and rubbed his brow before he said, "Line 'em up, John." That meant two Pabsts. Stevie occasionally asked after the "Missus and the childen," and liked to talk. An hour later, Jake, at that point a solitary drunk, would order another "Budweiser quart."

John always wiped down the bar between customers. *His* patrons would never go home with bar dirt on their shirts or sleeves.

John always wore a white shirt and blue tie. He was the waiter, the listener, the fetcher of beef jerky, beer nuts, potato chips, and pork rinds. At least he could predict what a day would be like.

The Smiling Lion's Teeth

For the time, Nadra gave up thoughts of leaving John. She also became unusually circumspect in her behavior, avoiding any gesture or remark that could possibly be misunderstood as funny, bold, sexual, or daring. She was weary of gathering her hair into a bun at the nape of her neck. But she would not cut it, hot weather and bother be damned. She would leave herself as is, even though her clothes were getting baggier. She wanted to look like a little old lady from Saidnaya.

Farid, however, was reveling in their success. He dressed like the Syrian flag, which consisted of three horizontal bands of red, white, and black with three green stars on the white band. His shirt was red, his apron white, and his trousers black. The three green stars were centered horizontally on his white apron, like a cummerbund. He was no longer lecturing, but he never stopped radiating charm, hospitality, and goodwill.

Neither of them again brought up the subject of opening a business in Charleston. Nadra had even stopped worrying about the possibility. Mr. Amour, however, had not given up on the idea. One Thursday when he came to pick up his usual order, complaining of a bad back, he left Farid to complete the loading. He sought out Nadra.

"You don't have to worry about Farid's wanting to move to Charleston, Mrs. Hanoun."

"He never told me he wanted to move."

"Mrs. Hanoun, is he going to say that to you?"

"We speak openly to each other."

"Mrs. Hanoun, the man is known for his graciousness...and gratitude... He is also ambitious, and single, he can go anywhere, do anything—"

"I'm sure he would say if—"

"Wait. Let me speak. Let me make it easier on both of you. I will lend you the money to buy him out. I know how much it would take."

"You think I don't know?"

"Forgive me. Of course you do. What I'm saying is Farid doesn't have to know the source."

Nadra wanted to tell him to get out.

"No. Don't answer now! We will say no more this year, Mrs. Hanoun. I know you need time. After all, you have a family to think about. Consider it for a while. After the first of the year you and I will talk again."

She knew another wall might fall on her. She hadn't known where or when. She hadn't suspected it would be Mr. Amour. Even though she was worried and afraid, she would deal with her daughter's needs first.

∽

At the end of summer Nadra and Aurelia reviewed the college expenses and savings again. They were ecstatic. Aurelia said, "Sister Alberta was sure our guardian angel would take care of us."

Nadra laughed and added, "Farid calls such a creature our good-luck ghost." Nadra even felt they could afford a mini shopping spree for Aurelia. They would not have to ask John for money, but Nadra did make it a point to keep John informed.

His reaction was always, "Why does our daughter have to leave us?"

Nadra expected Aurelia to be a little apprehensive, but she wasn't. Nadra had never seen her so excited. She was already making decisions about what to take. When Nadra entered Aurelia's bedroom, she noticed the red autograph dog tucked into a travel satchel. Nadra handed Aurelia the amulet, Kef Miryam, which she had put in a small velvet bag.

Slipping the amulet out of the velvet bag, Aurelia said, "Why are you giving me this?"

"It will always protect you," she said.

"Protect me from what?"

"Keep you safe," Nadra said as she sat on the bed.

Laughing, Aurelia said, "You mean from boys?"

"Don't joke! If Baba hears you..."

"My mouth is sealed, my tongue tied!"

"Sitto gave me that when I left the old country, in 1922."

Aurelia sat across from Nadra, on the small vanity chair. "Thank you, Mama. But I can't take it."

"Why not?"

"I don't need it."

"You don't need it?" Nadra asked.

"I don't want it, Mama."

She handed the velvet bag to Nadra. "Thank you anyway, Mama."

∽

Shanti offered to drive Aurelia to Mary Ward College. When they arrived, Nadra wished John could see the beautiful all-girls school and particularly the Sisters who hovered about, greeting the parents and helping the students. She knew he would feel a sense of relief, but all she felt was loss. Sonya was right. Every woman needed a daughter, particularly a woman who anticipated leaving the comfort of the only real home she ever had. Nadra cried all the way home and Shanti let her, occasionally patting her hand.

∽

Home wasn't the same. Billy and Tommy left early for their drive to college, and often spent additional time studying in the library. George seldom rose before noon, having spent his late nights with Wasim or his other newly mobile friends. Aurelia was gone. The tavern became John's retreat, The Oasis became Nadra's retreat. She made an evening meal, which might or might not draw the boys. But she and John ate dinner together.

Even though they sat no more than five feet away from each other, they acted like strangers. They didn't know what to say, and when they did speak, it was awkward and humorless. When he finished eating, she rose automatically to clear the dishes. One day he rose to help her. Astonished, she stared at him. The anger that once consumed Nadra was dissipating. The ache to get away was displaced by confusion. She would sneak looks at John in hopes of discovering what he was thinking, feeling, but she could not read him. She knew him well enough to know that his expression cloaked strong feeling that he had chosen not to express. The only thing that lifted autumn's chill from her heart was the knowledge that Aurelia would be home for Thanksgiving.

∽

Four days before they expected her, Aurelia banged her way into the apartment.

Surprising her parents in the middle of their usually forlorn dinner, she said, "So who died?" Embarrassed they said nothing, choosing instead to lather themselves in her good humor and abundant affection. Dressed in a wool skirt, matching twinset, and bobby socks, she looked like a preppy version of herself except for her hair, which she had corralled into a ponytail. Amused by their expression, she said, "I guess curly hair doesn't make it in a ponytail." She tried to push away the curls that framed her eyes and neck.

Nadra set a plate before Aurelia and began filling it with meatloaf, mashed potatoes, and peas. Aurelia wasted no time digging in.

"I thought you were coming on the Greyhound," John said.

"The parents of my roommate, Patricia, came for her and said I could come along too. We had an English paper due, but Sister said we could hand it in early."

"You like school?" Baba asked.

"I love it, Baba!"

To John, Nadra said, "Let George come up for his dinner."

Looking at her father's plate, Aurelia said, "Mama?"

Embarrassed, Nadra said, "I'm sorry. I thought you were finished, John."

John moved his plate to the side and left.

Nadra couldn't take her eyes off her daughter, all the while placing more food in front of her. Aurelia didn't mind, taking another slice of meatloaf.

"So how is the food there?" Nadra asked.

"It's okay. Institution food. Enough of it, but no flavor."

"Looking very American, Aurelia," a smiling George said as he entered the kitchen.

She got up to embrace him, then poking him in the stomach, she replied, "Still looking like yourself, stout Syrian."

"Find any good-looking men?" George asked.

"Don't make trouble, George," said Nadra.

"Home sweet home," Aurelia said, laughing.

"Home, but it's not been so sweet," George said with a wink.

"I noticed," Aurelia said.

The Hanoun tradition was to have their Thanksgiving dinner at noon, then go to Lila and Sami's for an evening meal for both clans. Nadra and Aurelia decided on a simple American meal for their immediate family. Presently they were making Syrian pastries ahead of time for the Zahir celebration. Mother and daughter worked in synchrony, exchanging gossip, jokes, and reflections, Nadra taking delight in their likeness. John smiled when he saw them working together, and most especially when Aurelia sat him at the table with Arab coffee so he could sample the *mamoul*, the walnut-filled cookies, to determine if she was making them right.

All seemed to be going well until the early evening when John entered the apartment and hissed at Nadra, "How dare you invite him!"

She was at the stove, browning ground beef. "What are you talking about?" she asked.

"You invited Farid Ferris!" he said.

"I did not invite him."

"Then why did he thank me and say another time?" he asked.

"I don't know. He told me he was going to Sonya's for Thanksgiving."

"Sonya's?" he said.

"Yes, Sonya's! So what the hell are you thinking!" Nadra added onions and garlic to the meat and continued stirring.

"He thanked me for the invitation and said—"

"I don't care what he said. Now shut up before Aurelia hears you."

Aurelia entered the kitchen with a laundry basket of her clothes.

"I already heard," Aurelia said. "What's going on?"

"Nothing's going on!" Nadra said.

"Nothing to worry about," John said.

"The boys tell me you have been like this for a long time now."

"You don't have to listen to the boys," Nadra said.

Again, John said, "Nothing to worry about."

"Nothing to worry about? Then why do you walk around each other as though the other doesn't exist? Why is there a chill in the air? Why is there no humor, no smiles...no love?"

"We missed you, Aurelia, we missed you very much," Nadra said.

"We don't know how to act without you, Baba," said John.

"It's the loss of you that we feel," Nadra said.

"Oh, I know you miss me, but that's not what makes you this way! The loss of me is so keen because you no longer have each other. Because you have abandoned each other!"

"We're here."

"Are you, Mama?"

Nadra felt a sudden wave of heat as her face turned red and her eyes tightened.

"You wouldn't feel the loss of me so much if you had each other!"

Aurelia left the apartment, slamming the door behind her. Nadra and John talked to each other long enough to agree to a feigned degree of civility between them. They would talk more, exchange gossip, be helpful to each other. They even planned a couple of humorous exchanges in the hope of creating an atmosphere of family harmony. The mere planning of these pretenses made them laugh, especially when John said, "Try not to frown when I enter the kitchen," and Nadra retorted with, "Do something with those sad sack eyes."

❧

Outside, Aurelia told her brothers that she wanted to talk to them privately, away from the apartment. George immediately suggested that they go to D'Amato's. Billy said he wasn't in the mood for an Italian meal.

"So who's talking about a meal! We're gonna have pizza," George replied.

"You guys go ahead," Billy said.

"What about you?" Tommy asked.

"I don't want to go."

"Why not?" George asked.

Billy started to say, "You know, you must have realized by now that..."

"Realized what?" Aurelia asked.

"I'm not talking about you, Aurelia."

"*What* are you talking about?" she asked.

Looking down first, then directly at George and Tommy, Billy said, "I don't like you, George, haven't for a long time."

"Nothing new there, Brother," George said.

"So why should I spend time with you?" Billy said.

"That includes me?" asked Tommy.

"Alone you're okay," Billy said.

"Thanks, Brother, as long as I'm driving the car, you're okay with me," Tommy said.

"I'm sorry but that's right," Billy said.

"So screw you, Billy!" Tommy said.

Aurelia said, "I can't believe this. You are brothers!"

George laughed, saying, "Maybe that's the problem."

"Come on, Billy! It's time you learned to bend a little!" Tommy said.

Billy said, "I can't be what I'm not."

"Everybody in the family has been hurting at some point, in some way, Billy! Mama and Baba are hurting really bad now, which is why I want us to talk about it," Aurelia said.

"You think I'm blind? But it's their problem and I'm smart enough to know I can't fix it!"

"Smart is all you are, Brother!" Patting his chest, Tommy added, "There's nothing ticking in there."

When they returned to the apartment, George stopped to relieve John in the tavern, Billy retreated to his room, and Tommy went looking for girls. Aurelia went upstairs and saw Nadra in the living room, watching television. Nadra looked at her, but Aurelia only acknowledged her with a smile. After being in her bedroom for a while, she returned to the living room where John had joined Nadra.

Like them, Aurelia pretended to be interested in the television program while she surreptitiously scanned their posture and their faces. They pretended there was nothing wrong. She decided to do the same.

1955

Thanksgiving

On Thanksgiving Day 'Am-moo arrived wearing his good suit and full of good cheer, declaiming, "Salaam aleikum!"

Nadra and John responded with, "And peace to you, too." The boys shook his hand, even Billy, who scowled in spite of himself. Aurelia smiled and nodded, knowing that women were not to touch the patriarch. He acknowledged her with closing eyelids and expanded hands, as though confronted with a beatific vision. Nadra beckoned them to the table with "*Tfaddalou.*" ("Welcome to the table.")

Before they began, 'Am-moo picked up a piece of bread, like it was a Communion wafer, looked at Nadra, and invoked, "*Yisslamou eydaki.* If Farid Ferris were here I would say the same to him. I invited him, but he could not come."

Nadra looked at John and John looked down at his plate.

Five hours later, after three servings of pastry and an afternoon nap, 'Am-moo Ike took an abundant stash of leftovers and went home. It was time to go to Sami and Lila's. The Hanouns walked single file, like prisoners being led to the execution chamber, carrying pies and Syrian pastries. The big house loomed in front of them, a large buff brick with a wraparound porch. After entering the hardwood foyer and removing their coats, the men went left into the spacious living room, which merged into a dining room. There they greeted Sami, Teddy, Wasim, Tina's husband, Oran, and Eva's husband, Barry.

Nadra and Aurelia went to the kitchen. Standing in the doorway, Nadra saw that this Thanksgiving was going to be like every Zahir Thanksgiving. The food wasn't ready, the table not set, her sisters fighting, and her mother, Lila, helpless.

The tile counters held an assortment of food, burghul, pine nuts, rice, cans of chicken broth, rolled grape leaves, salad, cranberries, and a large bag of pistachios. Several pans and a Dutch oven stood next to the six-burner stove. With some relief Nadra noted that the turkey was in the oven.

Eva was pulling out drawers to hunt for more cutlery. Tina shouted at her, "For God's sake, use the good stuff. It's Thanksgiving!"

"Where is the good stuff?" Eva asked.

Pointing to a large silver chest, Tina said, "There!"

Sami entered the kitchen to ask, "Where are the drinks?"

Wasim came alongside of him and added, "And the arak, we want the arak also."

Lila told Eva to get the men something to drink.

Eva said, "How come everybody gives me the orders?"

Nadra stood back and took it all in. She locked eyes with Lila, saw her expectant look, and resisted the temptation to make her plead.

Finally, Nadra put on an apron and told Millie, "Start browning that meat and throw in a handful of pine nuts. Then find the rice and chicken broth."

Millie told Nadra, "I don't cook."

"You do today!" Turning to Lila Nadra asked, "Did you buy some bones?"

"Yes, I think they're under the napkins," Lila said.

"Put those bones in the bottom of the Dutch oven, Tina. Rinse them first, and add salt."

"I always rinse them first!" Tina barked.

"Then layer the grape leaves crisscross over the bones," Nadra said.

Tina said, "I know that."

"Then why isn't it done?"

Nadra then turned to Lila and asked, "Do you have lemons?"

"Oh, I hope so. You can't make grape leaves without lemon," Lila said as she pushed things around in the refrigerator.

Aurelia checked the turkey and told Nadra it was probably close to done.

Nadra responded, "Thank God."

Lila lifted her head from the refrigerator long enough to say, "Don't forget about the kibbe." She took a large bowl of ground meat out of the refrigerator. "It's not Thanksgiving without kibbe."

"I can make it!" Tina said.

Taking the opportunity to needle Tina, Eva said, "The whole world knows Nadra makes the best raw kibbe."

"Well, I guess I travel in a different circle," Tina huffed.

Lila returned to her investigation in the refrigerator.

Again Sami entered the kitchen, long enough to demand, "Where are the pistachios?"

Millie said, "I saw them somewhere." Sami left while Millie hunted for the pistachios. When she found them, she poured them into a bowl which she handed to Aurelia. "Give these to your grandfather."

"No," said Aurelia.

"I beg your pardon?"

"No."

"I found the lemons!" Lila shrieked.

Millie, Eva, and Nadra stared at Aurelia, who busied herself folding napkins.

Within an hour and a half the women were carrying platters of turkey, dressing, Syrian rice, grape leaves, salad, kibbe, mashed potatoes, gravy, and cranberries to the dining room where the men sat, waiting eagerly.

Meanwhile, the women relaxed in the kitchen, drinking soft drinks and gossiping, occasionally peeping in the dining room to see if the platters needed refilling.

After about an hour, John said, "Let's go to the living room so the women can eat."

The men moved back to the living room. The women added more to the platters and sat as Lila said, "This is better. We can take our time and chew on the bones if we like."

Afterward, John and the three boys raced home while Nadra and Aurelia, exhausted, linking arms, trudged along together.

"Why did you refuse to serve your grandfather?" Nadra asked.

"I got sick of the masters and slaves routine," Aurelia said.

"You don't have to take it personally. It's just old country ways. Sitto Lila is old country. She was taught to wait on the men and she taught us to also."

"I think there's more poison in the pudding than that!" Aurelia said.

"What do you mean?" asked Nadra.

"Everyone knows Sitto Lila cut Jidoo Sami's balls off."

"I can't believe how you're talking, Aurelia!"

"I think you're all hypocrites. Like you and Baba with your funny little sweetheart routines…after being ready to kill each other!"

"All right. We didn't fool you. Baba and I can be like Lila and Sami sometimes and—"

"Baba is not like your father!"

Dropping Nadra's arm, Aurelia stormed ahead. Stunned by her daughter's reaction and anger, Nadra stood immobile. When Aurelia passed John, he turned and, mystified, waited for Nadra.

❧

When Aurelia returned to college and the boys were out of the house, Nadra found her tongue. It was late. They were in their living room/bedroom and John was taking off his shoes.

"Okay, John, what if I had invited Farid Ferris to Thanksgiving dinner?"

Immediately he raised his head and shouted, "If you want to leave me, leave! But I will not have that man in my house!"

"He's my business partner!"

"Maybe to you, but to him you are more!"

"More what?"

He threw his shoes across the room. "You're a woman he would like to have! I saw it in his eyes, the way he looked at you. When you raised your arms flinging the bread, your breasts swaying, your eyes dancing—he's taken with you."

"You saw that?"

"Yes, when I came over with Sergeant Cork."

Nadra laughed. "You're pathetic, John. Farid's a showman. It's all part of the rah-rah 'she has golden hands' act. Even good old 'Ammoo hasn't seen anything to get worked up about. You heard him. He thinks Farid and I have a great business, feels that we're making Syria known, that we are respected—"

"This is not about bread or respect or business!"

"Other than jealousy, what is it about, John?"

Ignoring her, John crossed the room to pick up his shoes, but she stopped him. "Well, what is it?"

He swung around and pointed his finger at her accusingly. "You left me out, Nadra."

"I what?"

"You left me out! You make bread for women, families, children. I hustle beer, sometimes to drunks who have hungry kids waiting at home!"

She studied him, her inquisitive eyes dancing between rage and amusement.

"And you would have been a willing partner? You, overcautious John, would have been willing to take a chance?" Nadra could not stop pacing as she tried to control herself. "*I* left *you* out! And what did you do, John?" Nadra began intruding on his space. "You and your 'incle were sending money to the old country when your children needed it."

"You always acted like ten dollars was a hundred!"

"In those days every ten dollars was a hundred! And I don't believe you! Ten dollars! You always handed me a lousy five dollars for shopping just so you could enjoy my expression before you dipped into your pocket again!"

"Stop shouting. Half of the east end is going to hear you."

"You think I care! You ran Oran off when he paid attention to me and made me laugh. You wouldn't let me work! You robbed me of that beautiful house on Woodland Drive! You never told me about the deal Michael proposed—you stopped talking to me, stopped trusting my judgment—"

"Your judgment was not always right!"

"My judgment was not right?"

John backed away from her, like a rabbit being stalked by a fox.

"How so? When, John?" she asked as her eyes pinned him.

He stepped in front of her, enraged, ready to turn on his predator.

"Sit down, Nadra!"

She sat, never taking her eyes off him.

"You lost respect for me when I refused to confront Simon Metrey. You looked down on me."

"I looked down on all of you! Sonya had no one to protect her."

"I tried, Nadra."

"What do you mean?"

"I talked to Simon!" he said as he turned away.

"You never told me that."

He went over to the sofa, sat, and buried his head in his hands.

"When did you talk to Simon?"

"The day he almost killed Alex."

"My God."

"Talking to him was a risk. It backfired," John said.

Nadra said, "It was my fault. I kept pushing."

John shook his head.

"But I was the one who went to Simon, against my better judgment."

Nadra rose and went over to him, put her hands on his shoulders.

"I'm sorry."

His voice full of anguish, his eyes brimming with tears, he said, "So am I, but it was Alex and Sonya who were hurt."

"I misjudged you."

He shook off her arms and turned to confront her. "I saw something far worse than that in your eyes, Nadra. You despised me. I saw contempt!"

"Forgive me."

Turning away he said, "An insult can be forgiven, but not easily forgotten."

"I'm sorry, John."

Reflecting, resigned, he replied, "You could not have acted differently."

"You did the right thing, John. You know that. Just as you did the right thing when you protected your mother!"

"No, I went against my better judgment. I know what men like Simon are like. Do anything, say anything, and they will turn on you or on their victims—on whoever is weaker—in this case little Alex. Men like that get meaner! Their power is in their meanness. There's a hole where their heart should be.

"Causing hurt to another, especially a child, never leaves you!

It makes me more cautious and afraid. It's no wonder you have stopped needing me."

For the first time in a long time her eyes embraced him with tenderness. "For you that's been the problem—I stopped needing you. The problem for me, John, is that I have not stopped loving you."

She picked up his shoes and placed them next to his feet.

"It's the first of the year. Soon there may be nothing for you to feel left out of."

❧

The next morning John got up the same time as she did to walk her to work. They did not speak and she was glad. She needed to gather herself, to reflect on the turmoil of the night before.

Somewhere between John's "You left me out" and, "You have stopped needing me," Nadra figured it out. *It isn't just Farid he's jealous of. He's jealous of the operation, the business! Now he blames me. "You left me out," he had sobbed. Why hadn't I seen it before?*

Perhaps it began much earlier, even with her engagement belt holding the gold coins. And the heavy gold bracelets that Lila insisted Nadra wear. At that time she felt they were handcuffs. Eventually she wore them all the time, when they were happy and in love. Before they became the ties that bound.

Those pieces are gold, valuable handmade items. Perhaps they are my answer. Where can I sell them?

She pondered all the possibilities—pawn shops, jewelry stores, individuals with money—but none seemed remotely safe or secret.

Cash. She needed readily available cash or credit to head off Mr. Amour's takeover.

Wound

Nadra arrived at Lila and Sami's house just as Lila returned home, unlocking the front door. Nadra, in her middle age, seemed taller than her normally imposing mother. Turning to face her daughter, Lila asked, "Why aren't you working?"

"Why aren't *you* working?" Nadra said.

"I began early." She stood aside so Nadra could enter and said, "Do you want to make us a cup of tea?"

"I don't have time to make tea."

Lila studied Nadra before she said, "Then I'll make it."

Nadra followed Lila into the kitchen. Nadra still envied the spacious kitchen, the many cupboards, tile counters, and six-burner stove. She also took note of the unwashed cups and glasses in the sink. When she spied several packets of Lipton Noodle soup, she smirked and said, "You've been cooking again!"

Lila didn't look at Nadra, but she acknowledged her snide remark with a frown. She filled the kettle and put it on the burner then fiddled around for the tea bags.

"On the right," Nadra directed her as she sat down.

"You want sugar?" Lila asked.

"Yes."

"Naturally. You have always needed a little sugar—to cover your anger—to sweeten your bitterness."

"Thank you, Mama."

Lila sat down at the table and leaned forward to touch Nadra's hand. "After all these years something inside you still stings, like a wound that won't heal."

Nadra moved her hand away. "The wound healed, but the pain remains."

Speaking softly, Lila asked, "Why, Nadra, why?"

"I was cheated."

"Has your life had no rewards?" Lila asked.

"That's not the point."

"You have a husband who can't take his eyes off you, children, three sons! Now a business that's yours."

Standing to address her mother, Nadra said, "I was cheated."

"How did we cheat you?" Lila said.

"I wanted an education. I wanted choices."

"You were not born into a world of choices! Nor were Feheema and Nesrin, but at least you got to America."

"Only because you needed someone to work for you, someone to take care of your babies."

"Nadra, I already had baby Tina and another on the way. I didn't deserve that help?"

"Did I ever refuse to help? Before you even thought to ask, I had it done."

"You have forgotten my suffering, my humiliation."

"Baba was your problem, not mine."

"Oh, he could have been yours also, daughter, but you were too young to see it."

"Of course I saw it. He made me his slave. I wasn't allowed to go to school. I spent my childhood working in the goddamn store!"

Shaking her head, Lila said, "That's not what I'm talking about."

"I don't care what you are talking about! He was guilty of broken promises."

"Yes, he broke many promises," Lila said.

"You were no innocent. He even cheated John and I'm sure you knew it."

"What could I have done?"

"You've managed to do a lot. You've taken over, taken care of yourself. Lathered yourself in revenge."

"Is that what you want?"

"I'm not like you."

Laughing out loud, Lila said, "That's what the daughters always say!"

Nadra fired back, "Mama, you were mean!"

Temporarily stunned, Lila was quiet before she responded, "You have wanted to say that for a long time."

"Perhaps."

"You know how to break a mother's heart."

"You never had one, Mama, at least not for me and perhaps not really for Feheema, Nesrin, Tina, Eva, and Millie either."

"I loved my daughters!"

"But you adored your sons!"

"Is that so unnatural?" Lila asked.

Nadra said, "The water's boiling."

Lila took the kettle off the stove, but did not pour the water.

She sat down, looking at the floor. "No matter what she does, a mother is always guilty. A daughter is forever flinging something in her face."

"Oh, I know that feeling," Nadra said.

Nadra put a tea bag in each cup, poured the water, added a spoon of sugar into one cup, and took them to the table. When she sat down, Nadra said, "I didn't come here to hurt you. You're the one who started all this, Mama."

"Why are you here, Nadra? What do you want?"

"Money."

"Aren't you making money?"

"I want to buy out Farid so he can move on to Charleston."

After the First of the Year

A week later, Farid excused himself after the morning rush to say that he had an errand to run and would be back in an hour. He apologized for not being able to help with the cleanup before the prep for lunch. Nadra told him not to worry about it. She was glad to have him out so she could review the figures she wanted to discuss with him later. From her satchel she took out the notebook that Aurelia had bought for her. It was called the All American Marbleback Composition Book—that made her laugh. Still far from being literate, she had trouble with some of the spellings, but the numbers were clear and accurate.

After Farid returned, she told him that before she left for the day she wanted to talk about their future. He said, "Of course," and seemed amused by her request. He was smiling.

When the time came they sat at the old desk in the corner of the supply room. Nadra showed Farid her calculations, saying, "I have the money to buy you out, Farid. Here's the list and numbers. Let's go over them so you can see if they are fair."

Farid burst out laughing.

"Why are you laughing? Am I insulting you?"

"No, no, I would never laugh at you. It's just that…"

"It's just what?" She took back her calculations.

"Everybody is throwing money at me! For the first time in my life everybody is throwing money at me. Well, not everybody, but—"

"I need to know what's going on," Nadra said.

"You are too late. I just agreed to sell my share."

"Farid, how could you!"

"It's all right, Mrs.! It's all right!"

"Damn it, who bought it? Mr. Amour?"

Farid said, "Never! Though he was the first to offer."

"I knew it!"

"Then who? I want to know who?"

"John."

Nadra was silent for a moment, then bent closer to Farid to ask, "John?"

"Yes."

"My John?" she asked.

"There's another John?"

"Where did he get the money?" Nadra said.

Farid shrugged. "That's not my business."

Nadra looked at him suspiciously and asked, "Who else is throwing money at you?"

"Mr. Amour, your husband, your mother, Lila, your son George, but evidently he doesn't have any money. Everybody wants a piece of the action!"

Agitated, Farid stood, walked around the table, and stopped finally to look at her while he made his point.

"We're just a small operation now. We have a powerful mixer and we have a huge furn and a fast system, but one day, one day,

Mrs. Hanoun, there will be machines that will do it all and do it all fast!"

Speaking softly, she asked, "And will the smell of baking bread still bring out people?"

Smiling, he answered, "Maybe. But Syrian breads won't be special anymore…though yours will be, Mrs. Hanoun. As your 'Ammoo Ike says, it's blessed by your hands."

"It's also the *expensive* mahleb," Nadra teased. He looked at her for a long moment before he dropped his gaze.

"Like I said, everyone wants a piece of the action. That's why they are throwing money at me. But you and I are going to keep control, Mrs. Hanoun. Let me tell you how."

Farid sat back at the table, facing her. "We're going to patent our idea—I should say your idea—so neither Mr. Amour nor any other slippery Syrian or angling Anglo can steal it. The patent and control will be in our names. It will be one idea and two locations, this one in Hedley, which you and John will manage, if that's how you want it, and mine in Charleston, which I will manage. Perhaps I'll hire George if he can work half as long and hard as his mother."

"I'm not taking any responsibility for George, Farid."

"Funny. John said the same thing."

Nadra inched closer and spoke very deliberately. "I'm still listening, but first I want to know something. Have you and John been plotting?"

Farid scooted his chair back slightly, leaned across the table to look directly at Nadra, fixing his eyes on hers. "Have I joined forces with your husband behind your back? Never! I would cut off my right hand first! Both hands! Today John came saying he had the money. Pleaded with me, said he wanted to save your investment, your work. I believed him. And I didn't want to see our business in Mr. Amour's hands, nor Lila's."

"I didn't mean to accuse you."

Farid raised his voice, saying, "Don't ever apologize, Mrs. Hanoun. You have a right to question, a right to mistrust. It is your idea and our work that is starting to pay off. You know what the Americans call it, our 'brainchild,' our 'blood, sweat and tears!'"

"You're getting worked up, Farid."

"That's what happens when people throw money at you. But now we have work to do. I think we can come up with a better name than The Oasis and we will need a logo. Do you want to call our business Golden Hands?"

"No, that won't translate in people's minds to a bakery."

"How about Nadra's? We'll call it Nadra's and use a picture or drawing of you and..." Farid saw that Nadra was having trouble listening to him. "It's late. Go home now and we will talk tomorrow."

John was standing by the front window, waiting. He could tell by her determined walk and angry expression that she knew. She came into the tavern, beckoned him to the side and demanded, "What the hell are you up to?"

George was working the bar, pretending he wasn't listening.

"Is this a game of checkers you're playing?" Customers sitting on the stools turned slightly to look at her.

"Keep quiet," John said. "Go upstairs and change so you can come with me."

"Why?"

Exasperated, he said, "Trust me, Nadra, just this once trust me."

She did as he directed. When she came back down, she and John walked up Miller Street, past 13th, to Woodland Drive. Finally they stood in front of a house that was similar to the one that John had refused to buy. It had a For Sale sign.

"This house is even better than the one on the corner that Charles bought. This one has a sun porch in the back and beyond it a grape arbor, a large yard where you can plant your vegetables and herbs. And this house is less expensive than the one Charles bought."

"So?"

"So put a down payment on it with the money Lila gave you."

"Don't tell me what to do!"

"Call it a suggestion," John said.

"How do you know Lila gave me money?"

"She called me, had me come over. She wanted to give the money to me because Sami cheated me."

"Then why did I get it?"

"Because I told her she owed you even more than me. She agreed."

"Did she really?" Nadra said sarcastically.

"Yes. She agreed. She was generous, as you know."

"Why am I finding all this out now?"

"You're the one who has been keeping secrets, Nadra."

She walked away from him, took a closer look at the house, then turned to accuse him.

"You dare say that when you just bought out Farid's part of the business!"

"I did it so that I can become a part of it! I want to work side-by-side with you once again…in a happy business!"

"How did you come by the money?"

"The bank."

"The bank? You…"

"I took out a loan."

"And the earth didn't open up and swallow you? The demons from hell didn't scream beware? God didn't shout, saying don't…"

"They left all that for you."

Nadra walked around, looking at John from several angles, while he stood perfectly still.

"And our savings? The money you hauled to the bank every month?"

"It's still there."

Finally, she said, "You don't even know how to bake bread."

"I can learn! I didn't know how to make nougat or peanut brittle, but I learned…or white cows and fizzy fruit drinks, but I learned."

Facing her, he said, "I want to take a chance, take a chance that you might need me again…and in needing me might also want me."

"You're suddenly full of courage, Mr. Hanoun."

Moving Day

Closing out of the tavern was easy for John because George was eager to take it over. George would call it "Hanouns: TV Pinball Vending." Learning how to make bread was harder for John, but he was enthusiastic. Considering how hard it was to take time away from the business, Nadra made moving them out of the apartment a fast job. She was almost done.

Armed with a good screwdriver, she climbed on a stepladder and carefully loosened the two bars over which the tapestries hung. Then she descended, poked her head outside sacred door one, and shouted, "John! John!" When she heard him on the steps, she climbed the ladder again.

As John entered, leering camels and sanguine Arabs plunged to the floor, releasing years of dust and railroad soot.

"They're all yours, habibee!"

Acknowledgments

Thank you to all my family and friends for helping me create *Sister of Saidnaya*. Delores Forge read and commented on those tortuous first drafts. I really appreciate her work and patience. Vicki Le-Fevre, Tony Marconi, Ursula Lanning, my knowledgeable readers, contributed insights and suggestions. I thank my dear colleagues in Writers Satellite, Francoise Bartram, Peg Hanna, Brenda Layman, and Rosalie Ungar for their continuing help and encouragement. George Allam, dear "cuz" and scholar, sent me books and myriad helpful items. He always had an answer or knew where to find an answer to my many questions. I thank my daughter Mari Kalister and my daughter-in-law Laura Kalister for all their ready assistance. My son Steve's expert help and loving encouragement have contributed greatly to my recent playwriting and fiction endeavors.

I thank publisher Brad Pauquette for all that he has taught me and for his ever "cheerful cooperation and communication." Many thanks to Emily Hitchcock for her thorough copy editing.

ABOUT THE AUTHOR

Rose Ann Kalister

Rose Ann Kalister first began writing short stories then concentrated on playwriting. She was awarded a Playwright Fellowship from the National Endowment for the Arts for *Silk Pongee,* a three-act comedy. The comedy was produced by the Ohio University School of Theatre. Gallery Players awarded her first prize and production for *Contours.* That two-act drama literally and metaphorically focuses on a cancer that is destroying the family. The West Virginia Centenary gave her first prize for *The Visionaries*, a play about the Burr/Blennerhassett conspiracy. She was also the recipient of the Letters Award from The National League of American PEN Women. Before she began writing her novel, she was working on *Double Dutch.* That play's subject is two families whose unity is being threatened by betrayal and divorce. The play's resolution is innovative and eminently suitable.

Sister of Saidnaya: A Syrian Immigrant's Tale is her debut novel.

Rose Ann Kalister lives in Columbus, OH. Learn more about her at www.RoseAnnKalister.com.